PRAISE FOR THE DAN CONNOR MYSTERIES

"McMillen is a solid plotter and there are no extraneous clues. What really makes this novel zing is her love for the scenery and setting. You can almost smell the salt air and feel the trees. That, along with some interesting characters, makes for a terrific weekend book. This is a perfect cottage hostess gift." —Margaret Cannon, *Globe and Mail*

"Authentic characters, terrific dialogue . . . Highly recommended for mystery buffs who yearn for Canadian settings and our inimitable dialogue." —Caroline Woodward, author of *Light Years*

"McMillen clearly loves every square inch of her mystery's wild setting, a distant region in British Columbia: the mists, the brooding trees, the mountains, the winds, and the waves. It's the settings and the atmosphere that will enchant readers . . . Recommend this one to unregenerate nature lovers." —Booklist

A DAN CONNOR MYSTERY

GREEN RIVER
FALLING

R.J. McMILLEN

TouchWood
Editions

The information in this book is true and complete to the best of the author's knowledge. All recommendations are made without guarantee on the part of the author or TouchWood Editions. The author and publisher disclaim any liability in connection with the use of this information.

LIBRARY AND ARCHIVES CANADA CATALOGUING IN PUBLICATION
McMillen, R.J., 1945–x, author
Green River falling / R.J. McMillen.

(A Dan Connor mystery)
Issued in print and electronic formats.
ISBN 978-1-77151-168-1

I. Title. II. Series: McMillen, R.J., 1945–. Dan Connor mystery.

PS8625.M56G74 2016   C813'.6   C2015-907634-X

Design: Pete Kohut
Editor: Linda L. Richards
Proofreader: Claire Philipson
Cover images: *Fishing Boat* by Michael Olson, istockphoto.com
Eagle by Aleksei Oslopov, istockphoto.com

We acknowledge the financial support of the Government of Canada through the Canada Book Fund and the Canada Council for the Arts, and of the province of British Columbia through the British Columbia Arts Council and the Book Publishing Tax Credit.

The interior pages of this book have been printed on 100% post-consumer recycled paper, processed chlorine free, and printed with vegetable-based inks.

This book is a work of fiction. Names, characters, places, and incidents are either products of the author's imagination or are used fictitiously. Any resemblance to actual events or locales or persons, living or dead, is entirely coincidental.

PRINTED IN CANADA AT FRIESENS

16 17 18 19 20   5 4 3 2 1

For Liam

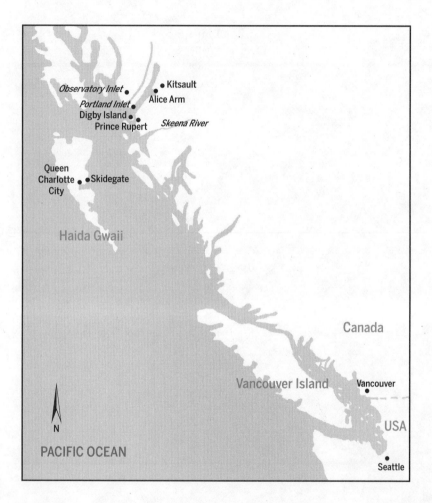

Observatory Inlet
Kitsault
Portland Inlet
Alice Arm
Digby Island
Prince Rupert
Skeena River

Queen
Charlotte
City
Skidegate

Haida Gwaii

Canada

Vancouver Island
Vancouver

USA

N

PACIFIC OCEAN
Seattle

► The scent drifted past the thousand-year old cedars. It wrapped around the soaring trunks, caught on the rough bark, slid softly across the moss-covered branches on unseen currents of air. Deep in the forest, a black bear sow lifted her head and wrinkled her snout. She had smelled man-scent before, when instinct had drawn her to the mouth of the great river to feast on the rich, red fish flesh that arrived every fall, but seldom had that scent reached this deep into her forest. She checked behind her for her two cubs. They were frolicking around a fallen tree, untroubled by this invisible, alien presence. She scented the air once again, and then, suddenly nervous, she called to them. It was time to move. This was man-scent, but yet not man-scent. It carried some element she had never smelled before, and now a strong metallic odor had melded into it. Blood. There had been a kill. As she turned to leave, a wolf started to howl. Then another.

► Andrew Horvath still could not believe his luck. Only six months out of university, with the ink on his master's degree barely dry, he was in exactly the place he had dreamed about for most of his life. He had grown up on the vast, open lands of the prairie, where no matter which direction he looked, the fields stretched out flat to the horizon. There were no valleys, no mountains, no rocks, just smooth, cultivated earth. Even trees were absent, except for a couple of straggly specimens his mother had planted beside the house, and they were more like tall shrubs. Trees took up space, and that space, unending as it seemed, was meant for crops. Fields of wheat, oats, barley, flaxseed and canola stretched out as far as his eye could see, painted a luminous green soon after the spring plantings, becoming a rippling emerald as summer took hold, turning to rich gold as seeds and blossoms ripened in the low sun of shortening days, changing to brown stubble later in the fall before snow clothed the land in white. The seasons were painted on the landscape, just like they were on the pages of the Farmer's Co-op calendar that hung on the wall beside the back door, and they had formed the pattern of his life. He had not imagined there could be any other until he had gone to visit his aunt on the west coast.

He had been thirteen, shy and awkward, tripping over his own feet as he tried to adjust to a body that seemed to change shape and size every day. He hadn't wanted to go, but his mother had insisted. It was his last chance, she said. By next year he would be old enough to work fulltime alongside his father in the fields and there wouldn't be time to take trips. She had helped him pack, driven him to the city and put him on the train. He could still remember watching her as she stood on the platform, her solitary figure diminishing with distance even as his apprehension grew.

Three hours later that apprehension had changed to wonder as the train moved into the foothills of the Rockies, and the flat land he knew started to heave and fold and twist in ways he had never imagined. Trees appeared, singly at first, then in clumps and groups and, finally, as dense forests that covered the slopes in a multitude of green. Rivers cascaded down valleys, and pale, glacial lakes shone in every hollow.

He stared out the window, so entranced he forgot everything else. It was the beginning of a love affair that would blossom into a passion bordering on obsession. On his return home, he had spent hours in the local library and read every book he could find on mountains and forests and trees, picked up tourist brochures and studied the photographs, haunted the magazine racks at the grocery store and bought every magazine that had articles on the mountain and forest environment. And it was there, in a magazine, he first learned of the Great Bear Rainforest.

"Stretching for more than two hundred and fifty miles along the northwest coast, the Great Bear is part of the largest coastal temperate rainforest on earth," he read. That statement alone was enough to entrance Andrew, but there was more: ancient trees, moss-covered meadows, waterfalls dropping down sheer granite cliffs into glacier-cut fjords, and, to top it all off, white Kermode or Spirit bears. He was hooked. And now he was not only there, in that incredible forest, but paid to be there. At the job fair he had attended in his last days on campus, he had been hired by one of the largest oil and gas companies in North America to be one of their environmental officers.

Andrew shook his head and stepped out of the Jeep. *Enough with the daydreaming*, as his mother used to say. That could come later. Now there was work to be done. He was following the planned route of the northern pipeline, noting the age and species of the trees, checking them for any cultural modifications that would indicate traditional use by the original inhabitants of the area, which might therefore involve talks and negotiations with the various Native band councils. The giant cedar he had glimpsed just off the edge of the dirt road he was traveling had a notch in its bark high up on the trunk that might be the result of cultural harvesting.

He reached back and pulled his backpack off the seat where he had left it, then changed his mind. Regulations said he had to take it with him at all times, but he was only going a few yards into the forest, and there were no bears in sight. No need to load himself down with the bear spray and the bear bangers and all the rest of the gear. He would just take the camera. Hell, he could be in, photograph the tree, and then get back to the Jeep in minutes. The head of the inlet was only a few miles away, and then he would be on a paved road. If he was lucky, he could be back in the village by five, join the rest of the gang for dinner, and catch the game on TV.

It took him longer than he had thought, but not much. Once he reached the tree, he saw two others, just off to the right, with similar modifications, and he went over and took photographs of them too. There was still plenty of time. He had the Jeep door open and was leaning in to place the camera onto the passenger seat when he heard the noise. It was very faint, yet it sounded close. Not in the forest, but right on the road. A footfall? Was there a bear here after all? His heart started to pound as adrenaline surged into his bloodstream, but he fought to keep his movements slow and steady. Even if there was a bear, there was no reason to assume it would attack him—unless it was a grizzly, of course. Grizzlies were completely unpredictable and often aggressive, and there were plenty of them around here, but there was no bear smell, and that was reassuring. Even though he was still relatively new to the job, Andrew had been out on the coast long enough to have already encountered a few bears, and the wet-dog scent was unmistakable and usually overwhelming.

He straightened up and started to turn, moving slowly so as not to startle whatever was there. He neither heard nor felt the cut of the blade that severed his head from his body.

▶ It was coming up on five in the morning in Small Inlet, on the north end of Quadra Island. Dan Connor poured himself a cup of coffee and padded, barefoot, out onto the stern deck. There was just enough light seeping into the eastern horizon to allow him to make out the shadowed contours of the trees against the dark sky, but above his head the stars still glittered in the vast bowl of night. This was his favorite time, when the world came alive around him: fish rising for the first insects, birds celebrating the return of day with a dawn chorus, the faint scurry of animals starting their search for food along the shore.

He rarely had the time to indulge himself in solitude these days. After his re-instatement to the RCMP the previous year, he had moved his boat, *Dreamspeaker*, from the remote west coast of Vancouver Island to Campbell River on the more populated eastern side. It satisfied the demands of his boss, Gary Markleson, that he be available to answer calls not only in the major towns, but in the small communities scattered across the nearby islands and inlets—and, if he was honest, it made it easier on him to have the convenience of stores and services just a short walk away.

But convenience came at a price. The Discovery marina was crowded, and the security lights that burned so brightly both up in the parking lot and along the floats took away any possibility of watching the stars. In fact, he had been forced to put a heavy curtain over the porthole above his berth just so he could get some sleep.

After a few months he had learned to ignore the constant rattling of the halyards and rigging on the other boats lining the docks, but it remained a background noise that drowned out whatever sounds nature provided—if indeed there was any nature left there. The mall that had grown alongside the marina had taken care of whatever wildlife there had once been.

Still, he didn't have to worry about any of that this morning, or for the next twenty mornings for that matter. He was on vacation, and this time it was a real one. He was not on call as he had been during the last couple of "vacations" he had tried to book. He had left the marina the previous day and moved north, up to a tiny inlet on Quadra Island. Tomorrow his partner, Claire, would join him, and they were going to head up to the mid-coast, where they had first met two years ago. He let the word "partner" roll around his brain for a few minutes, testing the texture and flavor of it. It tasted good. Certainly better than the "girlfriend" he had been using. More solid. Richer. Sweeter. Like their deepening relationship.

He drained the last drop of coffee from his cup and straightened up from the railing he had been leaning on. The light was getting stronger now, and he could make out a pair of eagles perching on a high branch. Below them a sea mist was forming, thin gauze ribbons twisting in the cool morning air that lay on the placid surface of the water; warm water that had barely enough depth to allow *Dreamspeaker* passage. The mist would disappear as soon as the sun rose, but for now it danced on the surface like a wraith, and Dan watched it, entranced.

A sound broke the spell, and he turned, frowning, as a powerboat entered the narrow gap at the mouth of the inlet. Not many boats found their way to this tiny finger of water, even though it was less than twenty miles north of Campbell River at the junction of Discovery Passage and Johnstone Strait. Small Inlet was aptly named. The entrance was neither wide enough nor deep enough to allow passage to most boats except at high tide, and at this time of year the water was so thick with spawning Moon jellyfish it appeared almost solid, which kept the recreational fishermen away.

So this was not a fisherman, nor did it look like some boater on his way north. This was an open boat with no room for accommodations. That meant it either had to be a local, which was unlikely as this end of Quadra Island was uninhabited, or someone specifically looking for him. And that could only be bad news.

Dan leaned down on the railing again and watched the boat approach, the calm of the morning gone, replaced with a growing sense of dread. It was only yesterday evening he had been talking with Claire. Surely nothing could have happened to her since then—although bad things did happen, as he knew only too well. But what other reason could there be for the office to send someone out here to find him? The only person who knew he was here was Claire, and she was—or had been—planning to join him later on today. Was she hurt? Ill? Surely if she was simply delayed by some technical or work problem she would just call him, but he had the phone turned off. And it was too late to turn it on now.

The light was too dim to make out who was in the boat, but it headed steadily in his direction. As it came closer, the engine revs dropped and the tiny outboard drifted in toward his stern. *Definitely bad news*, he thought. Dan forced himself to step down onto the grid to meet it. The operator was a corporal he recognized from the detachment at Campbell River, although the man was not in uniform.

"Phil," Dan said, forcing the words out through lips clamped tight with worry. "What brings you out here?"

"Hi, Dan. Sorry to disturb you, but you know how it is. They give the orders and you just follow them."

Dan nodded, unable to speak.

Phil coughed, obviously uncomfortable with the news he was about to deliver, then looked away. "They want you to turn on your phone. They've been trying to reach you since last night, but I guess you've got everything turned off."

Dan stared at him, confused by the unexpectedness of the message. "My phone?"

"Yeah. They need to talk to you. It must be pretty urgent. They called Claire and I guess she told them where you are."

Dan sucked in a lungful of air as the full import of what Phil was saying sank in. "Claire's okay, then," he said. It was a statement rather than a question.

Phil frowned. "Claire? Yeah, I guess so. At least they never said anything to me about her. Why? She been sick or something?"

Dan shook his head and smiled as a wave of relief washed over him. "No, she's fine. I was just wondering . . ." He changed the subject. "They tell you what this is about, or who I'm supposed to call?"

"Hell, they don't tell us anything. Just hand out orders. Do this, do that, go here, go there. You know how it is." Phil shrugged. "But this has to be something big because Markleson came in around six o'clock yesterday, just before shift change, and he and the boss were still huddled together when I left."

He reached back to start the engine, but turned again as another thought struck him. "Oh, and it's Markleson you're supposed to call. He's still in Campbell River. They said you can just call the office and they'll know where to find him."

Dan nodded and handed back the tie-up line he had been holding. "Okay. Thanks for letting me know."

"No problem." The roar of the outboard drowned out anything else he might have said.

▶ Back on deck, Dan made his way forward to the wheelhouse. He was relieved to know Claire was okay, but worried the three weeks of peace and solitude he had been looking forward to sharing with her were about to disappear. What the hell was going on? Gary Markleson was the commander of the North Island for the RCMP, and he was based in Tahsis, not in Campbell River. It was Markleson who had signed off on this vacation; he was not the kind of man who would easily cancel it, so why was he going to so much trouble to get Dan to call him? Phil obviously hadn't heard about any major happenings, or he would have been more than happy to say so. Despite his protests to the contrary, Phil was usually the first to hear—and repeat—any news. Dan thought it'd be nice to pretend the phone was broken, or that Phil hadn't showed up, but neither of those excuses were going to work. *Damn.* There was nothing he could do but call in and find out what it was all about—but if it was a recall, they were going to have a very hard time getting him to agree.

The phone sprang to life with the flick of a switch, the ready light instantly bright. Normally Dan would have been pleasantly reassured to see that the electronics were working so well, but this morning he had to fight off a shaft of disappointment. Another possible excuse gone. And of course his call was answered on the first ring. No help there either.

"Hi, Sara. It's Dan Conner. Is Gary Markleson there by any chance?"

"Dan! Good to hear from you. Yes, he's been waiting for your call. I'll put you right through."

Dan grimaced. Where was inefficiency when you wanted it?

"Dan!" The familiar growl at the other end of the line was unmistakable. Gary Markleson had a voice that sounded as if he had swallowed a load of gravel. "Sorry to disturb you. I know you're on vacation, and there's no way I would bother you if it wasn't really urgent."

"Urgent how? The guy you sent over said you've been there in Campbell River all night, but he hadn't heard of anything happening."

"It's not here. It's up north."

"North? How far north?"

"You been watching the news lately?"

"No, I haven't, but what's that got to do with anything?"

"You've heard about the plans to build a bunch of oil and gas pipelines out to the coast? Got all the environmental groups worked up?"

"Well, yes, of course I've heard about that," Dan answered. "You would have to be deaf, dumb and blind not to have heard about it. But what the hell does that have to do with me—or you for that matter?"

"Normally, not much, but I got a call from Mike . . ."

"Mike? Our 'illustrious chief down in Victoria' Mike?"

"The very same. He said he got a call from *his* chief asking if the Prince Rupert Detachment could borrow you. Seems they're up to their ass in murder and mayhem up there and have asked for help."

Dan held the phone away from him and stared at it for a moment before speaking again.

"Prince Rupert has asked for me?"

"Yep. Guess they've heard about our roaming, ship-based super-sleuth with his Native sidekick and want him for themselves."

"Whoa! Hold on a minute. How did Walker get into this conversation? He's got nothing to do with the RCMP."

"I have no idea. His name happened to come up in my conversation with Mike, so I'm passing it on. You can ask him yourself—he wants you to call him ASAP."

"Walker? Or Mike?"

"Mike, although I believe he said Walker was trying to reach you too."

The call to Mike went through as easily as the one to Markleson.

"So what's going on?" Dan asked as soon as Mike picked up the phone.

"Ah man, I'm sorry. I wouldn't call you unless it was really urgent—although there's a possibility it may be over soon, so it may not be as bad as it sounds."

"Really? So I still have my vacation, even though it's so urgent you had to get Markleson to chase me down?"

Mike ignored the sarcasm. "Yes and no," he answered. "It *is* urgent—very much so—but you just might end up with a longer vacation."

Dan didn't reply. He was used to Mike playing verbal games in order to get what he wanted, and this sounded like one of those games.

"You were planning on heading back up the coast anyway, weren't you?" Mike continued. "Markleson told me you and Claire were going up to see Walker again."

"That was the plan," Dan answered, his tone cautious. "Although we may not be able to connect with Walker. He can be pretty hard to find."

"Maybe not this time," Mike replied.

Dan frowned. "What are you talking about? Is Walker in trouble?"

"No. Walker's fine, but he called me yesterday to ask where you were."

"Walker called you? That's crazy. He never calls anyone. He doesn't even have a phone!"

"No, but Annie does, right?"

Dan focused his gaze on the scene outside, hoping that it would somehow provide an anchor in the strange vortex he now found himself in. Why was it, he wondered, that every time Walker's name came up, he felt as if he, Dan Connor, had stepped into some surreal fairytale, his reality altered to resemble a scene from *Alice in Wonderland*? It had been one of his favorite childhood stories, a story he had asked his mother to read him night after night, a story that he thought he had left behind long ago, together with his youth. But now he recalled an instance just a couple of years ago—and Walker and Mike had both been part of that instance—when he was so confused he thought he might have actually become the rabbit in that particular tale. It hadn't been a pleasant feeling, and now it seemed like Mike might be taking on the role of the Cheshire Cat.

"Yes," he answered, enunciating his words carefully. "Annie does have a phone. But she doesn't have your number, and you are not an easy man to find."

"True," Mike answered cheerfully. "But persistence—and a name like Walker—pays off. So Walker called me on Annie's phone and asked where you were. Seems he tried to call you, but couldn't get an answer. I told him I was having the same problem, but that I was working on it and hoped to have it solved by this morning. Which I did."

"I see," said Dan, not seeing anything at all. "And did he say why he was trying to call me?"

"Not exactly. But he did say he had a friend 'up north' who was in trouble, and he thought you might be able to help; it occurred to me that the urgent matter I wanted to talk to you about, and Walker's troubled friend, might just be linked."

Dan sighed. "Okay," he said. "You had better start at the beginning."

▶ THREE ◀

▶ There had been five murders so far, Mike explained, two women and three men, and all of them had been employed by one or other of the companies working on the pipelines. The latest had occurred just a couple of days ago. One of the men, a young biologist employed as an environmental officer, had been out checking an area of forest for "culturally modified trees," whatever they were, and had not returned to his hotel. A search had been initiated and they had found his body lying beside his vehicle. He had been almost decapitated. An autopsy would be conducted later today or early tomorrow, but there was little doubt it was the same killer. The other four victims had all been killed the same way.

"They got a suspect?" Dan asked.

"No, not exactly, but they think they might have a lead on something—and that's where Walker's friend may come in."

"I can't see Walker having a friend who goes round murdering people. Walker's a pretty peaceful guy—and he's very picky with his friends. Doesn't have that many of them."

"It may not be that specific. All they've come up with until now is that the same—or a very similar—weapon has been used in each case, and that there have been traces of seawater left in all the wounds. Now the coroner has come up with a sliver of wood. He says it's yew wood, and it's from some tool that had been worked or shaped, and then painted. He thinks it might have been a canoe paddle."

"A canoe paddle? So that's the link? This friend of Walker's paddles a canoe?"

"He might. I really don't know. Walker never gave me his name, so I don't know anything about him. What Prince Rupert is thinking is that the guy they're looking for might be Native. Specifically, that he could be Haida. The Haida are famous for their canoes; they often use yew wood for their paddles, they are very strongly opposed to the pipeline, and they live in the area."

Dan shook his head. "That's a whole bunch of pretty big jumps—from the wood of a yew tree to Haida to Walker's friend."

"They *are* big jumps, and I have no idea where—or if—the friend fits in. It must be pretty major if Walker feels that his friend's problem is big enough to go to the trouble of tracking *me* down just so he can get hold of *you*. And the timing is right."

"Yeah. But it's still pretty far-fetched. Probably just a coincidence."

"Could be," Mike acknowledged. "But as I recall, you don't believe in coincidence any more than I do, so I think you need to check it out."

"You want me to find Walker and ask him who his friend is so that Prince Rupert can question him?" Suddenly Dan's vacation plans seemed possible again.

"I want you to *call* Walker and see if you can find out what his problem is. He's still at Annie's. He said he would wait there for your call until lunchtime."

"Okay." Dan's optimism level dropped back down a notch. This seemed way too easy. "I can do that. I'll call you back afterward . . ."

"You can call me back when you're on the way. I want you to fire up that damn boat of yours and head north. You can pick Walker up when you reach Annie's place, assuming he wants to go with you—and I suspect he will—but you need to get up to Rupert as fast as you can. All hell's broken loose up there. They've got the company bigwigs and the politicians crawling all over them; the workers are so scared that some of them are talking about quitting, and the media is having a field day; no one can move without falling over one of them."

"So where do I fit in?" Dan asked.

"You're going to be the wild card. You don't even need to go into the

13

office, so the talking heads won't know you're there. All the reports will be routed through me, and I'll give you all the contact information. I'll even let them know when you arrive. It's a bit unwieldy but it will work."

"Whoa, hang on a minute. I've got Claire joining me in a few hours. What am I supposed to tell her?"

"Tell her whatever you like. You can still take her with you. In fact, she'll be a good cover—and she won't be in any danger as long as she stays on the boat. This guy is only interested in people working on the pipeline. She'll enjoy the trip—hell, you both will. I've heard that area is spectacular."

"Yeah, yeah, yeah. Mike, it doesn't work like that. Claire has to be back at work in three weeks. It'll take me a week to get up there, and that's only if the weather holds. I don't know the area, and it's going to take time for me to figure out who's who, let alone what's happening. I'm probably not going to have this sorted out quickly enough to get her back here on time, which means she'll have to fly, and that costs money, which she may not have. And then there's the fuel, and moorage, and . . ." He knew he was rambling and was almost grateful when Mike cut him off.

"We'll cover it. All of it. I'll get Rosemary to set up an account for you at one of the fuel docks, and arrange a berth at a marina once you arrive, but we need you up there, and we need you on your boat." Mike paused, and his voice took on a less stringent tone. "You can think of it as a long vacation of sorts."

"Gee, thanks." Dan's voice dripped sarcasm. "I should be so lucky."

▶ "He calls that a vacation?"

Claire had arrived an hour earlier. A friend had brought her up on his boat, and they had unloaded her beloved kayak onto the stern grid and strapped it on securely. Now she and Dan were sitting in the salon, looking at a chart of the British Columbia coast that Dan had spread out on the table in front of them.

"Mike has an odd sense of humor. He was trying to cheer me up—and the truth is if you're coming with me, he's not too far off the mark. Be kind of nice to cruise up the Inside Passage together."

She nodded. "It's a trip I've always wanted to take—I just didn't expect I'd be taking it while you were on a case. Five murders? That's just so horrible! And Walker's friend is tied up in it somehow?"

Dan shrugged. He had talked to Walker right after he got off the phone with Mike, and it had sounded as if the trouble Walker's friend was in might very well be related to what was happening in Prince Rupert, although exactly how was far from clear.

"It sounds like it, but Walker doesn't know all that much—just that the friend is in trouble and asked for his help. Maybe he'll be able to tell us more when we get to Annie's. He's going to hang around there till we arrive—assuming Annie doesn't drive him off."

Claire laughed. "Annie will enjoy having him around—not that she'll admit it, of course." She stopped as another thought struck her. "We'll have to stop at Dawson's Landing and get her some chocolate chip cookies. I hope the store has plenty."

Dan laughed. "Already done. There's a case of them stored up front under the V-berth."

▶ They spent the rest of the afternoon stowing the boat and waiting for the tide to rise high enough to allow *Dreamspeaker* to squeeze her almost eighteen-foot beam and nine-foot draft out of the entrance. At six o'clock, Dan fired up the big Caterpillar diesel, hauled the anchor, and nosed the bow cautiously through the narrow opening and out into the waters of Johnstone Strait. He and Claire were both familiar with this part of the coast and they had agreed they would take three-hour shifts through the night in order to make the best possible time, but for now, they were just going to relax and enjoy being together.

Ten hours later, with Hardy Bay still some thirty nautical miles ahead, the shrill ringing of the radiophone reverberated through the wheelhouse. Dan reached out and snatched the microphone from its hook.

"*Dreamspeaker.*" He kept his voice low as he glanced back toward the door of the cabin where Claire was sleeping, to make sure it was still closed.

"Where are you?" It was Mike again.

"Mike? What the hell are you doing calling at four o'clock in the morning?"

"Good question, but you haven't answered mine. Where are you?"

"I'm about thirty miles south of Port Hardy. Why?"

"Can you speed up?"

"Speed up?"

"Yeah, you know. Go faster."

Dan frowned. It wasn't like Mike to be sarcastic and at four o'clock in the morning he was in no mood for it.

"No, I can't go faster," he snapped. "I've been up most of the night, and I have to fuel up in Hardy. Nothing is going to be open until at least eight o'clock, maybe nine, so speeding up now would be a waste of fuel."

"Okay, okay. I'm sorry. I'm not trying to hassle you. It's just that things are really getting crazy up north and they need you there, like, yesterday."

Dan had never heard Mike sound so frazzled.

"Things sounded pretty crazy when you called last night. What's changed?"

There was silence for a minute, and then Mike came back, his voice more subdued.

"They might have another one."

Dan sucked in a breath. "Another murder?"

"Yeah. There's another woman missing—a journalist. Works for one of the Alberta newspapers. They sent over a bunch of them to check out progress on the pipeline, and four of them went out as a group a couple of days ago. Took one of those big crew-cab things that can go anywhere and has sleeping accommodation in a canopy on the back. Three of them came back late last night and they're pretty freaked. Said they were on this dirt road following the survey stakes and they stopped to check out the view. The woman walked back along the road to take a leak and disappeared. They went looking, walked up and down, called her name. Nothing. Then they found what looked like blood on some rocks beside the road. They were smart enough to mark the spot with some branches, and they used a spoon to scoop up some of the rocks and put them in a Ziploc bag so the forensic guys have them now. Man, if this turns out to be another one, it's going to turn into a complete circus."

The radio fell silent as both men contemplated just how crazy that circus could become, and how difficult it would make their jobs. It was Dan who spoke first.

"Is there any way you can call the guys in Port Hardy and get them to roust out someone on the fuel dock?" Dan asked. "Might be able to pick up a few hours that way."

"I'll call you back," Mike answered.

▶ The fuel dock was brightly lit, and with only a slight current and almost no wind, Dan had no trouble tying up to the dock. The silence as the engines were shut off woke Claire and she came out on deck to join him.

"You made good time," she said as she glanced at her watch. "I didn't think we'd be here until eight."

Dan looked at her. She was still flushed from sleep, and her short blond hair was tousled. The T-shirt she had pulled on was twisted, one edge of its hem caught in the waistband of her shorts. He would have liked nothing better than to spend three weeks waking up beside her every morning, but even if it meant her leaving the boat now, he owed her no less than the complete truth. That was a lesson he'd learned last year when he had tried to hide both his re-instatement to the police force and the nature of the case he was working on from her, and had spent days in an agony of indecision and worry. Now he pulled her close and buried his face in her hair.

"Things have changed. They think there's been another murder. I've been told to get up there as fast as possible."

She tilted her head back and looked up at him. "Another one? My God! What on earth is going on?"

He gave a short laugh. "That's what they want me to find out, and that's not going to be easy. It may not be dangerous, but it's certainly not going to be much of a holiday for you."

She frowned. "Are you saying you don't want me to come with you?"

"No! That's not what I'm saying. There's nothing I want more than to have you with me, but this is the last stop until Prince Rupert. You can catch a bus from here and be home in a few hours, but once we leave there's no other option but to go all the way, and I won't have time to do much of anything but work when we get there. Hell, I'll be working on the trip up. It's not going to be much fun for you, so if you want to leave now, I would understand."

She pulled away from him as the dock attendant came out on the wharf.

"Nice try, Dan Connor. I know you're a cop. You do what cops do. I made my decision last year when they dragged you back. I never thought I would be in a relationship with a cop, but here I am. You're stuck with me for the next three weeks!" She passed the line up to the waiting attendant.

▶ The long shadows of evening were reaching across the water when Dan checked the navigation screen one last time, set the depth alarm, and went out on deck. Claire was already at the stern, working the davit controls that swung the dinghy over the side. She smiled at him as he approached.

"Have you got the cookies?" she asked.

"I do," he answered, patting the duffel bag that swung from his shoulder. "Has she appeared yet?"

Claire smiled. "I saw her looking over this way, but she didn't come out. I think she might have gone back to the galley to put the kettle on. I saw a puff of smoke coming out of the chimney."

It had been almost two years since either Dan or Claire had seen Annie, and while they were both looking forward to visiting her, neither one of them could be absolutely sure of what kind of welcome they would receive. She lived alone aboard an old workboat moored in a tiny cove in the middle of a tangle of uninhabited islands, one of several loners and misfits scratching a living from the sea and land around her. She was not quite a recluse, like some others who called the area home, but she was certainly close. If it hadn't been for Walker, another solitary area resident who had since become a friend, they might never have met her.

▶ Dan started the motor and they headed over to the ancient boat. The old ladder that had hung down the side when they had last visited had rusted out completely, but the frame still provided a handhold to keep them steady while Dan rapped against the hull.

"Annie? It's Claire and Dan. Can we come aboard?"

There was no response. Dan looked at Claire and shrugged. "I'll try one more time, but she has to know we're here."

He leaned over, his hand outstretched, but then stopped as he heard the familiar sound of heavy boots clomping along the metal deck. Annie's face appeared above them, leaning over the railing.

"Hi Annie," Claire shouted above the noise of the motor.

Annie stared down at them without speaking, her gaze moving from one to the other, and then she turned and started back along the deck.

"Took you long enough." She tossed the words over her shoulder as she disappeared from view.

Dan laughed. "Well, she certainly hasn't changed! I guess that's the closest thing to an invite we're going to get."

▶ They found Walker sitting in the galley, a cup of tea in his hand. It had been a year since they had last seen him, two years since they had met on Annie's boat, but it could have been yesterday. He still wore his black hair in a long braid, and the same small smile lifted one corner of his mouth. Dan was tall—a couple of inches over six feet—but as he slid onto the bench beside Walker, he couldn't help but be aware that the man would have been taller than him if it had not been for the accident that had damaged both legs so badly he could barely walk. It was an accident that Dan had played a role in all those years ago, back in the city, when he had been chasing Walker over a roof after a bank robbery. Who would have thought then that the two of them would end up friends? But they were, and in spite of the way they met and the cultural divide between them, it was a friendship based on respect.

"Good to see you," Dan said. "I wasn't sure you would wait."

"He's been hanging around here for two days!" Annie muttered as she pulled two more mugs off their hooks and slammed them down on the table. "Figured he was never going to leave." She reached up into a cupboard, and took out a package of chocolate chip cookies.

"Damn near ate me out of these!" she growled as she carefully counted eight out onto a plate. "Guess you're both gonna want some too." She slid the plate onto the table beside the mugs, and then reached for the kettle.

Dan's glance caught the quick, conspiratorial smile that Claire shared with Walker, and he turned away before he too broke into a grin. Annie's gruff exterior didn't always respond well to humor.

"Thanks, Annie," he said with a straight face. "Chocolate chip are my favorite."

. Her only reply was a harsh snort.

▶ They were all on their second cup of tea, the cookies long finished and the local gossip, such as it was, put aside before they got to the real reason for their visit.

"You heard any more about this friend of yours?"

Walker shook his head. "Nope—and I'm not going to unless I can talk to him directly."

"You know where he is?"

"I can find him when I get there."

Dan nodded. "So you're planning to come with us?"

"Yeah. Too far to paddle."

"You know about the murders?"

"Yeah. I heard. Three of them, right?"

Dan shook his head. "Not anymore. There are five definite, and maybe a sixth."

Walker stared at him, then turned away to look out the window. "All done the same way?" he asked.

"Yes. At least the five they're sure about. Why are you asking? Do you know how they were done?"

Walker looked back at him, his face expressionless. "They had their heads cut off, right? And they found saltwater—sea water—in the wound."

"Yes, they did, but where did you get that information? The only people that should know that are the RCMP and the guy who's doing it. If you're getting this from this friend of yours, maybe he is the one."

This time it was Walker who shook his head. "I did get it from my friend—or at least a friend of his—but he didn't do it. The police told him all that when they dragged him in for questioning. He figures it's how the guy who did do it is trying to frame him."

"The police have already questioned this friend?"

"Yeah."

"And they let him go?"

"Yeah. Didn't have anything to hold him on, I guess. Just grabbed the first Indian that came along."

Dan raised his eyebrows and stared at Walker without saying a word. He wasn't about to acknowledge that kind of comment, and after the silence dragged on for what seemed like a long time, Walker finally shrugged.

"Okay, maybe they thought they had a reason," he conceded. "Although it would have to have been a pretty pathetic one. Joel paddles a canoe, so he has a paddle, and he's Haida, so he obviously opposes the pipeline, but he is also one of the quietest and gentlest people I have ever met—and not all RCMP are like you." He glared at Dan, his face defiant and his tone challenging. He was angrier than Dan had ever seen him, even all those years ago when Dan had arrested him and put him in jail.

"Thank you . . . I think," Dan answered. "Although there are a lot more 'like me,' as you put it, than you recognize—or will admit. But that's not the issue here. If they let this guy go, why did he send a message to you? What is he so worried about?"

"They let him go, but they warned him not to leave the area. Said they wanted to talk to him again, that they had more questions to ask him. It scared the hell out of him, so he asked a mutual friend to contact me. If there have been more murders, they might have already pulled him in again." He frowned. "Didn't they tell you who they're looking at when they talked to you?"

Dan shook his head. "They haven't told me anything yet. They don't want me too close. The whole idea is to have someone who's free to move around without the media watching every move and getting in the way."

"Huh." Walker's reaction was typically skeptical. "Gonna be pretty hard to figure out what's happening if they don't tell you anything."

"They're sending me the file by email. We're routing everything through Victoria to avoid any possibility of the media hacking in. I'll read it on the way up—and speaking of which, we should get going. Where's your canoe? I didn't see it when we arrived."

Walker's face twisted into a lopsided grin. "Still have those same lousy observation skills, huh? You need to practice them some more, white man. You're gonna need them up in Rupert." He inclined his head toward the shore. "It's right there under the ramp. Up against the hull."

"Huh. I must have been too busy making sure I didn't drop these," Dan said as he lifted up the duffel bag he had placed on the floor beside him, pulled the boxes of cookies out, and piled them on the table. "Here you go, Annie. We figured you might be able to find a use for these. Sorry it's taken so long to repay you for all your help, but it was much appreciated."

Annie stared down the boxes, a look of complete shock on her face. When she finally raised her head, her eyes were unnaturally bright, her mouth was compressed into a thin line, and she was frowning. With an abrupt shove she pushed herself away from the table and headed out onto the deck, muttering something under her breath. Dan watched her go, then glanced across at Claire, raising his brows in an unspoken question, but Claire just shook her head and followed Annie out of the cabin.

"Well, that went well." Dan was talking more to himself than Walker, who had been watching it all with an enigmatic smile on his face. "She looks like she's pissed off. I thought it would make her happy."

Walker shrugged. "She's not used to receiving gifts," he said. "Give her some time."

The two men sat quietly, looking out over the water, just as they had two years earlier when Walker had asked Dan to help find a missing friend. The friend had been Claire, and Annie had been central to the success of their search, sharing not only her boat, but also her treasured stash of cookies. The boxes that now covered the table were their way of repaying her.

Claire's return ended his musing.

"She okay?" he asked.

Claire smiled. "She's fine. You surprised her, that's all. She wasn't expecting it and she didn't know how to respond. I think she's feeling a little embarrassed."

"Do you think it would be okay if I went out and talked to her?"

"Sure. Why not?"

Dan found Annie leaning against the railing at the stern, and he leaned down beside her without speaking. He had learned long ago that there were times when silence worked far better than words at opening the doors of communication. It was several minutes before Annie spoke.

"Thanks."

Dan turned his head to look at her. "You're welcome," he said, smiling. "And thank you."

She nodded once, and then straightened up.

"Claire said you have to leave."

"Yeah. They've got a problem up in Rupert, and they want me up there."

"Walker going with you?"

"He says he is."

"He's a good man, that."

"Yes, he is."

She nodded again, but still didn't look at him. "Stop by when you come back," she said, her voice muffled as she turned away.

Dan smiled again. "Thanks, Annie," he said. "We'll do that."

As Walker followed Dan and Claire down the rough plank walkway that led to the beach, a lone raven landed on the railing above them. It watched their progress with curious, black eyes and remained there until Dan hauled anchor almost an hour later and pointed *Dreamspeaker*'s bow north.

FIVE

▶ Days merged into nights as they moved north through the winding channels of the Inside Passage, daylight fading into the long, northern dusk, and dusk merging into brief darkness before an early dawn. Walker refused Dan's offer of a stateroom and instead slept on a settee in the salon—when he slept at all. Most of the time he sat out on the stern deck, watching the shore as it slid past. Namu, Bella Bella, Klemtu, Butedale. The tiny communities slowly emerged from the trees, only to disappear again as *Dreamspeaker* moved steadily north.

Dan contacted Mike soon after they left Annie's cove, and was connected with Prince Rupert via a conference call on a secure line. After a brief, carefully worded conversation with the detective in charge of the investigation there, he got the emailed reports. The five murders had all occurred in remote, heavily forested areas within eighty miles of the city, and all the victims had been working at the time. Two had been alone, but the other three had been either part of a group or one of a pair that had somehow become separated. Most had been surveyors, but one had been a geologist; the most recent—assuming the missing journalist was simply missing and not among the dead—had been an environmental officer.

Dan read and reread the pages, shuffling them back and forth as he tried to absorb all the information. The victims had worked for three different companies, but all of them were contracted to one or other of the big corporations that were building the pipelines.

The first murder had occurred a little less than two months ago, the most recent just over a week. All were committed using an identical weapon, and all the victims had traces of salt water in their wounds. Only the most recent had the sliver of yew wood.

"That's all they've got?" Walker sounded incredulous. "Why the hell are they trying to finger Joel?"

Dan had shared the reports with both Claire and Walker. It was not standard RCMP operating procedure, but then he was not exactly operating in the standard way, and he figured they deserved to know.

"I haven't got the interrogation report yet," Dan said, checking the stack of paper again. "My guess is that he is what they call 'a person of interest.' He's opposed to the pipeline, he's part of a group that has stated their intentions to stop it, and he was in the area."

"They?" Walker asked.

"They? They what?"

"You said '*they* called him a person of interest.' Does that mean that you don't consider yourself one of *them*?" Walker's voice was quiet, but it commanded complete attention.

Dan stared at him, unable to answer. It was a very perceptive question and one he should have asked himself long before this. Did he really think of himself as an RCMP officer? There had been a time when his answer would have been instantaneous and unequivocal, but that was before he had returned home and found his wife brutally murdered by a man whose trail he had been following at the time. He had lost himself then, lost himself so completely that he no longer knew who or what he was. No longer knew if he had a life, let alone a career.

Three years on the water aboard *Dreamspeaker*, spending most of his time alone, had healed many of the wounds Susan's death had caused and had given him back a sense of identity, but he was not the same man he once was. Working to resurrect some of his old skills in order to work on the cases he had run across, as well as witnessing Walker's courageous journey from troubled youth to confident maturity, had added to the change. Whether that was good or bad he couldn't say. He only knew he was different.

It certainly hadn't been his intention to re-enlist in the RCMP last year, but he had not refused the invitation when it was handed to him and now he had the badge again. It was the same one he had worn proudly for almost twenty-five years before his resignation. Officially, he had both the rank and the authority. That was confirmed in the insignia that adorned the red serge dress uniform stowed in the hanging locker in the master stateroom. And he certainly had the case. That was documented very clearly in the paperwork that Mike had sent him a few days earlier while he was on his way to Port Hardy. So why did he hesitate? His response should have been automatic.

He looked out across the water, letting his gaze wander over the steep shoreline with its dark blanket of cedar and spruce. This was Walker's territory—his people had lived here for thousands of years. They knew every creek and every river and every cove. They knew what lived there and where it lived. They knew the pattern of the seasons and the rhythms of the days. They were an integral part of the land, as it was an integral part of them.

Dan was a newcomer who had come here not out of any particular knowledge or desire, but only to escape his memories, and yet it had become his home too. This tangle of islands and inlets with its swelling tides and serpentine currents, its towering cedars and twisted pines, had worked its magic on his soul. It was where he felt most comfortable now, certainly more at ease than back in the city where he had spent most of his adult life. While that didn't change the job, it had certainly changed the way he did it. He knew he could never go back to being a member of a squad, always on call, following orders, rushing off to emergencies, but he could still do what he loved to do: protect and serve. He would simply do it in a different location, and in a different way—and perhaps for a different reason. A better reason. A less selfish reason.

He turned back to Walker. "Yes," he said, his voice firm. "I do think of myself as an RCMP officer, although maybe not in the same way I once did. But that's okay."

He scanned the water ahead and altered course to put *Dreamspeaker* on a heading to enter Wright Sound.

▶ The weather changed soon after they entered the narrow confines of Grenville Channel, the clouds lowering until it seemed as if
Dreamspeaker and her crew were enclosed in a gray tunnel, the air
they were moving through thick with the weight of presaged rain. The
wind had yet to arrive, but Dan increased speed, preferring to burn
fuel rather than risk the wrath of a storm. Grenville was a fjord-like
body of water, in places less than a quarter of a mile wide, the steep
shore plunging to depths of up to three hundred feet. There was no
possibility of anchoring anywhere within its forty-three-mile length,
and no coves or bays to pull into for shelter, unless he could squeeze
into Lowe Inlet, and that seemed unlikely. The southwest winds that
usually accompanied bad weather in this part of the world would
create a following sea that would make steering a nightmare, lifting
Dreamspeaker's wide stern and twisting her like a corkscrew. To make
matters worse, the current was about to reverse, and that would put the
wind against the water, making the waves steeper and closer together.

The change in engine revs brought Claire up to the wheelhouse,
and the three of them sat quietly peering out into the gloom. The
rain started as a fine drizzle, but quickly grew to a steady downpour,
reducing visibility even further. The sound, as it drummed on the
coachroof, added to the steady rumble of the big diesel and acted as
a soporific, stealing all desire to talk, or even to think. The slopes and
cliffs of the shore slid past unseen, even though they were only a few
hundred yards away, marked only by the changing tracery of green
lines the radar painted on the computer screen.

"Is your paddle made of yew wood, Walker?" Claire finally broke
the silence.

Walker shook his head. "Nope. I mostly use birch, but I've got
a couple I carved out of spruce too. Yew is a really hard wood. The
trees grow very slowly, and there's not too many of them around any
more, at least until you get up north."

"Up north as in Haida Gwaii?" Dan asked.

Walker looked at him and nodded. "Yeah. Haida Gwaii probably
has more than most places—except for the Prince Rupert area. Yew
likes the climate there."

"So do the Haida use it for paddles?"

"The Haida, the Tlingit, the Tsimshian, the Gitxsan, the Nisga'a—everyone on the north coast used it. Good wood for spears and harpoons."

"Yeah, but nobody uses spears and harpoons anymore. So I guess that leaves paddles, right?"

Walker sighed and nodded. "Yeah. That leaves paddles."

"And the Haida still make them?" Dan was persistent.

"Yes," Walker said, his voice hardening. "They do."

Claire reached out a hand and touched his arm. "I've been reading about the Haida," she said. "They're amazing people! They could navigate across Hecate Strait in a canoe just by reading the waves and the sky. It made them incredibly powerful because they were the only ones who could do it. The book said there used to be over forty thousand of them, maybe more, but after smallpox and flu and all the other white man's diseases decimated their villages there were only six hundred or so that survived." She shook her head. "Six hundred! I just can't comprehend that level of loss."

"Yeah." Walker nodded, glaring over her head at Dan. "They were way too busy just trying to survive, never mind build canoes and make paddles out of yew wood." His voice softened. "But they're getting stronger again, teaching their kids the old language and the old ways. Joel told me he helped carve a traditional canoe at a work shed up near Masset. Said they had this big red cedar tree they'd cut down, and he was part of the team that worked on it. Said they did everything the old way: dragged the tree down to the ocean with cedar ropes. Floated it to check which was the heavy side so they knew where to split it. Adzed it out with traditional tools. Smoothed out the inside with a curved knife. Filled it with water and then dropped hot rocks into it until the water was boiling. Steamed the wood and pushed boards into the top to stretch it out. He said it widened out nearly two feet!"

Walker turned his head and looked out the window into the curtain of gray, his eyes unseeing, and let his voice drop to a whisper.

"They had the canoe blessed so the Creator could breathe life into it. Joel said it was the best thing he'd ever done. Made him feel real. Like he was whole again."

Dan looked at him. "Ah, man. I'm sorry. I'm just trying to get a handle on the yew-wood thing."

Walker shook his head. "It's okay. But you have to realize that a Haida canoe is maybe thirty or forty feet long. Takes a long time to build one and a whole bunch of people to paddle one. And a yew paddle would take a long time to carve. They would be mostly ceremonial now. Probably only see them in the museum. Joel has a canoe like mine—fiberglass. And he probably has a paddle like mine too."

Dan was scanning another report. "Sure will make it easier if he does. They . . ." He looked across at Walker and smiled. "The Prince Rupert guys . . . sent it off to forensics for testing."

Walker turned away without speaking.

▶ The current split halfway up Grenville Channel, and they battled three knots of flood until they emerged into the silt-stained waters of Telegraph Passage. The rain had eased to an intermittent drizzle, and the clouds had lifted enough that they no longer felt claustrophobic. They passed the brackish outflow of the Skeena River, skirted Port Edward and headed for Rushbrook Marina, where Mike had reserved a berth for them.

"Hope he was smart enough not to put it on the RCMP tab," Claire said. "If the wharf community there is anything like the ones down south, the 'kelp vine' would have spread the news of your arrival all over the waterfront. Maybe all over town. That would sure ruin your wild card status."

Dan nodded. "Yeah, it would, but Mike booked it himself, not through the office, so we're okay." He gestured to the stack of faxes and emails in front of him. "The info is all in there. Rushbrook is the biggest marina in town, and it's got all the bells and whistles, including good internet. At this time of year there should be enough boats there to ensure *Dreamspeaker* will barely be noticed."

"You figured out how you're going to get around once we're there?" Walker asked. "You can't poke around in this big-ass boat, and Claire's kayak is a single."

"I'll have you know *Dreamspeaker* does not have a big ass," Dan retorted. "She is a well built lady with excellent lines, who has done a fine job of carrying your skinny butt up here! And for your information, I am planning on doing what any good tourist does: I am going to rent a Jeep." He glared at Walker with mock ferocity.

Walker grinned. "In that case, you can give me ride."

"And why would I do that?" Dan asked. "You planning on taking in the sights downtown?"

"Nope. I'm going to go find Charles."

"Charles? I thought you said your friend's name was Joel."

"It is. But *his* friend—actually it's his uncle, not just a friend—is called Charles, and Charles will know how to find Joel."

"Wouldn't it be easier just to phone this Charles guy?"

"Yep, probably would if he had a phone."

Dan stared at him for several seconds, and then shook his head. "Okay, no phone. But I assume he at least has a regular house? Is it here in town?"

"Kitsumkalum."

"Kitsum—what?"

"Kitsumkalum. It's out toward Terrace, but Charles lives off the reserve. It's not that far, and you'll get to see some of the area you're going to need to see anyway."

Dan sighed. "Fine, and what happens once you get there? You want me to wait around and drive you back?"

"Nope. Charles has a boat. We'll come back down the river."

▶ They found the marina and located their berth. Mike had been right. Nobody was going to take any notice of a converted fish packer among the jumble of boats that shared the floats. By seven they had tied up, unloaded both the kayak and the canoe, and eaten a meal of fresh shrimp that Claire had purchased from one of the fishing boats.

"When do you want to go to . . . wherever Charles is?" Dan asked. "It's pretty late now. How about we just relax here tonight and I'll book the Jeep for tomorrow morning?"

31

Walker shrugged. "Sounds good. I'm going to check out the harbor." He turned to Claire. "You want to come? Leave the man in peace to check out his reports?" The printer had started up while they were eating, and hadn't stopped since.

Dan watched as the two of them walked toward the stern rail, Claire easily adapting her stride to suit Walker's slow pace. When they were out of sight, he sat down and lifted the first report off the top of the growing pile.

► S I X ◄

► The drive out to Charles Eden's house took less than an hour.
The two-lane strip of smooth blacktop followed the Skeena River
east and Dan made good time. Signs along the way pointed to small
communities and distant lakes, but there was no sign on the tiny dirt
access road that Walker pointed out.

"Doesn't look like anyone uses it," Dan said as he bounced down
the narrow lane trailed by a cloud of dust.

"Probably don't," Walker replied. "He's right on the river. Doesn't
need a road."

"Might be nice to have one in winter," said Dan.

Walker gave him one of his infuriating grins. "Us Indians heap
tough."

Dan couldn't hold back his laughter.

The lane curved and dipped and they followed it until they saw a
small wooden house. Set right on the bank of the river, its deck of old
wooden boards jutted out over the edge, the land below dropping steeply
down to the water. It appeared deserted except for a pair of ravens sitting
on the roof. Dan approached as close as he could get, then switched off
the engine and watched as Walker opened his door and struggled out.

"You want me to wait here while you see if he's in?"

"Nope. It's fine."

"What if he's not here? You're miles away from anywhere. You
can't walk back to town."

Walker shrugged. "Then I'll wait," he said as he hobbled toward the house.

He was still standing at the door when Dan topped the rise and the house disappeared from sight.

On the way back through town, Dan picked up a good map of the area from a store that specialized in hunting and hiking equipment.

"You heading anywhere in particular?" the clerk asked. "I've got some good topographical maps if you plan on going off-road. They've got the GPS coordinates on them."

Dan started to shake his head, but then thought better of it. The bodies had all been found on one or another of the many old logging roads that criss-crossed through the forests, but if the Prince Rupert guys were looking at someone who paddled a canoe, maybe they were also all near the water. Perhaps a topo map would come in useful.

"Sure," he said. "And you had better throw in some bear spray and bear bangers while you're at it." He wasn't planning on straying far from the Jeep, but if he had to check things out, he wanted to have the right equipment with him.

▶ *Dreamspeaker* was quiet when he returned, and Claire's kayak was missing from its normal place on the stern grid. He wasn't surprised. Claire's love of being out on the water was almost as great as Walker's, and she had told him the previous night that she planned to explore more of the harbor while he was gone. Dan carried his purchases into the salon, loaded the bear spray and bear bangers into his backpack, added his binoculars, a notebook and several granola bars, and then spread the maps out on the table. He took a bottle of Corona out of the fridge, unwrapped the thick pastrami on rye sandwich he had picked up at the marina grocery store, and ate his lunch while he studied the locations of the murders.

It didn't take him long to realize the topo maps had been not only a good buy, but also a necessary one. Outside the city of Prince Rupert itself, there were almost no gazetted roads, and the regular maps were almost useless. With no way to identify a specific address, and with most of the vast network of logging roads decommissioned and therefore lacking even basic forestry identifiers, the location of each victim had been described using GPS coordinates. Painstakingly sorting through the RCMP reports, and shuffling back and forth through the sheets of the topo map, Dan carefully identified each of the crime scenes with a red *x*. Then he traced out the road each victim must have been following in green pencil. He was using a blue pen to highlight the creeks and rivers when he heard Claire return.

"What on earth are you doing?" she asked as she took in the mounds of paper scattered around the salon. "Have you taken up coloring?"

Dan turned the map so she could follow it as he explained. "It's the only way I can think of to be able see the big picture," he said. "I can't ask the guys who are working the cases directly, because then I would blow my cover. I thought of asking Mike, but trying to figure out the details over the phone would be way too cumbersome, so I'm just going to have to find my own way in."

She nodded and bent down to look at something more closely. "What are these?" she asked as she pointed to the thin blue lines he had drawn in.

"They're creeks. They're so small you almost have to have a magnifying glass to see them, but if you look at the contours, they make sense. And you have to remember that Prince Rupert is the wettest city in Canada. They have over one hundred inches of rain a year here. There are creeks everywhere."

"But why do you care? You're going out in the Jeep, right?"

"Yes." He nodded and started to trace one of the creeks down to the ocean with his finger. "But I have to figure out how the bad guy got to the murder site. No one that was there at the time saw a vehicle—and there were other people out there with three of the victims when they were killed. That's odd, and it seems to me it means there's at least a good chance that whoever did it traveled to the sites by water. That's why the local guys have been looking at Walker's friend. It's because he paddles a canoe."

"So are there creeks near every site?"

"Looks like it so far. I still have one to do."

Claire straightened up and moved to the galley. "Well, if you hurry up, you can take me out to dinner. I'm starving. I didn't have any lunch." She looked regretfully at the empty plate and beer bottle sitting on the counter.

"How about we order in," Dan said as he reached for the pen again. "Walker said he might bring Charles Eden over here tonight. I don't want to miss him."

▶ It was ten o'clock, the sun just starting to slip beneath the horizon when Walker and Charles Eden arrived. Dan and Claire were sitting out on the deck, each sipping on a glass of wine as they watched the clouds ignite with color so bright it seemed as if the sky was burning. They barely noticed the arrival of yet another boat until they felt the gentle bump against the side of the hull.

Dan reached over and took the tie-up lines, wrapping them around a cleat. "Welcome," he said to the man who stood beside Walker. "Thank you for coming."

The man nodded, and glanced at Walker. "My friend here says you want to speak to me about Joel. He says you are a good man, who only wants to help. But he also says you are with the police. In my experience it is not likely that both things can be true."

Dan smiled. "How about we sit down and talk about it? You've come a long way. You must need something to drink. Wine? Beer? Maybe a cup of tea?"

The man looked at him for a minute, and then turned to Walker and nodded. "Perhaps you are right," he said, and climbed over the rail. Walker followed him by using his powerful arms and upper body to lift himself up, pivoting himself so that his legs were dragged behind him.

▶ Charles Eden looked nothing like Dan had expected him to look given the retired fisherman designation Walker had given him. If Dan hadn't known better he would have thought the man had spent his life as a teacher or a doctor, even a banker, rather than in some demanding physical job. His skin was smooth and taut and he was taller than any native man Dan had ever met, with a slim build and the sinewy muscle of a long-distance runner. Certainly someone who kept himself in very good shape. His hair was cut short and was streaked with just enough gray to add to his look of quiet authority. He was wearing blue jeans and a white polo shirt under a dark blue rain jacket.

"Have a seat," Dan said, gesturing to the benches that lined the outside wall of the cabin. "Or we can move inside if you prefer."

"Outside is fine," Charles answered. "I haven't liked being inside since they let me out of the residential school."

"You were in residential school?" Claire had said nothing since Charles and Walker arrived, but now she was leaning forward and staring at the man who had just arrived. "But you don't look old enough!"

He turned toward her and nodded. "Unfortunately for me, I am indeed old enough." He leaned toward her and held out his hand. "Charles Eden," he said, "And I was there for over ten years."

"My God! That's awful!" Claire said, and then caught herself. "I'm so sorry. I've forgotten my manners. I'm Claire." She reached over and shook the outstretched hand. "I'm not usually this rude. Welcome aboard, and let me get you that cup of tea." She stood up and disappeared into the cabin.

Dan watched her go, his face puzzled, and then he sat down and joined the other two men who had seated themselves around the deck.

"Walker says you may know where Joel is," he said to Charles Eden.

Eden waggled his head. "I know where Joel likes to go," he answered. "I do not know where he is."

Dan nodded. "Did Walker tell you why I'm up here?"

"All he told me is that you are the 'wild card' for the police, and that you are a good man who will search for the truth."

Dan looked across at Walker. "Walker is a good friend. I'm honored by his trust."

Eden nodded. "He is both a good friend and a good man—but I believe you and he were not always friends?"

Dan laughed. "No. We were certainly not friends to start out with, but things change. I think we've both learned a lot since then." He looked at Walker and smiled. "He's taught me much, although I'm sure he thinks I'm a poor student."

Again, Eden nodded. "Has he told you about Joel?"

"Only that he's a gentle person. Not capable of these crimes."

"Yes," Eden said. "That's true. But you need to know him to understand." He nodded toward Walker. "Walker met him at a special camp that helps Native youth regain their heritage. It was not an easy time for either of them."

Dan looked at Walker. "Percy?" he asked.

Walker nodded, but didn't reply. Dan had met Percy two years earlier, when Walker had enlisted the man's help to disable a ship whose crew had not only murdered Claire's boss, but tried to kill her as well. According to Walker's description, Percy's camp taught young aboriginal men "how to be Indian again."

Charles Eden turned and looked out over the water. He seemed to be lost in thought, and for a moment Dan wondered if he should say something to bring him back to the subject of Joel, but courtesy and respect made him hold his tongue. The man had come here voluntarily in response to Walker's request, and he was a guest, not a suspect.

The minutes stretched out until Claire returned with a tray containing four mugs, bowls of sugar and milk, and a large pot of tea.

"Thank you," Eden said as she passed a mug to him. "So. Joel." He looked from Claire to Dan and shook his head. "It is a long story, and difficult to explain to people who have not lived it, but I will try to be quick.

"Joel is my nephew, my sister's son. In my culture that means that I am the one who must teach him what he needs to know: the songs, the dances, the traditions, the skills—all of it. It is a privilege and a duty that I am happy to have, but there is another reason I took responsibility for Joel. I mentioned the residential school." He nodded at Claire. "And you said it was awful. It was. Unbelievably so. But it was worse for my sister. Much worse. She was abused in the worst possible way, and she has never been able to find a way to deal with that. She uses alcohol to help her forget."

"Does she live with you?" Claire asked, her voice gentle.

"No," Charles replied. "She lives in Skidegate, over in Haida Gwaii. It was our home when we were small."

"And Joel?" Dan asked.

"Ah, Joel. He lives everywhere and nowhere. Joel was never comfortable anywhere—not at home, not at school, not with other kids. I took him to a potlatch when he was very small and he ran out screaming when the drums started. He couldn't stand any loud noise. Couldn't be in any large group of people. He screamed when someone he didn't know came near him. Screamed when people touched him. Sometimes he screamed when my sister tried to dress him. The teachers could do nothing with him. If they tried to comfort him, or even approach him, he would throw things at them to keep them away. My sister couldn't deal with him, even when she was sober. When she was drunk . . ."

He was quiet for a long time, his eyes closed and his face lined with remembered pain, and then he continued.

"He would follow me when I went into the forest. Walk where I walked. Sit when I sat. Touch the trees and the plants. After a while I started to tell him stories. Our stories. Stories of Yaahl, who you call Raven. Or Kaiti, the Bear woman. Or Foam Woman. I wouldn't look at him, just sit and talk. And he listened. Never spoke. Then one day he started to ask me about the stories—what they meant, where they came from. So I told him that too. And I told him about the trees, and how our people used the bark, and the roots, and the wood. I gave him wild berries to eat, showed him how to find clams and oysters, where to harvest herring roe, how to smoke a salmon—all the things that he needed to know.

"It helped him. I don't know how or why, but he became calmer. Stopped screaming. Stopped running away from people, although he never spoke to them unless he knew them really well—and even then, it was only a few words. After a while he started going out into the forest by himself. Sometimes he stayed out there for days. At first I was worried that he would get lost or hurt himself, but he always came home. One day I found him out there and he was doing some kind of dance. I asked him what it was and he said he was honoring a deer." Charles Eden shook his head and smiled at the memory.

"Because of the residential school I never learned the dances, so I took him to the Heritage Center; we call it Sea-Lion Town, *Kay Llnagaay* in our language. I showed him the masks, and the totems, and the canoes, and that night I took him to the performance space where they were dancing."

He paused, and when he looked up, his eyes were bright with unshed tears.

"There were a lot of people there. It was summer and it was hot, and there was drumming and singing. I thought he would run away, but he just sat down on the bench beside me and took it all in. When the dancers came in, I could feel his body start to move and sway in time with the drums. I could hardly believe it."

It was dark when Charles Eden finished speaking, the deck bathed in light reflected from other boats. The four of them continued to sit there, unmoving, until finally Dan spoke.

"Have you talked to him since the police questioned him?"

Charles nodded. "Yes. He came to see me. He was terrified. He didn't understand what they wanted. Why they were talking to him. Why they stole his paddle."

Dan looked at him. "Do you know where he got the paddle? Did he buy it, or did he make it himself?"

"He made it himself. He likes to follow the traditional ways whenever he can. He had one of the carvers over in Skidegate help him carve it, but he was the one who painted it. Did a really good job with it too. It's beautiful."

"I don't suppose you happen to know what kind of wood it's made of?" Dan asked quietly.

"Yew wood," Charles replied. "All the traditional Haida paddles are yew wood."

SEVEN

► Charles Eden left them a little after midnight. They sat in the soft darkness and watched his boat move away across the harbor, its passage marked by a trail of silver ripples.

"He's not going to try to go back up the river tonight is he?" Claire asked.

Walker shook his head. "No. He'll go out to the islands to look for Joel."

"Do you think he'll succeed?" asked Dan. "Joel sounds like someone who might be hard to find unless he wants to be found."

"Charles will find him. Whether he can get him to agree to talk to you is another matter altogether."

Dan nodded. "I can understand that, but it's going to be a whole lot easier to talk to me than to talk to the guys who talked to him before, and if his paddle comes back as being made of yew—and it sounds like it will—those same guys are definitely going to want to talk to him again."

"He didn't do it," Walker said, his voice quiet. "You heard what Charles said. Joel would never hurt anyone. I spent nearly three years with him. We lived together, fished together, paddled together, even hunted together. I know him better than anybody except Charles Eden. It was me he asked Charles to find after the cops talked to him. There is no way Joel could have done this," He pulled himself up and made his way over to the railing. "I'm gonna take off for a while."

Dan checked the time. "It's almost two in the morning. You and Charles are both going to be out there on the water in the dark. Don't you guys ever sleep?"

Walker smiled. "Percy asked Joel that same question once."

"And what was Joel's answer?" Dan asked.

"When it's moonlight, I go for a walk."

Dan looked at him in confusion, but there was nothing more and he could only watch as Walker used his powerful upper body to lower himself down to the grid and into his canoe.

▶ "What do you think about Joel?" Claire asked as they made their way through the salon to the master stateroom.

"Hard to say. Walker and Charles are both obviously convinced he didn't—couldn't—do it, but according to Charles, he used to have violent episodes where he threw things at people he didn't like. He certainly doesn't like the pipeline. If he's as anti-social as they say, he might have decided he didn't like the people working on it either. Might not take all that much to progress from throwing a book or a hunk of wood to wielding a paddle."

"I think he sounds autistic," Claire said. "A friend of mine has an autistic son, and some of the behaviors that Charles described sound awfully close to Sean's."

"Yeah?" Dan pushed open the door to the stateroom and ushered her in. "Well how about you research that tomorrow while I'm out searching for clues in the bush, and we'll discuss it over a glass of wine at dinner?"

Claire arched her eyebrows. "Maybe I should follow Walker's example and do the research while it's moonlight?"

"Exactly what I was thinking," said Dan as he pulled her down onto the bed with him. "Although it's possible I have a somewhat different kind of research in mind."

▶ Dan woke first and lay, warm and comfortable, watching the rain slide down the glass in the portholes. It was going to be a lousy day to do anything other than stay warm and dry; the softness of Claire's skin against his body and the gentle sound of her breathing made that proposition seem even more attractive. On the other hand, the weather was unlikely to improve, which left him no justification for delaying things. While June was one of the better months in this part of British Columbia, it still had an average of over sixteen days of rain. And it wasn't like he had a choice anyway. Mike had made the importance of this case very clear, and the stack of crime-scene photographs he had sent added an extra layer of urgency.

He glanced at the clock. Six fifteen. He could at least make himself a decent breakfast before heading out. He folded back the covers and slid out of the bed, careful not to wake Claire.

The coffee pot was already prepped. He switched it on, then listened for the promising gurgles it made as it started to brew the Veracruz coffee beans Susan had introduced him to that he had developed such a liking for, enjoying the rich aroma as he mixed the eggs for an omelet. The maps he had been studying the day before still lay on the table and he glanced at them as he worked. It was going to be a long day. The murders may have all occurred within an eighty-mile radius of the city, but the roads he needed to take to get him to the murder sites all required driving out along the highway toward the city of Terrace, and then heading roughly north on the Nisga'a Highway past Kitsumkalum Lake toward New Aiyansh, the largest of the Nisga'a communities. From there, he would be traveling on rough forestry roads that wound through some very rugged terrain, including across some lava fields. There was no way he was going to be able to reach more than one, or if he was lucky maybe two, of the sites today.

The smell of fresh coffee had drawn Claire from her bed. She reached around him to lift a cup off its hook, and then leaned over to peer out the window at the rain.

"Not exactly great weather for driving or kayaking," she said. "Or canoeing for that matter. Did Walker make it back last night?"

"Not unless he's sleeping on the stern grid," Dan answered.

"Well, with Walker that's definitely a possibility, although not too likely." She smiled and took a sip of coffee. "Mmmm, that's good. So are you still planning to spend the day driving the back roads?"

"Today, tomorrow, and maybe the next day. I need to see where the murders happened. It's the only way I can even start to get a handle on what's happening."

She nodded. "Okay, but I'm holding you to that promise you made—dinner and a glass of wine—so don't go getting lost, or stuck in the mud."

He pulled her to him and kissed the top of her head. "And you look after yourself too. I don't want to have to search the harbor after I get home."

▶ He was on the road before eight, driving into a slanting sheet of rain. Four hours later, he was bouncing and sliding along a narrow track that clung to a ledge above a fast-flowing creek. He had no idea where he was. He was blindly following the GPS navigation device mounted on the dash, praying that it was not leading him into a dead-end that would require either backing up or turning around.

A shrill beeping from the GPS told him he had arrived at his destination. He stopped the Jeep and turned off the engine, then sat and listened to it tick as it cooled. The rain had eased, and he put the window down, inhaling the clean wet scent of the forest. As he became accustomed to the silence, he heard the spatter of raindrops falling onto the ground beneath the trees and the chuckle of water coming from somewhere below the lip of the bank. The creek he had seen when he first turned on to this road was still there, but it sounded considerably calmer now.

He slung his backpack over one arm, checked that the can of bear spray was easily accessible, patted his shoulder holster to confirm his gun was in place, and stepped out of the car. The track—you could barely call it a road—stretched out for a couple of hundred yards both ahead and behind him before it disappeared into the murk, and a length of police tape fluttered from a tree, confirming that this was the right location. A minute later he crossed the road and found the creek. It was both wider and deeper here, and the surface was calm, only faint ripples portraying the water's progress. There was no beach. The rocky bank rose straight out of the water, and while it had a steep slope, he thought the twisted conifer trees clinging to life on its surface would make climbing it relatively easy.

His next stop was nearly twenty slow miles further along the same road, and it was almost a perfect replica of the first: massive, old-growth cedar and spruce mixed with a few mountain hemlock on one side, and a difficult climb down to a slow-running creek on the other. If the sites he visited the next day were the same, then it was certainly possible that the murderer had traveled by water, but he would have had to be in very good shape.

▶ A droning voice and the rich aroma of beef stew wafted out to greet him as he stepped onto the deck of the boat that evening. For a moment both things confused him. They were the sounds and smells of home and while *Dreamspeaker* was where he lived, in the three years since he had moved aboard he had always returned to silence, to emptiness. The voice and the aroma both belonged to a previous life—one with a house and a wife. A life with Susan. He felt a momentary wave of panic as the unwanted memory threatened to overwhelm him and then he pushed it back. Susan was gone, but Claire was here, and *Dreamspeaker* was no longer just a place where he lived; an empty hull that kept the water out—she was becoming a home.

The voice turned out to be the television, tuned to the evening news.

"There you are! I was about to send out a search party." Claire was lying on the settee, a blanket draped across her legs. The table was set, and a bottle of wine and two glasses sat on the galley counter. "Why don't you pour us both a glass of wine? The stew's ready, but it can wait."

He did as she asked, then sat down beside her, pulling her close. "You're very nice to come home to," he said, as he clinked his glass to hers. "And thank you for the stew. It smells delicious."

She laughed. "So it should. It cost a small fortune. I would love to take the credit, but the truth is I'm a pretty lousy cook. I bought it at a restaurant in town. Boeuf Bourguignon and a loaf of French bread. I figured it was perfect for a day like today, and I didn't have to worry about what time you got back."

"So what are we watching?" he asked. He took a sip of Merlot and felt the smooth liquid warmth slide down his throat.

"The local news," she answered. "There was an interview with the bigwigs from the pipeline companies talking about the murders. I thought they might have something interesting to say, but it was just the same old stuff. You wonder why they bother."

"Well, they have to say something."

"Yes, but saying it's the work of the lunatic fringe or that there's a homicidal maniac on the loose isn't much help. One of them even tried to hint he thought it was someone from an environmental group, which is really going to endear them to those people!"

"It's quite possible, even probable, that it is," Dan said. "It's hard to see any other reason behind this than trying to stop the pipeline, and that has to be related to an environmental issue."

"Odd that they would pick the most northern route," Claire said as she moved to the galley to serve their stew. "That other one is much more controversial, and it's just a few miles south of here."

"Yeah," Dan said. "It doesn't make any sense. At least not to me. But I'm sure whoever is doing it thinks it's perfectly logical. They always do. And I'm going to have to figure out just what that logic is if I'm going to sort it out."

He gathered up the dishes and took them to the galley, then started a pot of coffee before he headed to the wheelhouse to download the day's messages. He was less than halfway through them when the phone rang.

"They've got another one." Mike's voice was grim.

"The journalist?" Dan asked.

"Yeah. A couple of game wardens were out there and found some body parts. Guess the grizzlies had been at work, but they've got enough to know it's her. Got her jacket with her phone and wallet, but here's the thing: it wasn't the same as the others. They found her head and it's still attached. It looks like she was knocked unconscious and then strangled."

▶ EIGHT ◀

▶ At latitude 54°18.3' N, the sun rose just after five in the morning, and it would set a little after ten in the evening. Dan planned on using all seventeen hours of daylight to check the remaining four murder sites. He was on the road by five fifteen, and with almost no traffic on the highway, he made the turnoff in less than an hour. By eight thirty he was at the first site on his list and by mid-afternoon he was heading to where the body of the journalist had been found. All of the locations were on narrow, wilderness roads that had been carved out of the forest by some giant machine and then covered with a loose bed of gravel. All of them also followed creeks or rivers that appeared to be navigable by a small boat.

Dan got out of his car and pushed his way through the trees to the yellow crime-scene barrier. There was little undergrowth here. The old-growth trees stole the light from anything trying to grow beneath them, and the forest seemed empty and silent except for the occasional call of birds.

He knew that scavenged body parts had already been found in two other nearby locations, but this was where the forensics guys figured the journalist had been murdered. He didn't have the autopsy results yet, but the initial report said it seemed likely she had been attacked when she was on the road, then dragged or carried into the trees and strangled. Why? Why her? Why here? There were questions he needed answered, but he had no way to ask them.

He returned to his vehicle, retracing his route back to the junction with the Kitsault road, carefully checking for anyplace someone might have pulled a car off the track and hidden it, but there was nowhere. Even in the few places where there was space to fit a car between the trees, there was neither a way of leaving the road nor a way of concealing anything.

Kitsault was the last place on his itinerary for the day. Dan wasn't sure what he would find there, and he would be lucky to make it back to the relatively well-maintained Nisga'a highway before dark, but he had to see it and he didn't have another day to waste. Kitsault was where all of the victims except the journalist had been staying; According to the research he had done the previous night, it had been an instant town built by a mining company back in the early eighties to house twelve hundred people, and then abandoned just two years later. It had sat empty except for a caretaker for twenty-five years, until it had been purchased in a private sale. The new owner had dreamed of turning it into a resort, but saw a better return on his investment with the announcement of the proposed pipelines. The route of one of those pipelines would take it right past Kitsault and the workers would need a place to live.

Dan bounced and skidded down the ungraded road snaking through the desolate rainforest, grateful for the Jeep's four-wheel drive. The thought of trying to make the return trip in the dark spurred him on to greater speed than he would normally risk.

He emerged from the forest onto a flat plateau. Ahead of him the land stepped down through clusters of buildings to a fjord, its jewel-bright water painted with the reflection of snow-covered mountains. That had to be Alice Arm, one of the long fingers of water opening off Observatory Inlet, which in turn led down to the ocean just north of Prince Rupert. The view was breathtaking, but he didn't have time to appreciate it. Instead, he drove through the manicured streets, past an empty park where a black bear was grazing on lush grass, weaving his way through an empty town. It was eerie. There were well-kept houses and apartment blocks, a shopping mall complete with an empty grocery store and bank, a swimming pool and cinema, even a community center, but no people. It wasn't until he reached the pub that he found any vehicles.

He pulled into the parking lot, picked a space between a green pickup truck with a company logo stenciled on its door and a faded red Jeep Cherokee that had seen better days, and headed into the dim interior. Except for a placard under the bar that advertised smokes for seventy cents a pack, the place could have been shut down only weeks before, but most of the shelves behind the bar were empty, and only one of the tables was occupied. The three men and one woman who were sitting there all looked up when he entered, but it was the woman who stood up and approached him.

"Hi," she said. "Welcome to Kitsault. I'm Marjorie Wakeshaw. My husband and I manage the place. I don't think we were expecting you?"

"No, I guess not. My name's Dan Connor. I was just out exploring." He looked around the room. "And I certainly didn't expect to be here, or to find anything like this. What is this place?"

"Well, that would take a long time to explain, but it was built back in the early eighties, and then abandoned. Now its being used it to accommodate the folks that are doing the preliminary work for the pipelines."

"Really? It looked kind of empty when I drove in. I figured it might be a ghost town except it looks too good. I didn't think there was anybody here until I saw the pickup and the Jeep outside."

Marjorie Wakeshaw glanced quickly at the three men still sitting at the table before looking back at him. "I guess you haven't heard about the murders."

"Murders?" Dan hoped he had injected the right amount of surprise and trepidation into his voice. "There have been people murdered here?"

She shook her head. "Not here, no, but in this area, and all of them were working for the pipeline companies at the time." She looked over at the men again. "Why don't you join us? You might as well have a drink while you're here."

"Sure. That would be great."

Three pairs of eyes watched them approach the table.

"This is Dan Connor," Marjorie announced to the waiting men. "I asked him to join us."

The men all nodded a welcome and introduced themselves.

"So what brings you all the way out here?" Bill Caversham introduced himself as the personnel manager for a surveying company. He was wearing an open-necked shirt with a blazer and casual slacks, and his florid face held a faint sheen of perspiration. Dan figured him for more than a few pounds overweight, with a severe case of hypertension that was not being helped by the beer he was drinking.

"Simple curiosity, I guess," Dan answered. "This is my first time up north. I came up by boat and then rented a Jeep so I could see the area."

"You're kind of off the beaten track, aren't you?" The man seemed naturally outgoing, but Dan got the feeling that perhaps there was more than idle curiosity in his question. Given the circumstances it would be impossible for any of these men not to be suspicious of strangers.

"Guess you could say that," Dan answered. "But I like getting out of town and exploring. I'm not what you would call a city kind of guy." He sipped his beer. "Of course, if I'd heard about the murders I might not have been so adventurous. Marjorie here was saying there have been several?"

"Five." Kent McGilvery was easily the youngest of the three. Marjorie had said he was managing environmental assessment teams for the company that owned the pickup parked outside, and he looked the part: wiry and bearded, with faded blue jeans, canvas jacket and heavy-duty hiking boots.

"Six." The third and last of the men joined the conversation.

"Six?" The others turned to stare at Ridley MacPherson, media relations manager for one of the major pipeline players.

"Yeah. They found that journalist that went missing."

"Jesus!" The single word hovered over the table like a dark cloud. "They got any suspects yet?"

"Nothing definite, but they're looking at a Native guy. Haida."

"Haida?" Kent McGilvery frowned as he considered the possibility. "I think the only Native folk I've run across around here have been Nisga'a—which makes sense because this is their territory—and maybe a few Tsimshian and Tlingit, and I think some of them are okay with everything, at least officially. We've managed to sign a few contracts with them."

"Yes," answered MacPherson. "But Haida makes sense too. A lot of them live around here, they're all fanatically opposed to the pipeline, and they don't hesitate to let everyone know they'll fight it any way they can." His voice was heavy with resentment.

"Well, fighting it is one thing, but six murders? Seems like a pretty extreme way of making a statement." Bill Caversham pushed himself away from the table, gathered up the empty beer bottles, and made his way behind the bar. "Anyone need another one? Dan? Marjorie?"

Both Dan and Marjorie shook their heads.

"No thanks," said Dan. "I'd better not. I've got to drive back into town, and I think I had better have all my wits about me on that road."

"You're welcome to stay here," said Caversham, continuing the conversation as he returned to the table with three fresh bottles. "God knows there's plenty of room. We gave the crews a week off and sent them all into Rupert for some R & R. Better to let them blow off some steam than have them all quit on us—or worse still, have another murder." He looked at MacPherson. "Sure hope this Haida guy is the one. We're losing a helluva lot of money and time with this."

"They say he looks good," MacPherson replied. "He's got a canoe and he's got one of those Haida paddles. The cops sent it to forensics, and it came back as yew." He turned to Dan. "They found a piece of yew wood in the wounds of one of the victims, and it had been shaped like in a paddle. In the old days, the Haida used to use them to cut the heads off their enemies."

"Yeah? That's pretty gruesome, but it certainly sounds like they might be getting close," Dan said. "What's with the canoe, though?"

It was Caversham who answered. "That's Ridley's theory as to how the killer gets in and out, and he might be right. Some of the victims were out there as part of a team, but none of the other team members saw a vehicle. You drove in on one of the roads, so you know how narrow they are and how open the forest is. Pretty hard to hide a vehicle anywhere out there." He looked at MacPherson. "But you said you didn't see a canoe on any of your trips in either, so maybe you're wrong."

"Pretty easy to hide a canoe," MacPherson replied. "And you can hear me coming from a long way away. That baby of mine can make thirty—forty knots easy, and she's not quiet about it. Besides, I come straight up Observatory and into Alice Arm. I don't go into any of the little creeks and I'm not on the water that long. Pretty unlikely I would see a small boat like that."

Caversham laughed and turned to Dan. "Ridley here's got a big Bertram that's his pride and joy. You probably saw it down at the wharf when you came in. My boat's down there too, but it's not nearly as grand. The old Chris-Craft?"

Dan shook his head. "Didn't even know you had a wharf. I didn't get down to the water. Saw this place and thought I would come in and see what was happening."

"You should take a look around." Marjorie Wakeshaw picked up the thread. "It's quite an incredible place. We have nearly two miles of waterfront here, just teeming with fish and crab. And if you like fishing, there are eight salmon streams within a twenty-minute walk. You could even bring your boat up here if you like. There's plenty of room, even when the crews are here."

In other circumstances it could have been a sales pitch, but there was no one present to sell to, and nothing to sell. Instead, Dan figured it was simply an expression of a genuine love for all this unique place offered. Fleetingly, he considered enquiring into what it was that had brought Marjorie Wakeshaw and her husband to this remote outpost, but it would be only idle curiosity and now was not the time. He had to get back to Rupert.

"That's a pretty impressive offer," Dan said as he stood up. "I just might do that. Thanks for the invite—I really appreciate it, but right now I've got to go. My partner will be waiting for me back at the marina, and I'd like to get off that road before it gets too dark."

► NINE ◄

► A watery moon dodged between scudding clouds as Dan made his way down the dock at the Rushbrook Marina. Because of her size, *Dreamspeaker* was tied on an outside float. As he approached, Dan could see Walker's canoe bobbing gently off the stern grid beside Claire's kayak.

It was well after midnight and there was no light in the salon, but he could hear faint strains of music drifting out over the water. As he got closer he could make out the clean sound of Coltrane's saxophone. It seemed Claire and Walker were still up, and they were listening to one of his favorite pieces of music. For some reason that made him feel good.

"Keeping late hours for a white man."

The voice emanating from the dark caught him by surprise and he climbed aboard to find Walker sitting on the deck with Claire perched on the rail beside him. Dan sprawled out on a bench seat across from them. "Keeping late hours for any man. I'm beat. Those roads are really tough."

"Learn anything?"

Dan took his time answering. The truth was he had learned a great deal. He had learned that the old-growth forest could be both hauntingly beautiful and yet desolate at the same time. That the waters of remote northern inlets and fjords shone with a depth and intensity that he had thought reserved for rare gems. That the land was fed by a thousand, perhaps a hundred thousand creeks and rivers, all of them home to a multitude of fish and animals and birds. That ghost towns not only existed but could come to life again. And that the killer had to be intimately familiar with the area.

But that wasn't what Walker was asking.

"No, not really, but I think I've figured out one of the reasons they're looking at Joel."

"That's not too hard. He's Indian. They don't need much more than that."

"Walker, give it a rest. That's not what I meant, and I'm too tired for this shit right now."

Walker fell silent, and the three of them sat and listened to the music, letting themselves be carried along into the night on the serene melancholy of "Blue and Green" by Miles Davis. As the last note fell, Dan heard Claire get up and move into the salon. Minutes later she returned and a bottle of beer was pressed into his hand.

"Thanks," he said, smiling up at her.

"So what was it you figured out?" Walker decided to rejoin the conversation.

"I figured out that the killer had to have traveled by water. All the sites are right beside creeks or rivers, and there's no way to hide a vehicle anywhere nearby. That's why the police are looking at Joel."

"Lots of people can travel by water," Walker pointed out. "There are over two hundred boats in this marina alone."

"He's got a canoe, and that means he can get up those small creeks and waterways that drain into the inlet. Add that to the fact that he's already known for his opposition to the pipelines. And then there's the yew-wood thing, although I've got to admit I don't understand why they think a paddle can take someone's head off."

"It's what the Haida were known for." Walker's tone had become subdued, resigned. "You ever see a picture of a Haida longhouse? They built them with real small entrance holes, placed down low. Anyone coming in had to stoop down—hell, it would have been more than just stooping down. Those doorways were so low you would almost have to bend yourself in half to get into them, which means that your head went in first, and if they didn't like you, there'd be a Haida warrior standing inside with a club or a paddle ready to make sure you didn't make it."

"So they'd hit you on the head as you came in?" Dan asked.

"Not exactly," Walker drawled. "Remember I told you that yew was a hard wood? It's so hard it can take an edge, and the Haida would sharpen those yew paddles so they had an edge as sharp as a knife. They say they could take your head right off."

▶ Sunrise found Dan awake again and staring at a pile of emails and faxes he had just downloaded from the computer. The forensic report on Joel's paddle was one of them. The paddle was definitely made of yew, and it had the same kind of paint as the paint traces on the sliver found in the fifth victim's wound. It also had several gouges and nicks and was missing some splinters, although none could be matched exactly to the one found. Once he had read the report, Dan knew what most of the other messages would say. They would ask him to find Joel.

Moving cautiously so as not to wake Claire, Dan crept back through the salon to the aft deck. Walker was lying on one of the bench seats.

"They send you the results on the paddle yet?"

"Yeah, they did."

"And?"

"It's yew, and the paint's the same."

Walker stared silently up into the swelling light of early dawn. "So I guess they're really looking for Joel now," he said finally, as he glanced at the stack of papers Dan was carrying.

"Yep."

"They tell you to bring him in?"

"No. They won't do that. It would totally blow my cover. They just want me to tell them where he is so they can go get him."

"And are you going to?"

"I can't. I don't know where he is. Do you?"

"I know where he was yesterday. He won't be there now."

"Did you tell him he should talk to me?"

Walker looked at him then turned to stare out over the dark water. "Yeah, I told him. I even said you were my friend." He turned back and fixed his eyes on Dan's face. "You want to hear what he said?"

"Sure."

"He said, 'But is he mine?'"

"And?"

"And I didn't know how to answer him. Are you?"

"That kinda depends on whether he's murdered six people or not."

"I already told you he didn't."

Dan sighed. "Walker, I know you believe that, but I'm a cop. I can't just accept your word that your friend didn't do something. I have to check it out."

"How are you going to do that? He's just one guy out there in a canoe. He's not going to be able to come up with an alibi."

And that was exactly the problem that Dan had been wrestling with for the last few days as he visited each scene. No matter who had ended those lives, they had taken great care to make sure there were no witnesses, not even the other people who were out there with the victim, and that had to have taken both stealth and planning. There had been no vehicle, no evidence left at the scene. Nothing except the salt water in the wounds and that single sliver of yew, both things circumstantial and both pointing subtly but directly at Joel.

"I don't know how I'm going to do that. But what I do know is that he needs to talk to me. If he keeps running away it's just going to look worse and worse, and he can't hide forever."

Walker nodded. "I know. And that's exactly what I told him. He doesn't like the idea, but he said he would think about it. But you would have to go to him. There's no way he'll come here."

"That's fine. I don't have any problem with that, but where would I have to go?"

"Haida Gwaii. He's gone home."

▶ TEN ◀

▶ Emily Caruthers snipped the last threads from the loom, carried the finished piece over to the table and laid it out. It was good work. The edges were straight, the interlocking threads of warp and weft smooth and tight, the colors rich, the varied textures leading the eye as they curved and swirled within the pattern. Here, a river flowed, green and peaceful, past a grassy bank. There, the glint of rapids over smooth rocks. A glimpse of speckled fish deep within a pool. The eye of Raven, glittering from within a stand of cedar.

He shouldn't have been there, of course. She shouldn't have let him come out, but perhaps it didn't matter. The pieces she wove were for the tourists who arrived here every summer. They bought her work from the local galleries and gift stores, leaving behind the money that allowed her to survive the long, dark days of winter. They would surely never notice that quick, bright eye as it peered out at them. A Haida might, though, and that could cause all kinds of trouble—trouble that she did not want.

She glanced quickly at the door she kept closed and locked. They were getting stronger. She could hear them muttering in the daytime now. Their calls were louder, their screams more shrill, their laughter more raucous, their demands more insistent. She didn't know if she could keep them in much longer, but she feared what would happen if they broke out. They didn't belong to her. She had no right to them, and yet they seemed to need her.

She rolled up the new piece and carried it across to the sink, carefully avoiding passing too close to the locked door. She had been here almost five years and knew she could never leave. She had known it was her home the instant she had arrived, driven by loss and grief, and some unknown yearning for a place she had only read about. She spent a week wandering the streets of Old Massett, staring at the soaring house poles that should have looked alien, but instead were only familiar. She roamed the windswept beaches of Naikoon Park, hearing the faint whisper of ancient voices in the swaying branches of the trees. She explored the lazy, green river at Tlell, lost herself in the mystery and history of Sea Lion Village at Skidegate, visited the stores and coffee shops of Queen Charlotte City—and then the house had found her.

She hadn't been looking for it. She had simply felt its presence behind her as she sat on a piece of driftwood among the tall sea grass at the edge of the inlet. She had turned, and a flash of sunlight from an open window had called her in. The door had been open, and as she neared, an old man appeared.

"You've come to look at the house."

It was a statement, not a question, and she found herself nodding.

"Yes," she said as she stepped inside.

▶ The house was perfect of course: small and cozy, with a brick fireplace and wood floors polished by years of footsteps and love. There was no garden, just a narrow, stone path that led from the front door down through the sea grass to the beach, and both the kitchen and living room windows faced toward the ocean beyond. There was even a light-filled studio, its wide windows looking out through the trees to the curve of the inlet. The walls of the studio were covered with sketches, and two benches held an array of carved masks. The air was full of the pungent smell of cedar, mixed with turpentine and paint. An unfinished painting sat on an easel in the center of the room and she walked over to look at it. It showed a raven looking down from a spruce tree to the shore below, and she thought she had never seen a painting that seemed so vivid and lifelike.

"Is this yours?" she asked the old man, who was still standing in the doorway.

He shrugged. "They say it is," he answered. "But I'm never sure."

She smiled. "I know what you mean. I'm a weaver. Sometimes I don't have any idea where the patterns come from."

They looked at the rest of the house together, and then returned to the kitchen.

"You like it," he said.

"I love it," she replied as she looked wistfully at the tiled counters and the bright crockery stacked on the shelves. "But I don't have enough money to buy it. My husband was sick for a long time. I don't have much left now."

They walked back toward the door and she stepped out and turned to him. "I'm sorry. It would be perfect."

He nodded. "You have enough. Go and see Margaret tomorrow. She will help you."

She frowned. "Margaret?"

"My granddaughter. She's a real estate agent. She has an office in town." He nodded in the direction of Queen Charlotte City.

"Oh," she said, looking out over the swaying grass to the water lapping on the beach. "Well, I don't want to waste her time, but thank you anyway."

She turned to offer her hand, but the door had closed.

▶ But she did go and see Margaret. She hadn't planned to do that either, but the next day the office seemed to appear right in front of her, with a large sign she hadn't noticed on any of her previous ramblings through the little village. Chiding herself for her stupidity, she pushed open the door. A slim woman with long, lustrous black hair caught with an ornate barrette rose from the single desk and came to greet her.

"Welcome," she said. "My name is Margaret. What can I help you with?"

Emily smiled and shook her head. "I'm sorry. I really shouldn't be bothering you, but I saw this house yesterday, and the owner suggested

I come and talk to you." She shrugged. "I know I can't afford to buy it, but perhaps I could rent?"

"Perhaps." Margaret sounded doubtful. "Although not many people rent here on the islands. Where was the house?"

Emily pointed toward the west. "Past the town. Maybe a mile down that trail that follows the beach. It's the only house along there."

Margaret was looking at her intently, her expression cautious. "You said you spoke with the owner?"

"Yes. He was such a nice man—and his paintings and carvings are amazing. He showed me through the house, and of course it would be perfect, but I'm afraid I don't have much money."

Margaret stared at her, then got up and went to the door. "Would you mind waiting here for a couple of minutes? I need to go next door and speak to someone. I'll be right back."

A few minutes later she returned, accompanied by a tall man with short, gray hair.

"You are interested in Chinaay's house?" he said.

"Well, yes, if that's the owner's name," Emily stammered. "But as I told Margaret, I can't afford to buy it, only to rent."

The man ignored her statement. "You liked his paintings?"

She smiled. "Oh yes! All of them are wonderful, but the one he is working on is magnificent."

He bent his head to stare at her with piercing eyes. "Which painting was that?" he asked.

She frowned as she heard the question. "I don't know if it had a name," she answered. "But it was a raven. Its eye was so bright it looked alive, and it was sitting in a spruce tree, looking out over the grass to the inlet."

The man inhaled a deep breath, straightened up and glanced across at Margaret before moving deeper into the office and opening a door.

"Did it look like this?" he asked, nodding his head toward something Emily could not see.

She glanced at Margaret too, perhaps hoping for some kind of reassurance, then moved slowly across the room to join him. Her eyes followed his gaze to the wall beyond, and her breath froze in her throat. The painting that hung on the wall was unmistakably the same painting she had seen in the house, but now it was finished, every detail of the shore perfect, every rock and blade of grass shaded and outlined, every ripple of water caught with light, and the raven glossy and so vibrant with life it appeared ready to fly off the canvas.

"That's it!" she exclaimed. "That's the painting!" Her voice faltered. "But he couldn't have finished it overnight. Was he making a copy?"

The man stared at her a few moments, then he seemed to make a decision and his face relaxed.

"No," he said. "There are no copies. That's the original. My grandfather took almost a year to create it, and he died the day after it was framed."

She stared at him. "But I don't understand! He's not dead. I talked to him yesterday, and it wasn't finished." She looked at Margaret again, a pleading look on her face as she searched for an answer. "It must have been someone else I spoke with, someone who is trying to make a copy."

Margaret reached down and picked up a framed photograph from her desk. She looked at it for a second, and then held it out. "Is this him?" she asked. "Is this who you spoke with?"

Emily took the photo with trembling hands. The face that looked out at her was the face she had seen the day before.

▶ Everything moved swiftly after that. Margaret insisted that Emily revisit the house, and warned her that it would not look the same. She had been both right and wrong. It looked a little older, felt less alive. The counters were bare, there were no logs in the fireplace and the studio was empty, the carvings and paintings all gone, but as she trailed her fingers along the stained wooden surfaces Emily felt a subtle shift in the air. The house was coming alive around her. It was welcoming her. As she walked past the open door, she heard a raven call.

She and Margaret returned to the office to discuss the price. It was lower than Emily had believed possible and although it still took almost everything she had in the bank, she didn't hesitate. She moved in a week later. Raven and his friends were already there.

► She soaked the woven piece in water, moving it back and forth to wet the strands and fix the interlocking threads. As she carried the dripping fabric out to the line she had strung between the trees, she passed the door she always kept locked. The voices paused as she passed, then called to her as they always did, murmuring her name, but this time their tone had changed. They were softer, cajoling perhaps. Or pleading. It was time. She reached out her hand and turned the key.

ELEVEN

► A storm was building somewhere in the west. Out toward the horizon, thick, gray cumulus clouds were massing, and the air was laced with a fine mist as Dan stepped out on deck to watch Walker clamber into his canoe. They had agreed to meet at the marina in Queen Charlotte City later in the week, although how Walker was going to cross the hundred or so miles over the treacherous waters of Hecate Strait Dan didn't know. He didn't know how Walker would find Joel again either, but he had no doubt that the man would do so. Walker always found a way to do what he said he would do, although he seldom shared his methods.

Over coffee, Dan read and reread the emails detailing the interviews and research conducted by the Prince Rupert detachment. It was obvious that Joel was their only suspect. Other than soliciting input as to routes and schedules from company management—including people whose names Dan recognized, like Bill Caversham and Ridley MacPherson—and taking statements from the other workers who had been out there when the murders took place, the only serious questioning had been with Joel, and that had resulted in almost nothing except an acknowledgment by the young Haida that he owned both a canoe and a paddle. The detectives had spoken with Charles Eden twice, once at his house and once on his boat when it was tied up at a marina in Cow Bay, and both times Charles had told them—truthfully, Dan thought—that he had no idea where Joel was, and rarely saw him.

Dan leaned back from the table and rubbed his eyes. There was nothing there he could get a hold on. Nothing that even pointed him in a specific direction, although he could see why the Prince Rupert guys had latched onto Joel: he had all the necessary attributes. Being in the area and spending all his time in a canoe gave him opportunity, his stated opposition to the pipelines gave him a motive, and the paddle gave him a weapon. Of the three, the painted yew paddle provided the strongest evidence, although it was still circumstantial. Forensics had found no trace of blood—not surprising if it had been immersed in saltwater for an extended period of time after the crime—and that made the link tenuous. So while there was certainly not enough evidence for charges to be laid, there were enough pointers to ensure that Joel would remain the focus of the investigation.

But over the last couple of days Dan had come up with several questions of his own that were still unanswered, and the one that he was most troubled by was the paddle itself. Was it really sharp enough to completely sever a human neck? It seemed unlikely, even impossible, that a wooden paddle was capable of doing that, in spite of Walker's description of the old Haida custom of defending their longhouses. He pushed his empty coffee cup aside, stood up, and headed to the wheelhouse. Sitting in front of a computer was not his favorite activity, but at times like this he was very glad he had one, and that it was connected to the Internet.

▶ The clatter of dishes and the smell of frying bacon pulled him back to the galley.

"Good morning." Claire was breaking an egg into the frying pan. "I wasn't sure if you had already eaten, but I can add a couple for you if you like."

"That would be great," Dan answered. "I could do with some breakfast now I think about it. I'll make us some toast."

They ate in companionable silence, watching the local news on the television screen mounted high on the salon wall. The big news of the day was the protest rally against the pipelines that several environmental groups had scheduled for noon down at the waterfront park. Police were expecting a large crowd and were blocking off several roads.

"Are you going to go?" Claire asked.

Dan nodded "Yes. I can't pass up an opportunity like that. It will give me a chance to see who the local opponents are without letting them know I'm around."

"Is it okay if I come?"

"You want to go to a protest?" He stared at her in surprise.

"Sure. Why not? I've never been to one before, and this is something I'm really interested in."

Dan shrugged. "I don't see any reason why you can't. You won't be in any danger there, and it would be nice to have you along." He looked at her quizzically. "We've never talked about it, but how do you feel about the pipelines?"

Claire smiled. "I'm with Joel," she answered. "How about you?"

▶   They arrived early to find the park already jammed with people, and more pouring in every minute. It had the feel of a party, and, like the protests Dan had attended back when he had served as a constable in the city, it reminded him of photos he had seen of Woodstock. Groups of young men and women, many wearing tattered jeans and tie-dyed shirts, wandered aimlessly through the crowd, some sporting lip- or nose-rings along with their tattoos. Others gathered around a pair of musicians, one of whom was strumming a guitar while his partner kept time with gourd rattles tied to her ankles. Over by the stage, which had been set up as close to the water as possible, a group of Native dancers and drummers were performing a round dance, their hand drums beating out their own powerful rhythm. Surrounding them, wearing earth-colored T-shirts with environmental emblems and brandishing placards, were the serious protesters. Further back, the politicians and business people hovered. Dan and Claire joined them.

"Come to join the circus?" A loud voice in his ear startled Dan, and he turned to find Ridley MacPherson standing behind him. "You would think the lunatic fringe would find some better way to entertain themselves," MacPherson continued in a disparaging tone, inclining his head toward a trio of young women who were dancing barefoot on the grass.

"Ah, they look pretty harmless." Dan smiled as he introduced Claire. "We just dropped by to see what was happening."

"They may look harmless to you," MacPherson snarled. "But they're a damn nuisance to those of us who are trying to make a decent living up here." He glared at the round dancers, many of whom were wearing their red and black button blankets and cedar hats. "Murdering bastards."

He heard Claire's sudden intake of breath and turned to her with an apologetic smile. "I'm sorry. I shouldn't be venting my frustration on you. You've heard about the murders, of course? I was telling Dan about them when he visited us up in Kitsault."

Claire nodded. "Yes, he told me. It's really terrible. Were those people working for you?"

MacPherson nodded. "Some of them were. Good people too." His voice changed again. "I just hope the police can nail that little bastard. Might teach the rest of them a lesson."

"They know who it is?"

Dan had been listening carefully to the conversation, ready to jump in if it veered in a direction that might reveal what he was really doing there, but he was impressed with the way Claire injected just the right amount of innocuous interest into her question. She might have made an excellent detective.

"They know," MacPherson had total conviction in his voice. "They just can't prove it yet. I sure hope they figure it out before he kills someone else."

A loud cheer interrupted their conversation, and they turned to see five people mounting the stage. Three were Native men wearing their full ceremonial regalia, while the other two were white, the logos and lettering on their clothing clearly marking them as environmentalists. It was one of the environmentalists who took the microphone, but screams and shouts of "No pipelines" drowned out whatever he was saying.

Dan leaned down and spoke into Claire's ear. "How about we wander through the crowd. See who's here."

She nodded her agreement and he turned to MacPherson. "We're going to head out. I think we've seen and heard enough."

"You're right," MacPherson had to shout to be heard. "Same old, same old. Wish I could leave, but this kind of shit comes with the job." He looked at Claire and smiled again. "You and Dan should come over to Cow Bay later. I've got a boat over there." He handed her a business card. "If you can't make it today, have Dan give me a call. I'm usually there in the evenings." He clapped Dan on the shoulder and disappeared into the crowd.

Dan and Claire wandered though the throng of people, all of whom now seemed focused on the words being said by the speakers standing in front of them. The round dancers had moved to a position just below the stage, and their singing and drumming punctuated each pronouncement. They were accompanied by a waving sea of placards.

"See anyone interesting?" Claire leaned into Dan's side as she spoke.

"Nope. No one that stands out anyway, but there are a lot of cops wandering 'round, so I may learn more when I get the reports." He looked toward the back of the crowd and nodded his head. "They've got a couple of them taking photos too, so if there's anyone they're suspicious of here, or who has a record, I'll be able to match the name with a face."

Claire followed his gaze. "How on earth do you know they're cops? I can't see anyone in uniform."

He laughed. "You would have to ask the crooks that question. They can recognize a cop half a mile away. I just know they're here, and I know they planned on filming the whole thing. It was in one of the reports they sent." He looked around again. "I hope I've lost whatever it is the crooks look for!"

Claire laughed, and started to speak, but was distracted from whatever she was going to say by the sudden pall of silence that fell over the crowd. They both turned to face the stage, where the group of speakers stood as if transfixed, staring at one of the Native men who was now covered with what looked like red paint. Or blood.

"Murderers!"

It was impossible to tell exactly where the voice came from, but heads were turning toward a small group directly in front of the stage. A figure darted forward and threw some kind of container. More red liquid arched up to splatter on yet another Native speaker.

A murmur raced through the crowd, and within seconds, it swelled into an angry roar. Bodies pushed against Dan as people surged toward the disturbance, and he pulled Claire to his side, holding her tightly against him as he forced his way toward the road.

"We need to get out of here. All hell's about to break lose."

They broke free from the crush, but Dan kept them moving until they were completely out of the park and across the parking lot, and then he stopped and turned back to look at the scene behind them. The five speakers were being escorted from the stage by three uniformed police officers assisted by two other men Dan assumed were plainclothes RCMP. They in turn were being guided by some of the Native dancers. Below them, people were pushing and shoving each other and at least two fights had broken out, while over to one side a scuffle between a television media crew and a group of perhaps six or seven T-shirt-clad young people looked like it was about to become nasty. The shouts and screams could be heard even over the noise of slamming car doors and revving engines as those who wanted no part in what was quickly becoming a riot rushed to leave.

"My God! This is insane!" Claire was still clinging to Dan, her arm wrapped around his waist. "I don't understand. What on earth happened?"

"It was planned," Dan answered, his voice grim. "Someone wanted to start a riot, and whoever it was knew the police were looking at a Haida, or at least at a Native. The whole thing was staged, right down to the paint or whatever it was they threw." He looked down at Claire. "Let's go back to the boat. We can see what happened later. I'm sure it will be all over the news."

She nodded, still shaken by the speed with which the mood had turned from carefree innocence to violence, and started toward the Jeep, only to jump back as a bright red Porsche Cayenne roared past on its way out of the lot.

"Did you see that?" She exclaimed. "I think that was the man you introduced me to. I don't think he even saw me, he was laughing so hard. I don't know why he should be so darn happy considering what's happening here."

▶ TWELVE ◀

▶ The bank of seagrass ran along the edge of the shore, stretching along the inlet as far as he could see and reaching back almost seventy feet to where the path from the old house stepped down. The slender green stalks arched and billowed, lifting with the breeze, catching the light like a school of moon-silvered fish. Joel sat quietly, surrounded by the whispering blades of grass, letting the day grow around him. The early morning air was soft, almost weightless on his skin, and the pale sky was streaked with high cloud. An otter brought her family of two kits down to the edge of the ocean, chittered briefly at him, and then scampered over his feet. Joel smiled. He was home.

A raven landed in a tree branch above his head, talking loudly in his harsh voice. A few years ago, Joel would have accepted the invitation it was offering to him to go up to the house and spend time with Chinaay, but the old man had gone to join the ancestors many moons past. Now there was someone new living there, someone Joel didn't know. Raven called again, and Joel peered through the grass. A woman was coming down the steps toward the beach, a white woman, and Raven was calling to her too. Joel had never known Raven to call to a white woman before.

The woman stepped down onto the beach, turned, and walked toward where he sat under the arching grass.

"Hello," she said.

Joel nodded cautiously.

"Would you like to come up to the house? I was just going to make breakfast. You're welcome to join me."

The mention of breakfast made Joel aware of how hungry he was. He hadn't eaten since the fish boat he had hitched a ride on had dropped him and his canoe off at the wharf at Queen Charlotte City, and that was many hours ago. Breakfast would be good.

"Okay," he said, and followed her up the path. Raven gave a bell-like call of approval.

The house felt as it always had. Weavings had replaced the paintings and masks, and the furniture had changed, but the walls still held the same quiet, welcoming warmth and the air carried the faint smell of cedar and paint that he remembered. The spirit of Chinaay still lived here. He turned to the woman, who was putting plates out on the table.

"I'm Joel," he said solemnly.

"Hello, Joel," she answered. "I'm Emily."

He sat down and watched as she heaped scrambled eggs and bacon onto his plate, then added some toast. They ate in silence, only looking up when a raven flew onto a low branch outside the window.

"The police are chasing me," Joel said as he ate the last of the toast. "I should go."

Emily nodded. "If you must, but you're welcome to come back any time."

Joel looked at her. "Will you tell them I was here?"

She shook her head. "No."

He looked out the window to where Raven was waiting. When he turned back his eyes were brimming with tears. "They stole my paddle."

Emily looked at him for a moment and then she stood up and beckoned him to follow her into the studio. The air inside was still and quiet, yet it seemed to hold within its silence the echo of many voices talking at once, laughing, even singing. The walls were empty except for a tapestry where Chinaay's painting of Raven had once been, and two woven panels, one of which evoked the cedar forest behind the house and the other the seagrass and ocean out in front of it. Raven was in both of them. Joel turned to look for Emily and found her over in the corner, between the two big windows. She was holding a paddle. It had an eagle feather tied to it with a leather thong.

"I think Chinaay left this for you," she said as she held it out toward him.

He reached forward, took it into his hands and sank down to the floor. Gently he stroked the feather, ran his fingers up and down the smooth wood of the paddle and traced the figures painted on it. There was Eagle, the master of the skies, the one who bestows truth and strength. Here was Raven, the Transformer, the Trickster, his strong bill holding Frog, the spirit helper, liaison between the land, the water and the spirit world of the deep forest, the one who sings the song that brings the rain to replenish the earth. They were all part of him, as they had been part of Chinaay, and he was part of them. He was Raven moiety, his father had been of Eagle lineage, and his crest was Frog.

The sun was high in the sky when he finally stood, the paddle grasped firmly in his hand, the eagle feather tied into his braid. He could hear the rhythmic clacking of a loom out in the living room as Emily worked on her weaving, and outside the window Yaahl was still sitting on his branch on the cedar tree. The loom slowed briefly as he entered the room, then resumed its steady beat.

"I packed some food for you to take," Emily said, inclining her head to indicate a basket that sat on the counter.

"Thank you," he said. "Haaw'a."

▸ There was no sign of activity on the inlet when he pulled his canoe from its resting place in the seagrass and slid it into the water. The paddle felt perfect in his hand, a gift from his grandfather, who had reached out from the spirit world with his blessing. An eagle feather could only be worn by someone who had earned the privilege. It was always given, never taken, and wearing it not only transmitted strength, but also gave the wearer the ability to speak honestly, from the heart. Now, with this acknowledgment of who he was, Joel knew he would finally be able to speak his truth.

His destination was Haina, where his ancestors had lived before the sickness came. No one lived there now, but Joel visited there often. He liked to wander through the remains of the old longhouses, to listen to the voices that were carried on the breeze, to share the land with otter and weasel and mink. He felt safe there. It was his home, and the ravens kept him company.

It was dusk by the time he pulled the canoe up onto the beach, hid it in a jumble of logs above the high tide line, and made his way up into the trees. Once he was deep in their shadow he was invisible to anyone out on the water or down on the shore, but the elevation was high enough that he could see out between the massive trunks. He would know if anyone was coming long before they arrived. Even at night, the curve of the bay captured and echoed sounds, providing ample warning in the unlikely event that anyone should try to approach during darkness.

The moon was close to setting in the west when the splash of oars woke him. He had made a bed out of cedar branches placed inside the rotted out trunk of a giant cedar tree, just a few feet away from the remains of an ancient longhouse beam that lay half-buried on the forest floor. A small dinghy was approaching the shore, its pale wooden hull lit by a thin ribbon of moonlight, and behind it Joel could just make out the outline of a small fish boat, a troller, its poles and lines glinting faintly as it bobbed on the waves. He smiled, but didn't move out of the shadows. His uncle had taught him well. Assumptions and guesswork were dangerous. He would wait until he was certain, until the owl called to tell him that it was safe to announce his presence. He didn't have to wait long. The dinghy scraped up onto the gravel, and the man who had been rowing it turned and gave two soft hoots. Joel went down to the beach to greet Charles Eden.

▶   "You have met this man, Uncle?" Joel asked.

The two men were sitting on a fallen log at the edge of the forest.

"Yes. He's a friend of Walker's. Walker traveled with him to Prince Rupert in order to help you."

"Walker trusts him?"

"He does."

72

Joel shook his head. "But he's with the police!"

"Yes, he's with the police, but he's different. He lives on his boat. He doesn't spend time with the ones who questioned you."

Joel looked down at the paddle he held in his hands. "If he comes here, will he want to take this paddle? I cannot give him this. It was a gift from Chinaay."

Charles Eden stared at the dark shape that Joel was holding. He had heard the story of Joel's visit to his grandfather's house earlier, when he had first arrived, and of the paddle and the eagle feather the woman had given him, and while he did not doubt Joel's sincerity for a moment, he also knew that the police—and perhaps Dan—would not believe it.

"There have been more murders since the police questioned you and took your paddle. It may be that they will want to check this one too." He had never been less than truthful with Joel and he was not about to start now.

They sat in silence as the sky slowly lightened and the stars winked out. Finally, Joel took a deep breath and stood up. "I can do this," he said, his voice stronger than Eden had ever heard it. "Chinaay gave me the eagle feather to tell me he knows I am strong enough to do whatever is needed. I will talk to this policeman—but he must come with Walker, and I will not let him take Chinaay's paddle. It is sacred." He looked at his uncle and nodded, and then sat down beside him again. "When will he come?"

"I don't know for sure. Perhaps in two days. Maybe three. He will have to bring his boat over to Queen Charlotte City and then he and Walker will have to paddle over here, but I think he is under pressure to talk to you soon."

Joel nodded. "It would be better if he came soon. I think there's another storm coming. The birds are restless."

Eden smiled. Joel read the weather better than any meteorologist he had ever listened to. If he said there was a storm coming, then it would come.

"Will you be all right here?" he asked the young man, knowing that Joel would be fine, but needing reassurance anyway.

73

"Sure." Joel looked surprised at the question. "Emily gave me some food, and there is the ocean and the island." He swept his hand out in a semicircle that encompassed everything in front of him. "The ancestors will look after me."

"Emily?" Eden asked.

Joel nodded. "The lady who lives in Chinaay's house."

Eden nodded and made a mental note to visit this Emily when he got back. Perhaps she could give him a clearer explanation of how Joel got the paddle and the eagle feather, but in any case it would be good to see the house again.

▶ THIRTEEN ◀

▶ Dan watched the video the Prince Rupert detachment had made during the protest for perhaps the fifth time, stopping it occasionally to fix a face in his mind, replaying the section just before the riot started, tracking MacPherson and Caversham, who were both present, although apparently not together, and even identifying Kent McGilvery as one of the crowd of onlookers. Mike had also sent him a stack of still photos taken at the event, presumably by a plainclothes cop wandering freely through the park with a hidden camera. The photos identified each of the speakers up on the stage, as well as known environmentalists and activists who had been present in the crowd. They also showed local troublemakers who had a reputation for causing or participating in disturbances. There were a lot of them, but as far as Dan could see, none of them had been involved in this particular fiasco.

He ran the video yet another time, this time carefully tracking MacPherson's movements. He was still angry at how close Claire had come to being hit by the man's car, and he was bothered by the fact that he had been laughing. It could have been nothing of course—a joke he had heard, a phone call from a friend—but still, it was odd timing.

"You fancy following up on that invitation?" he asked Claire, who was idly flipping through a book.

"From that MacPherson guy?" she asked. "I'd certainly like to give him some advice on his driving habits!"

Dan grinned. "So would I, but maybe we had better let that rest this time. It would bring out the cop in me, and I would rather he continue to think I'm just a tourist."

"Why do you want to visit him?" she asked. "He doesn't seem like the most interesting guy to talk to—and he sounds so angry."

"Yes, he does, and that's part of why I want to talk with him. He also works for one of the pipeline companies, and he's got a boat that he uses to go back and forth between Rupert and Kitsault. Not only that, but he's got some kind of inside track into what's happening in the investigation that bothers me a little. He seems to know a lot about it. I think it might be worth spending a little time with him."

"Couldn't you go without me?"

"I guess I could, but I think it would be better if you come with me. It was you he offered the invitation to, and it might look a little odd if I showed up without you."

She raised her eyebrows, dropped her chin, and put on her best Marlene Dietrich voice. "Ah, *mein lieber,*" she drawled. "So you vant to use me as your decoy?"

"Something like that," he laughed. "But please, please, don't talk like that when we get there. That has to be the worst German accent I've ever heard!"

Claire threw a cushion at him.

▶ It was a couple of hours later when they made their way to Cow Bay—the cushion throwing had evolved into some more vigorous calisthenics that had required the use of the master suite and then the shower—and Dan wasn't sure if MacPherson would still be there, but he figured he could at least get a look at the Bertram the man was so proud of.

Cow Bay was only a short distance southwest of their moorage in Rushbrook Marina, an easy ten-minute drive back toward the center of town. Set in a tiny indentation in the shoreline shown as Cameron Cove on the charts, Cow Bay had earned its name back in the early 1900s when cows were made to swim ashore to reach a dairy. The dairy didn't last long, but the name stuck and now the area had become a trendy shopping district with art galleries, restaurants and coffee shops. It was easy to see why MacPherson had chosen the place to keep his boat.

"Want a coffee?" Claire asked as they drove past a coffee shop with a sign saying "Cowpuccino's." "That place looks good."

"Yes, but let's save it till later," Dan answered. "I would rather get this visit over and done with first."

They found Bill Caversham before they found Ridley MacPherson. Caversham was sitting on the stern of an old Chris-Craft that had seen better days. He had a beer in his hand.

"Dan!" he shouted as they walked along a float. "Over here! Can I get you a beer?"

Dan winked at Claire and led her over. "Hi, Bill. Actually we're looking for Ridley. We saw him up at that protest this morning and he invited us over."

"He's just run into town for something. Should be back in a few minutes. Come on aboard. You can wait for him here."

It was an invitation they couldn't refuse without being churlish, and Dan helped Claire climb onto the small deck.

"Quite the show this morning, wasn't it?" Caversham said as he handed them both a beer. "Thought it was really going to get out of hand for a while, but the police did a good job getting it under control."

Dan nodded. "Seemed like it might have been a put-up job," he said.

Caversham nodded. "Could be. Could be. There are a lot of people pretty upset about these murders—hell, we all are. There are a lot of jobs on the line. Wouldn't take much to get something like that going, not with the town full of pipeline people and those environmentalists and their Native friends spouting off about all the disasters waiting to happen if the pipeline goes ahead."

"Yeah, I guess you're right." Dan sipped his beer. "Ridley was certainly pretty upset with them."

"Ridley hates them. Makes no bones about it either." Caversham laughed. "He's always bitching about them. Calls every Native he sees a 'murdering savage' and says they're costing both us and the government millions of dollars. He thinks the whole lot of them—Natives and environmentalists—should be thrown in jail." He stood up and headed toward the cabin. "Gotta use the head. You guys want another beer while I'm in there?"

Dan and Claire both shook their heads.

"Back in a second." He bent his head to clear the low door lintel, and then straightened up again. "Hey, there's McGilvery. Kent! Come on over here."

Dan followed his gaze and saw Kent McGilvery slide a kayak up to an old motor cruiser tied to the other side of the float.

"McGilvery has a boat here too?" he asked Caversham.

"Sure. A bunch of us do. It's the easiest way to get up to Kitsault. Kent lives aboard his. He keeps it tied up at the dock and drives his truck in, but most of the rest of us have places in town; we just use our boats for fishing and to run up there when we need to."

Dan watched as Kent McGilvery climbed out his kayak and made his way over toward them.

"So how do you get around once you get to Kitsault? Or do you just have the crews come back in when you need them?"

"Hell no. They'd never get any work done that way. There's a bunch of vehicles we keep up there for use by anyone who needs one. There's always some around."

"Huh. I only saw a couple at the pub when I was up there," Dan said. "I guess I just assumed all you guys drove in and out."

"No. That road's too damn rough and it takes too long. We had already sent all the guys into town when you were up there, remember? That's why you didn't see all the transportation. It should all be back out there again in a couple of days—assuming the cops find that guy they're looking for anyway."

Caversham disappeared into the cabin, and McGilvery arrived to take his place.

"Hi, Dan. Good to see you again." He shook Dan's hand and introduced himself to Claire. "I met Dan up in Kitsault when he was there."

Claire nodded. "He told me about it. Sounds like quite the place."

"It is. You guys should take your boat up there. Not many people get the chance to see it. It's really beautiful."

"I saw you coming in with a kayak just now. Do you take it up there with you when you go?" Claire asked. "I have one on board our boat. I love using it to explore the places we visit."

"So do I," McGilvery answered. "But I don't take that one up there with me. I drive in and out so I leave it here. Marjorie and Jim—they're the folks that run Kitsault—have a couple of Kevlar kayaks they brought in. They're incredibly strong and light. I would buy one myself if I could afford it, but they let me use one of theirs when I'm up there, so I guess that's the next best thing to owning my own."

"Didn't Ridley say you guys figured the murderer must have used a kayak or a canoe or something?" Dan asked. "Seems like kayaking by yourself in that area might be a pretty risky proposition."

McGilvery shook his head. "That's Ridley's theory, not mine. How could you get a kayak or canoe up there? Marjorie and Jim brought the ones they have there in by car. It's too far to paddle from Rupert, and there's nowhere to camp up there except Kitsault because the shoreline is so steep, so we would know if there was anyone there who shouldn't be—and there hasn't been anybody."

"Could bring it up on a power boat," Dan said. "Launch it from that and then load it back on afterward."

"Yeah, could be done I guess, but the power boat would have to come up Observatory Inlet and then Alice Arm. There's a lot of traffic going up and down there, including Ridley and Bill, and no one's seen anything like that. Anyway, I don't go up those little creeks too much. I mostly just go out for an hour or so after I finish work. Ridley and Jim probably both go out more than I do. Jim even has an inflatable kayak he takes out with him when he goes hunting."

"So did McGilvery convince you to take your boat up to Kitsault?" Bill Caversham re-emerged from the cabin with another beer. "We figure he's angling to become the Kitsault tourism promoter once this pipeline's built."

Dan shook his head. "It's tempting, but we've got a trip over to Haida Gwaii planned. There are people there expecting us, so we can't put it off and I don't know if we will still have time after we get back."

"Haida Gwaii? Isn't that where the guy the cops are looking for comes from?" Caversham asked. "Better watch your step over there!"

Dan laughed. "We'll do that, but I don't think we have too much to worry about." He reached for Claire's hand. "And on that note, I think we had better get going. We have to stow the boat for an early start tomorrow. Thanks for the beer. If you're around when we get back, I'll give you a call and repay the favor on *Dreamspeaker*."

"No problem." Bill Caversham was starting to slur his words, and he made no move to stand up. "Take it easy."

Kent McGilvery stepped off the boat with them. "I'll walk up with you," he said as they started up the float. "I need to pick up some groceries."

He didn't speak again until they reached the gate at the top of the ramp, and then, as he was turning away to go to his car, he said, "Don't mind Bill. He's a good guy."

Dan nodded. "Does he always drink that heavily?"

"Not when he's on the job, but here on the boat that seems to be how he copes. We—Ridley and I and some of the other guys on the floats here—keep an eye on him. He's carrying a pretty heavy load right now. His wife left him a few months back and I guess she emptied out the bank account and maxed out the credit cards. The boat and this job is about all he's got left, and this work delay is killing him."

"Yeah, guess that's hard on all of you," Dan said, shaking his head. "Hope it's sorted out soon."

"Me too," McGilvery answered. "Well, I've gotta get moving. I'll maybe see you again if you make it up to Kitsault. Have a safe trip." He walked over to a battered pickup and climbed inside.

Dan and Claire walked the other way and followed suit, but Dan didn't start the engine. Instead, he simply sat, his hands resting on the steering wheel as he stared unseeingly out of the windscreen.

"Dan? Are you okay?"

"Huh? Oh, yeah, I'm fine. I was just thinking about the boats and kayaks and stuff. It's weird how things work. I came over here thinking that maybe Ridley having a boat might give me some way to balance out Joel's canoe, and I end up with another half-dozen boats and a bunch of kayaks that are available to anyone."

"Well, at least it means that Joel is not the only person who could get in there by water."

Dan nodded and reached for the ignition key. "Yeah, you're right. Well, what say we grab some dinner before we head back to the boat? I'm starving. How about you?"

"Oh, yes. I thought you would never ask. Let's get some fish and chips."

"Sounds good to me," Dan answered, and drove out onto the street. "You watch for a place we can get some."

Dusk had started to darken the sky by the time they got back to the boat. Walker was waiting for them, sitting on the stern grid, his legs dangling over the edge.

"Joel said he'll talk to you," was all he said.

▶ FOURTEEN ◀

▶ *Dreamspeaker* let go her lines at five o'clock the next morning. Dan let the wind and the current push her off the dock and carry her out into the channel before he engaged the engines, not wanting to disturb the other occupants of the marina. It would take the better part of the day to reach Queen Charlotte City, and there was a gale forecast to arrive late in the evening. There was no way he wanted to risk crossing the dangerous waters of Hecate Strait in anything less than calm weather, and neither did he want to enter a strange inlet in the dark. Claire and Walker both joined him in the wheelhouse, and they left the doors open to the fresh salt air and the sharp cries of the birds that wheeled above them. This was a trip they were all looking forward to, and their anticipation and excitement was contagious. None of them had been out of sight of land before, and none of them had visited Haida Gwaii, although Dan and Claire had spent a lot of time reading about it, and Walker had spent countless hours listening to Joel's descriptions and stories back in Percy's camp. But most important, at least for Dan and Walker, was the fact that Joel was there and had agreed to meet with them.

They threaded through the islands that formed the harbor at Prince Rupert, and made their way out into Chatham Sound. Ahead, through the wide gap of Brown Passage, they could see past Dixon Entrance to the open waters of the Pacific. From this distance, still within the enclosing embrace of land, it looked calm and welcoming, the surface undulating gently, the horizon a distant line separating the dark sea from a sky that carried the first faint promise of a new day. Dan hoped it would stay that way for long enough to reach their destination.

"What time do you figure we'll get there?" Walker was scanning the empty horizon.

"Maybe five or six o'clock this evening if the weather holds. I'd like to be tied up well before it gets dark. Why?" Dan asked.

"Just thinking. Charles said he figured it would take about three hours to paddle there."

"Paddle where?"

"Sunshine Island. It's called Haina on the charts. That's the Haida word for sunshine."

"And that's where Joel is?"

"Yep. At least for now."

"Why can't we go in the dinghy? It would be a hell of a lot quicker."

Walker shook his head. "Joel won't come out unless I'm there, and I need the canoe. I'm going to spend some time with him."

"So if I go with you, just how, exactly, will I get back? Or am I supposed to stay over there?" asked Dan.

Walker looked at him and grinned. "Well, you could, but I'm not sure you would like it. You would have to sleep on the ground and find your own food like us savages. No nice soft mattress and frozen pasta like you've got here."

Dan sighed. "Uh-huh. So I guess that wasn't you I saw eating my snack bars and sleeping on my settee last year at Louie Bay?" He raised his eyebrows and narrowed his eyes in mock ferocity. "But you haven't answered my question."

Walker smiled, completely unrepentant. "Charles Eden is there. He'll bring you back to the marina."

▶ The trip over took longer than Dan had thought it would. The forecast gale held off, but it was presaged by a long, rolling swell running from the southwest, and when he altered course after passing Butterworth Rocks, *Dreamspeaker* was heading directly into it. In many ways the slow climb up the face of the smooth green mounds of water, and the corresponding slide down the other side, was more comfortable than the rolling motion they had experienced earlier, but it slowed them down. Not that it mattered. From the look of it, a couple of hours were not going to make much difference, and it gave them longer to enjoy their surroundings. The air was full of birds none of them had seen before. Storm petrels and shearwaters, Parasitic jaegers, Caspian and Arctic terns, Ross's and Sabine's gulls all wheeled and dove around them. Claire and Walker tried to identify them all with the help of a field guide Dan had purchased before he left Campbell River, one of them using the binoculars and calling out identifying markings while the other studied the book. The cabin filled with their laughter as they argued back and forth about specific species, and read out descriptions.

"Tufted puffin!" Claire pointed out through the windshield at a small black bird bobbing on the surface.

"Horned puffin," Walker stated, looking up from the book. "Its beak is too fat for a tufted."

"But it's got those long, blond ear tufts," Claire protested. "And it doesn't have the black line over its eye."

"Huh. Okay, maybe you're right, but I still think that one we saw a few minutes ago was a Rhinoceros auklet."

Claire laughed. "You just want to be able to say you saw a Rhinoceros auklet because you like the name. I think it was a puffin."

"Nope. It had a yellow bill. Puffins have orange bills."

Dan interrupted the chatter. "If you two are through arguing about auklets and puffins, there's what I think might be an albatross over on this side."

"An albatross?" Claire rushed across to the other side of the wheelhouse. "You've got to be kidding. Are there actually albatross up here?"

"Looks like it," Dan replied. "It's got a wingspan nearly as wide as a 747 and I haven't seen it flap once."

"Oh my God! I think you're right!" Claire ran back and grabbed the book. "Where'd it go? I can't see it anymore."

"Over here," Walker called. "Damn. That thing's huge!"

"It's a Laysan," Claire said, holding the open book out to him. "It says here they're rare but regular up here—and now we've seen one!"

The delight in her voice made Dan smile and he turned to look at the two of them. They were both staring out the open door, Claire's hands resting on Walker's shoulders, their heads close together and moving in unison as they followed the gliding path of the massive bird. Looking at them, Dan was suddenly struck by the realization that this was the first time he had ever seen Walker allow himself to be touched. Even at Annie's, he had always remained slightly aloof, and he had never offered a handshake that Dan could recall. Dan's smile grew wider and he turned back to watch the sea ahead. It felt good to see Claire work her magic on his friend, and even better to see that friend responding.

They made their way steadily south, the eastern shore of Graham Island slowly appearing as a distant blur on the western horizon. They passed Naikoon Park and Tlell, then approached closer to land at Dead Tree Point before altering course as Skidegate Inlet opened up ahead of them. It was almost seven when they finally turned west and passed close in front of the village of Skidegate.

"That's where Joel made his paddle," Walker said as they motored slowly past a row of totem poles standing in front of a long wooden building. "He told me about it. He called it Sea-lion Town, like Charles mentioned the other night. Joel took a workshop there."

"Is it open to the public?" Claire asked. "I would love to see those poles up close."

"I'm sure it would be," Walker answered. "Joel said part of it's a museum."

"Maybe I can kayak over tomorrow. It's not that far from Queen Charlotte City and it sounds like you two will both be gone all day."

"I'll probably be gone longer than that," Walker answered. "But Dan should be back."

Dan nodded. "Yeah. I can't see it taking more than an hour or two to talk to Joel, so a couple of hours to paddle over with Walker and then a quick trip back with Charles. I should be home for dinner." He smiled at Claire. "Maybe you can find us a good restaurant."

▶ It was almost eight by the time they had tied up to a slip at the Queen Charlotte City marina and turned off the engine, and all of them were eager to stretch muscles that had seen little use all day. They offloaded the canoe and the kayak, and then parted company, Walker paddling west along the shoreline while Dan and Claire walked up the wharf into the town. The rain had not yet arrived, but the air felt damp ahead of the coming storm, and dusk was already muting the daylight as dark clouds massed overhead. Looking at them, Dan thought there was a good chance he and Walker would not be going to talk to Joel the following day. Surely a trip across Skidegate Inlet in a storm was not something even Walker would undertake, and Dan certainly had no wish to try it, even though he knew the need was urgent. There were questions that only Joel could answer, and if the detachment in Prince Rupert decided to mount a full-scale manhunt for him, not only might the elusive man completely disappear, but both Walker and Charles Eden could be caught up in it.

Dan and Claire didn't walk far. It had been a long day, and the little town had long since closed up for the night. A cup of coffee back onboard while Dan caught up on whatever correspondence had been sent that day, followed by an early night, appealed to both of them.

The cup of coffee became two cups, and the early night became early morning as Dan read and reread the information that had spewed from his computer. He had asked for a list of all locally based employees of all the companies with pipeline-related contracts that operated in the area, as well as everyone who had access to the work schedules of the victims. He figured that if the five murdered workers had been targeted, it had to be by someone who knew their schedules in advance—someone who knew they would be on a particular road at a particular time; that could eliminate Joel.

The reports Mike had obtained and sent to him showed that the first five victims had worked for three different companies, and the list of who knew, or had access to, their work schedules, was long enough to be almost useless. Added to that was the fact that the workers were all housed in Kitsault. They would have certainly talked among themselves, perhaps over a drink in the pub after work, and may well have shared information. Their schedules would probably have been common knowledge, which meant that whittling down the list of possible suspects would be a long and arduous job. To make matters worse, the nature of the work meant that predicting exactly which road any given man would be on at any given time, or even any given day, was almost impossible.

That left the possibility that the murders had been random. The victims could simply have been in the wrong place at the wrong time, and the killings had been opportunistic rather than planned. If Joel—or someone like Joel—was, in fact, the murderer, then he would have had to pick a waterway at random and wait for someone to show up, but the more he thought about it, the more unlikely Dan thought that was the case. Even a quick glance at the map showed so many rivulets and streams flowing like worry lines down from the mountains that the chances of anyone showing up on any one of the roads while the murderer was on a nearby creek would be ridiculously small. Unless, of course, the murderer was working with someone else, someone who had access to the schedules and routes and who passed the information on. But that would involve a pretty sophisticated method of communication, and cell phone towers were few and far between in this remote area. More stuff that needed to be checked out. Dan leaned back, twisting his head and neck to ease the stiffness brought on by hours of sitting, and made a mental note to check out radio and satellite communications in the area.

It was well past midnight and the rain had started, although he had been so involved in reading and analyzing he had been unaware of it. At least there didn't seem to be much wind, so perhaps the trip over to Sunshine Island could still go ahead. Claire had gone to bed two hours earlier, and Dan wanted to join her, but there were only a couple more reports to go and then he would have a clean start in the morning. He picked up the next piece of paper, and the words he read there cleared any thought of sleep from his mind.

Kent McGilvery was missing, presumed drowned, after his kayak was found floating upside down off Digby Island by a woman walking her dog. Witnesses said he had gone out shortly after nine o'clock that morning, and the report had come in just after two o'clock in the afternoon. The police sent divers out, but neither they, nor a search of the shoreline, had turned up any sign of him. The search had been called off because of darkness, but it would resume in the morning assuming the storm didn't prevent it. While the report didn't spell it out, written between the lines was the assumption that with the tides and currents that swirled through the passes, it wasn't likely that his body would be found quickly.

Dan read the report again and again, trying to reconcile the information it contained within his mental image of watching McGilvery bring his kayak up to the dock in the marina. The man had obviously been an experienced paddler, totally at ease with the tiny vessel. In fact, McGilvery's expertise had reminded Dan of both Claire and Walker; he had the same unconscious skill that could only come from years of practice. The kayak had been well equipped too, now that he thought about it. There had been a spare paddle, a paddle float and some other gear lashed onto the bow, and McGilvery had been using a spray skirt and wearing a life jacket—Dan remembered him shedding both of them after he climbed up onto the dock. He also clearly remembered McGilvery approaching Caversham's boat. The man had been wearing a wetsuit with a Gore-Tex jacket over the top, and he had tight-fitting rubber boots on his feet. He had looked like someone both at home on the water and well prepared for any mishap.

Dan went up to the wheelhouse and pulled out a paper chart of Prince Rupert Harbor. Digby Island was right across from the marina, largely enclosed by the harbor itself, and therefore protected from the worst of the weather—although there hadn't been any bad weather yesterday. What the hell could have happened? Perhaps it had been a collision; it was a busy harbor with freighters loading coal and wheat, ferries arriving and departing, fish and pleasure boats constantly on the move, but collisions were rare. He checked the reports again. It was obvious the Prince Rupert detachment was treating it as an accident; there wasn't even a mention of a possible collision. So were they right? Could it have been an accident? A moment of inattention. An unexpected wake from a passing boat that had not been handled properly. Either of those was possible, but somehow they didn't seem likely, and the timing was, to say the least, odd. It was only yesterday they had spoken with Kent McGilvery. Had they said anything that had set this in motion? The only other person there had been Bill Caversham, and he had been so inebriated it was unlikely he would have remembered anything.

Dan needed to talk to Walker, and to Claire. They both would be able to provide valuable insight into the likelihood of this being an accident, but Walker still had not returned and Claire was sleeping. He fought the urge to go in and wake her. Quite apart from wanting her thoughts on the dangers of kayaking, he wanted her to reassure him that this would not, could not, happen to her.

▶ FIFTEEN ◀

▶ A gray dawn found Dan still trying to reconcile the news of Kent McGilvery's death with his memory of their conversation just thirty-six hours ago. He knew he could be reading too much into it, but if it hadn't been an accident, then it changed everything.

Walker arrived just as it was getting light. Dan had spent the night checking charts and tables, making notes, and trying unsuccessfully to connect at least a few of the facts he had been given. He was making yet another pot of coffee when he heard the sound of the canoe rubbing on the grid, and he went out to greet the man who had become both a friend and a valued partner.

"Coffee?"

"Thanks," Walker said as he accepted the cup Dan held out. "Thought you would still be tucked up in bed." The black eyes narrowed as they took in Dan's haggard face. "You look like shit."

"Gee, thanks," Dan replied, rubbing his hand over his face. "Can't say it's been the greatest night. I guess it shows huh?"

"Claire okay?" Walker made his way over to one of the benches and sat down.

"Yeah, she's fine. Still sleeping." He took a sip of coffee. "Let me ask you something. How likely do you think it would be for you to tip your canoe over in Prince Rupert Harbor?"

Walker stared at him over the rim of his cup. "I've never tipped my canoe over anywhere. Why? You worried about Claire?"

"No, not really. I'm trying to figure out if a guy we met yesterday had an accident or was murdered."

"He was out in a canoe?"

"Nope. He was a kayaker—and a pretty good one, I'd say. Had all the right gear too: clothing, PFD, safety stuff, the works."

Walker shook his head. "If he was in the harbor, he should have been okay. Can't get too far from shore, and there's lots of traffic."

"Yeah." Dan sighed. "That's what I thought too."

"What do the cops think?"

Dan smiled. It wasn't that long ago since Walker had asked him if he thought of himself as a cop. He had answered in the affirmative, but now it seemed as if Walker was the one who thought of him as being in a different category.

"They're treating it as an accident, but without a body, there's no way of being sure."

"They don't have the body? I thought you said he was wearing a life jacket."

"A PFD. Yeah. At least he was when we saw him."

"Huh. Sounds wrong to me." Walker's eyes scanned the shoreline, then lifted up to check the sky. "We should get going. Gonna be more rain later."

▶ There was more rain, a lot more, and by the time Walker pointed to a faint blur appearing through the mist, Dan was soaked to the skin.

"That's Haina."

"How the hell can you tell? We could be anywhere by now." Dan made no effort to hide the discomfort he was feeling. Not only was he cold and wet, but his back was aching from sitting hunched over on a narrow, wooden seat for the past three hours.

Walker didn't answer, but after a few moments he lifted his paddle out of the water and let the tiny vessel drift in the waves.

"We'll be there in about five minutes," he said. "You ready for this?"

Dan glared at him. "Hell no, I'm not ready. I'm cold, wet, and stiff all over. I'm not even sure I'll be able to stand up once we get there. Joel's going to think I'm the sorriest-looking white guy he's ever seen. He'll probably take one look at me and disappear again."

Walker looked him over with a critical eye. "Yeah, you're a pretty sad sight," he said. "But don't worry about it. Looking miserable is probably an asset. Makes you more like a regular guy instead of a cop."

"Great! That makes me feel a whole bunch better. Maybe a regular guy won't get pneumonia!" Dan shivered as a gust of wind rocked the canoe. "Can we at least get this thing up onto the beach? If I don't stand up soon I'm going to be permanently paralyzed."

Walker looked at him a moment longer and then grinned as he thrust his paddle back into the water to send the tiny canoe slicing through the waves.

The hull touched the gravel of the shore and Walker drove it up onto land as far as he could, then waited as Dan forced his aching body to move.

"Don't you grind the bottom off when you do that?" Dan asked, his ears still flinching from the sound of rocks grinding on the hull.

"Nope. Had a guy put a couple of strips of metal on it."

Dan nodded. He should have realized that Walker would have figured out a practical solution to the problem of getting the canoe ashore. Given the amount of time the man spent on the water and his mobility issues, he would have destroyed a lot of canoes if he hadn't.

The beach was a narrow strip of shingle that sloped gently up to a row of logs that were wedged along the base of a low bank. Above them, huge cedar trees soared into the sky, stately branches draped above the moss-covered ground. There was almost no undergrowth, but here and there fallen tree trunks and tangled limbs gave testament to the passage of years. The rain had eased to a fine mist, and below the soft lapping of waves on the shore and the faint sigh of wind high up in the branches, there was an intense, brooding silence. The sense of presence that silence carried within it was almost palpable. It appeared to emanate from the island itself, yet Dan could see no sign of life.

He swung his arms wide, shrugged his shoulders and stamped his feet, telling himself he needed to get his blood flowing and some warmth back into his cold limbs, but he knew it was more of an attempt to distract himself from the strange and haunting feeling of stepping into some ancient awareness, of endless patience, of a vast, eternal watchfulness.

"Is Joel coming with Charles Eden?" he asked Walker. "Do you know when they're going to arrive?"

Walker glanced at him, then lifted his eyes to focus on something in the trees. Dan followed his gaze and saw a shadow disengage from a tree trunk and move toward them. The shadow took form as it moved out into the light, and a man of indeterminate age stepped down to meet them. He was of medium height, with a slight build, and he moved with a fluid, supple grace that reminded Dan of a young animal, perhaps a river otter or mink, surefooted and agile, and completely at home in its environment. Above his head a raven lifted from a branch and flew down to the rocks below.

The man went over to Walker, who had made his slow way up the beach and was sitting on one of the logs.

"Walker," he said, his voice soft as he inclined his head in an oddly formal gesture.

"Joel." Walker smiled. "I've brought the man I told you about. His name is Dan Connor." He nodded toward Dan, who was still standing and rubbing his arms as he tried to get warmth back into them. "He is a friend. He will listen to you."

Joel turned slowly toward Dan, dark eyes set deep into the smooth yet sharp planes of his face, but he made no move to approach or utter a greeting. He looked almost as if he had stepped out of a painting. His features were unlined, so perfect that they seemed unreal, like a three-dimensional holograph that could disappear at any moment. Some instinct told Dan not to offer his hand, and to keep his voice quiet.

"Joel," he said.

Joel remained motionless and silent for several moments, and then inclined his head slightly before he turned back and sat down beside Walker. Walker gave a nod to invite Dan to join them. He did so, hunching his shoulders to still the shivering of his muscles as he sat down on the other side of Joel, close enough to hear and be heard, but far enough away to ensure he was not intruding into the space Joel's body language was demanding be given.

They sat in silence for a long time, until the soundless life of the island reasserted itself, and then Dan spoke.

"Joel, do you know why the police wanted to talk with you?"

"Yes," Joel answered, his voice surprisingly clear and strong. "They think I killed some men."

"Do you know why they think that?"

Dan sensed rather than saw the shrug.

"I am Haida, and I have a canoe."

Dan smiled. Walker had said almost exactly the same thing.

"Do you know where these men were killed?"

Another shrug.

"Near the place you call Kitsault?" It was as much a question as an answer. "The police said they all worked on the pipeline."

"Yes," Dan agreed. "They did. And yes, they were killed near Kitsault. Do you know that area well?"

"Yes. I paddle there often." For the first time Joel turned and looked at Dan, his eyes alive and his face intense. "It is still as Creator made it. The animals are happy. They talk to me." He turned away again, his voice dropping. "But the men from Kitsault frighten them. Now there are only a few places left quiet, and some of the animals run away."

"What do you think about those men?"

"I don't know them. Perhaps they are good men, but the pipeline they want to build is not good. It will kill the earth."

"So you would like to stop the pipeline?"

Joel stared at him, frowning in puzzlement. "Of course! All of my people want to stop the pipeline."

"Do they have a plan to stop it?"

Joel turned away to look out over the ocean. "They have meetings, and there are lawyers. Sometimes people from the television come. I don't go to the meetings. It's too noisy and I don't understand what they say there, but I hear people talk—and they have given me papers and stickers. I have some on my canoe!" He gestured to the east, where the beach curved out of sight.

Dan sat quietly as he considered the answers this strange child-man had given him. He was beginning to understand why both Walker and Charles Eden had said Joel was incapable of committing murder. There was both a naiveté and a gentleness in him that was unmistakeable.

"Do you have a radio, Joel?" he asked, and watched as disgust and concern warred on the man's face.

"Joel lives a pretty traditional life." Walker reinserted himself into the conversation. "He doesn't use radios, or charts, or motors, or guns." He leaned toward Joel. "I think perhaps Dan would like to see your traps and fishing gear."

Joel hesitated for a moment and then stood and headed back up the bank. Dan followed. Ten minutes of fast walking over the soft, mossy ground warmed him up and brought them to a shallow gully. Joel stopped and held up his hand, then leaned forward and lifted a twisted braid of rope, made from what looked like strips of bark, out of a pile of dead grass and twigs. As he pulled on it, the rope jerked in his hands and the pile seemed to move. He reached into his pocket and pulled out a slim blade that shone black in the dappled light, intoned words that Dan could not understand, and then thrust his hands into the pile. Seconds later he stood up, blood dripping from the small, furred body he was holding.

They returned to the beach by a different route, stopping along the way to hang the rabbit carcass from a broken tree branch, and pick up an elaborate wooden hook from a cavity in an ancient tree.

"It's for catching halibut," Walker told Dan as Joel placed the hook on the log. "It's made from yew. All the tools Joel uses are traditional."

"Well, the knife he used to kill some animal back there wasn't traditional," Dan said. "It looked like plastic to me." The quiet efficiency of the killing had bothered him.

Walker shook his head. "Joel, have you got a plastic knife?" he asked.

Joel looked at him in confusion, shook his head, and then reached into his pocket to pull out the same knife Dan had seen him use. He passed it to Walker, who took it with great care—almost reverence—and held it out to Dan.

"Argillite," he said. "It's traditional Haida. There are only a few people who still know how to carve it, or where to find it. It's sometimes called black jade."

Dan took the tiny blade and let it lie in the palm of his hand. The hilt was intricately carved with miniature figures that looked much the same as the larger ones he had seen on the soaring wooden totem poles at the top of the wharf back in Queen Charlotte City, and the blade was razor sharp.

"Harder than yew." Walker grinned as he took in the look of admiration on Dan's face. "Could easily take off a head with that. Of course, it would have to be a pretty small head."

"Thank you, Walker," Dan said, infusing his voice with as much sarcasm as he could find as he handed the knife back. He turned to Joel. "What were you saying while you killed that rabbit?"

Joel turned to Walker without answering, his face puzzled.

"He would have been thanking it for giving him its life. Honoring its spirit," Walker answered. "It's something we all do, although the words may be different." He looked down the beach. "Joel's like me—he eats mostly fish and berries and roots and stuff. Whatever we find around us. Rabbits would be the only meat he eats. They're not native here, and they compete with the other wildlife, so it's as much about helping the environment as it is about food—and the skin makes good clothing."

Joel smiled and nodded, then sat down again.

Dan sat down beside him and the three men stared out over the ocean in silence until Dan spoke again.

"Did you ever see any other people when you were paddling near Kitsault? People in small boats, or canoes or kayaks?"

Joel nodded. "Sometimes," he said.

"Do you remember what they looked like?"

"I remember three," he answered. "They were all in kayaks. There was a man with red hair, but I only saw him three or four times. Mostly I saw this other man." He shrugged. "He was younger. Brown hair." He thought for a minute. "He was good on the water, and he liked the animals. He spent time with them. Watched them."

Sounded like Ridley MacPherson and Kent McGilvery, Dan thought. MacPherson had reddish hair, and McGilvery would certainly have watched any wildlife he saw. But who was the other one?

"You said you remembered three men," he said. "Can you describe the third?"

Joel smiled. "It wasn't a man," he answered. "It was a woman."

▶ Claire woke late and lay, warm and comfortable, in the big bed that took up most of the master stateroom, listening to the rain patter on the deck above her head. The pillow on Dan's side of the bed still held the imprint of his head, but the residual warmth of his body was gone, and she guessed he had been up early and had left with Walker as they had planned.

She got out of bed and padded out to the salon to put on some coffee, peering out of the window as she did so. The sky was gray, with low cloud hanging overhead and rain slanting down through the air, but off to the west there was a streak of light. It looked as if the weather was going to clear. She switched on the radio, turned it to the weather channel, and listened to the recorded voice announce the passing of one cold front and the approach of another that was scheduled to arrive sometime later that evening. Between the two there would be a brief period of fair weather.

She had hoped to visit the museum they had seen on the way in, to check out the row of carved house poles that stood sentry in front of the building, but today was not going to be the day to do that. She would be starting late on what would be a long paddle, and the return would be into the wind and waves generated by the approaching storm. Better to stay close to the marina and explore the shoreline east of the dock, and then maybe she and Dan could find a restaurant in town for dinner.

She took her time making breakfast, digging a bagel out of the freezer and sliding it under the broiler as she broke an egg into a pan of boiling water. A couple of slices of bacon on the bottom and a slice of cheese on top and she had herself an adequate eggs Benedict—not gourmet, perhaps, but it certainly tasted good. By the time she had washed the dishes and cleaned up, the clouds had lifted and the rain had stopped, although the air itself still felt moist on her skin. She pulled on her wetsuit, added a fleece top and a rainproof jacket, stuffed a couple of the snack bars that Dan always kept on hand into her pocket, and slid into her kayak.

Within minutes the town was left behind, and the shore became a mass of lush green seagrass that swayed in the breeze. There were birds everywhere. Green-winged teal and brightly patterned bufflehead dabbled in the shallows, vying for food with pintails, widgeons and scaup. Further out, sleek black cormorants dove for fish, while the stout red bills of oystercatchers lit up the rocks, and sandpipers ran along the shore on slender legs. All of them ignored her presence, either unaware or unafraid of her tiny boat, and she let herself drift slowly through their midst, moving slowly west with the current.

She had been on the water over an hour when the house came into view. It blended so perfectly into the landscape, its weathered wood half hidden behind the mounds of grass and dappled by the shadows of the surrounding trees, that she might not have noticed it except for a noisy group of ravens. There were three of them and they were sitting on the lowest branch of a large spruce tree, watching her approach. If she hadn't known better, she would have thought they were calling to her. As she paddled closer, the door of the house opened and a woman emerged. She looked straight at Claire and smiled.

"Welcome," she called as she walked down the path toward the water. "I'm Emily. I'm so glad you came. Is Joel with you?"

Claire stared at her in confusion. Charles Eden had said that Haida Gwaii was where Joel's mother lived, but surely this could not be her. This woman looked relaxed, happy, in vibrant good health, certainly not an alcoholic. Not only that, she had pale skin, light brown curly hair, and looked nothing like Charles.

99

"No," Claire replied as her kayak drifted into shore and brushed against the grass. "If we're talking about the same Joel, I think he's over on Haina. My partner went over there to talk with him. Are you a relative?"

"Oh no, dear. I'm just a friend. This was his grandfather's house and he comes to visit me sometimes." The woman looked back at the ravens that were still sitting on the branch, their eyes bright and curious although they had fallen silent. "They always tell me when he's coming."

Claire glanced at the watching birds then looked back to Emily, not sure what to make of either her or her strange statement. "They certainly seem to make good watchdogs," she said.

"That and a lot more," Emily answered. "At least where Joel is concerned. Would you like a cup of tea?"

Claire stared at her, confused by this odd, unpredictable woman, yet intrigued by the vitality and warmth she projected. "Yes," she said. "That would be lovely."

▶ While Emily made the tea, Claire admired the rich tapestries that lined the walls. A huge loom occupied one end of the room, and strands of brightly colored yarn stretched across the frame and draped down onto the floor where they were coiled onto upright wooden rods. A half-formed image of the shoreline was visible in the woven fabric, the curving blades of grass so realistic they almost seemed to move, the branches of an old cedar rough with lichen, and the eye of a raven glittering in the light.

"These are beautiful!" Claire exclaimed. "How on earth can you make them look so real?"

Emily came over and stood beside her, looking down at her work.

"I really don't know," she answered. "I've always been a weaver, but once I moved into this house, my weaving changed. It's much different now, and much better than it was before."

She went back over to the kitchen and lifted the kettle off the stove.

"It's Chinaay, of course. He drops by every now and then and gives me ideas and gifts."

"Chinaay?" Claire asked blankly. "Is he an artist too?"

"He was." Emily filled the teapot and took it to the table. "He's been gone a long time now."

Claire stared at her in puzzlement. "I'm sorry. I thought you said he sometimes comes by and gives you things."

"Oh, he does, dear. He leaves things for Joel too. He's such a nice man, and his paintings and carvings were amazing!" She laughed as she caught the bemused look on Claire's face. "You must think I'm a crazy old woman. I thought so too when I first got here, but it's just the way it is."

She poured tea into two cups and pushed one toward Claire. "I think the ravens bring him. They were living in the studio when I got here, and he always leaves his gifts there." She gestured to a door set in the back wall of the room. "Last week he left a beautiful paddle for Joel. I know he carved and painted it himself. His work is unmistakeable."

"A paddle?" Claire's reeling brain managed to focus on that single word. She remembered Dan talking about a paddle. That was what had first led the police in Prince Rupert to Joel. "Was it made from yew?"

"Yew? Oh yes, dear. I'm sure it was. All the traditional Haida paddles are yew."

▶ "She said someone called Chinaay had given Joel a paddle made from yew." Claire had returned to *Dreamspeaker* to find Dan and Charles Eden eating a late lunch of cheese and crackers.

Eden nodded. "Yes," he said. "I saw it. Joel showed it to me."

Dan looked from Claire to Eden and back to Claire again. "So you're telling me Joel has another yew paddle?"

"That's what Emily said."

"And this guy Chinaay gave it to him?"

She nodded.

"So maybe we need to go talk to him." Dan turned to Charles Eden. "Do you know where he lives?"

Eden smiled. "I know where he used to live. So does Claire. He lived in the house Emily lives in now, but he's been gone for more than ten years."

"Gone? Do you mean gone from Haida Gwaii, or just gone from the house?"

"Not just gone from Haida Gwaii. Gone to join the ancestors."

Dan stared at him. "You mean he's dead? That he's been dead for more than ten years?"

Eden nodded.

"But that doesn't make sense. How could he give Joel a paddle last week if he's been dead for ten years?"

Claire shook her head. "It didn't make any sense to me either. Emily kept switching back and forth from the past to the present all the time she was talking, and I thought perhaps she was just confused, but if Charles says Joel only got the paddle last week . . ."

"If the house belonged to this guy Chinaay, maybe he left it behind and Emily just found it," Dan said as he tried to find some kind of reasonable explanation.

"But why would she give it to Joel?" Claire asked. "How would she even know Joel?"

"Chinaay is Joel's grandfather. That's what the word 'chinaay' means," Charles Eden said. "And he was my father. He was a great artist and a very powerful man. I think you would call him a shaman in your language. A holy man." He paused and looked out toward the horizon. "Joel has the same power, but I don't think he understands it yet. The ravens speak to him."

"What is it with the ravens?" Claire asked. "I keep hearing about ravens, and they were certainly there at Emily's—the noise they were making was what made me go into shore in the first place."

"And did you think that perhaps they were calling to you?"

"Yes, actually, I did—but that's crazy. I think I just wanted to see what they were making all that fuss about."

Charles smiled. "Raven is many things, but mostly he is very powerful. In our culture, it was Raven who discovered us and fed us. He is a transformer and a trickster. He keeps secrets, and he brings messages from the spirit world. Chinaay used to call on Raven to help him see the truth. He said that Raven helped him understand, helped him stay in harmony with the world."

"So I guess you would say those ravens over on Haina were talking to Joel?" Dan had been listening to the conversation and thinking how similar this all sounded to Walker's stories about white wolves, and double-headed sea serpents, and lightning snakes. He was becoming so familiar with this panoply of spirits who seemed to slip in and out of everyday life that they were beginning to seem normal.

Charles nodded. "The ravens are always with him."

Dan shrugged. "There are ravens everywhere around here. There are always ravens."

Charles leaned back and looked up the wharf, then let his gaze wander out along the shore. "There's none here now," he said.

► SEVENTEEN ◄

► The wind was starting to pick up as Dan and Claire wandered up the wharf to explore the town. The cold front the meteorologist had predicted was coming in, and it looked like it was going to be considerably stronger than its precursor. Unless it changed course, it was unlikely they would be able to cross the strait until it had passed. In any case, Charles Eden had left to go and visit Emily, saying he would be back some time the following day, Walker was, as far as they knew, still over on Haina with Joel, and Dan wouldn't leave until he knew what their plans were.

Claire linked her arm with Dan's as they turned onto the street.

"You're very quiet. Is something bothering you?"

He looked down at her and smiled, grateful for her presence at his side, and for the warmth of their deepening relationship.

"You mean other than the reappearance of a man who's been dead for ten years, and a bunch of spirit birds that bring paddles from the other world?"

She laughed. "It does all sound a little weird when you put it like that."

"Yeah. And difficult to put into a police report."

"I hadn't thought of that! Do you really think it's all related?"

He didn't answer right away. On the surface, the whole thing seemed absurd. A dead man somehow returning to the place he had lived and leaving a paddle as a gift for a grandson. A young man who not only suffered from some form of autism but also spent most of his time either on the water or deep in the forest, living off the sea and the land. Ravens that talked to people and brought messages from the spirit world. Carved wood paddles that could sever a head. It was all crazy and yet somehow it all seemed to be linked.

"Yeah, I do, although I have no idea how."

He suddenly found himself wishing Walker were there. Walker would have no problem accepting the stories, and in his quiet, laconic way, he would help Dan make sense out of all of them. The man seemed to have effortlessly bridged the gap between the two cultures, comfortable in his own immediate and intimate relationship with nature, yet at ease with both the hard-edged world of the city and the more fluid, spiritual-based world of his ancestors.

"I think I need to talk to Walker, see what he thinks about it."

He pointed ahead to where a window gleamed with a warm yellow light through the thin gray mist of the oncoming storm. "How about getting dinner there?"

▶ The storm hit just after midnight. Rain lashed the waters of the inlet, churning it to a maelstrom of white foam, whipping the branches of the trees, and bending the seagrass low along the shore. It beat along the decks of the boats tied to the wharf, pounded on the roofs of the buildings in the village, and ran down the paths and streets of the town. Out in her small house, protected by the overhanging branches of ancient spruce and cedar, Emily stirred in her sleep, her mouth curving into an unconscious smile as her brain registered the murmur of the ravens who had taken refuge in the porch. In a tiny cove two miles down the inlet, Charles Eden went out on deck to check the anchor before he returned to the wheelhouse to continue contemplating his recent conversations with Joel and Emily. On Haina, Joel lay quietly on a bed of cedar boughs inside the hollow trunk of an old tree, listening to the patter of the rain on the deep moss and inhaling the fragrance of the wet earth. Two hundred yards off the shore of the town, Walker huddled lower in his canoe, and drove his paddle deep into the waves, driving the little vessel toward the faint loom of lights that glimmered through the murk. Onboard *Dreamspeaker*, Dan and Claire were woken by the furious drumbeat of the raindrops on the cabin and deck; they both got out of bed and made their way to the salon where the larger windows gave them a better view of what was happening.

"It sounds as if the sky itself is falling," Dan said as he peered out into the gloom. "I can't see a thing. There's no way we're going to get any more sleep until this is over." A flash of lightning and a crack of thunder accompanied his words.

"I'll make us some hot chocolate," Claire said as she headed for the galley. "We may as well be warm and comfortable."

The noise was so loud it masked the sound of Walker's arrival, and it wasn't until he appeared at the cabin door, water streaming down his jacket and jeans to pool on the deck, that they were aware of him.

"Jesus! Did you paddle over in this?" Dan pulled a couple of towels out of a cupboard and handed them to his bedraggled guest.

"It was okay most of the way. I'm not as familiar with the weather here so I was a bit off on the timing."

Dan eyed Walker's sodden clothes. "Let me see if I can find you something dry to wear. Hang on a minute." He went forward to the master stateroom and returned a few minutes later with a T-shirt, a sweatshirt, and some old sweatpants.

"Why don't you have a hot shower?" Claire asked. "I'll have some hot chocolate ready when you're finished, and I can throw your clothes in the dryer."

Half an hour later, with the dryer humming in the background, the three of them sat around the table, their hands wrapped around steaming mugs of cocoa.

"Is Joel still over on Haina?" Dan asked.

"Yeah. I think he plans on staying there for a while. It's where his family's village used to be, back before the white man's sickness wiped them out."

"Did he show you his new paddle?"

"Yeah. It's beautiful. He said his grandfather gave it to him. Gave him an eagle feather too."

"Walker, his grandfather has been dead for more than ten years."

Walker shrugged. "So he left it behind when he died."

Dan glanced over at Claire. "Did he happen to mention a woman named Emily?"

Walker shook his head. "Nope. Why?"

Claire told him about her visit to the house that Joel's grandfather had once owned, and about Emily's story of finding the paddle.

"If it had been left behind, she would have had to see it when she first moved in. That room was Chinaay's studio. She doesn't use it. She keeps it empty. She said it's where he comes back to when he visits."

Walker smiled. "She sounds like a good lady."

"She is. She's a weaver, and her work is amazing. She says it's better since she moved into the house because Chinaay helped her, which doesn't make sense either, because he must have already been dead a good few years before she bought the place five years ago."

"Were there ravens there?" Walker's question caught her off guard.

"Ravens? Yes, there were ravens. There were three of them sitting in a tree beside the house. That's really why I went in. They were so loud and insistent I thought something might be wrong. Why?"

Walker sighed and shook his head. "I am not Haida and I can't tell you the Haida stories—you need Joel or Charles Eden for those—but for the Haida, Raven is who discovered them, who released them, who made them human. He can pass through the boundaries between the worlds." He looked out at the rain streaming down the windows. "Joel is double Raven—both moiety and family. The ravens are always with him. He says the ravens speak to him. I believe him."

"What is it with all this stuff about ravens?" Dan's voice betrayed both his puzzlement and his frustration. "There are ravens everywhere. There was a raven sitting on the rail of Annie's boat when we left. There were ravens when I took you to Charles's house. There were ravens over on Haina. What's so special about them?"

"Depends on the raven. Yaahl has many faces," Walker answered with the infuriating grin that tended to drive Dan crazy. But Dan was learning; this time he simply changed the topic.

"You sure this paddle Joel has now is new?"

"Yeah. I guess he used it to paddle over to Haina, but the wood is dry and the paint is bright. Why?"

Dan looked at him. "If he had access to another paddle, the guys in Rupert are going to want to check that one too."

"It's new. Emily can testify to that."

Dan shuddered as an image of Emily telling the Prince Rupert detectives how she had found the paddle formed in his brain.

"Okay, well, it probably doesn't matter anyway. A new paddle— wherever it came from—can't have anything to do with what's been happening over there in Rupert."

"His old paddle has nothing to do with what happened in Rupert either," Walker retorted.

Dan nodded slowly. "Yeah, maybe you're right. He doesn't seem like the kind of guy who would commit murder—although for someone you say is so gentle, he sure didn't have any trouble killing that rabbit."

Walker grinned. "He has to eat. No freezers out there on Haina."

Dan rolled his eyes. "I'm going to see if I can get through to Victoria. I need to check a few things."

He switched on the electronics in the wheelhouse, thankful that the storm hadn't taken out the shore power he had plugged into. As the warm light from two brass lamps filled the space and reflected from the polished mahogany of the wheel, the black night outside the windows disappeared from view. He knew it would be morning before Mike read his email and relayed his questions to the investigators in the Rupert office, but the sooner they received them, the sooner they could answer—and Dan needed those answers.

▶ EIGHTEEN ◀

▶ Dawn broke calm and clear. The storm had blown itself out in the early hours of the day, and the sky was a freshly washed blue scattered with high cloud. With Walker already on board there was really no need to wait for Charles Eden to appear, but Dan was reluctant to leave without at least telling the man what he was doing. For some reason it seemed inconsiderate, and Eden had been the model of consideration.

"Does Charles have a radio on his boat?" Dan asked Walker.

Walker shrugged. "I guess so, but he doesn't use it much. Why?"

"He said he would be back this morning. I told him I would be here, but I'd like to get going. Take advantage of this good weather."

"He'll figure it out," Walker said. "He'll probably head back across as well."

"Yes. I guess so. Just doesn't seem right, that's all."

"He's Raven too. They'll probably tell him." Walker made no attempt to hide the amusement in his voice.

"Thank you, Walker," Dan retorted, his voice heavy with sarcasm. "Perhaps you would like to give me a hand getting your canoe up. Somehow I don't think the ravens are going to do that."

Haida Gwaii was a faint smudge of green far to the west when the computer signaled the first email of the day. Half an hour later, Claire took over the wheel so that Dan could concentrate on the growing mountain of printouts covering the table in the salon.

Mike had obtained lists of names and schedules from two of the three companies that billeted staff at Kitsault, but it was going to take time to match the names to the dates of the murders, and even longer to cross-check them against the logs the workers submitted to their supervisors documenting where they were working on any given day. Dan set them aside and concentrated on the background information he had requested on Marjorie Wakeshaw and her husband. There wasn't much. They had been hired as caretakers for the town two years previously, when the owner had first signed a deal with the pipeline companies and had presumably needed someone with more of a business background than their predecessor who had simply been a handyman, hired to do maintenance on the buildings. Prior to Kitsault, the couple had run a remote fish camp for several years, and before that, they had managed several logging operations. Neither Marjorie nor her husband, James Wakeshaw, had a police record.

There was a copy of a curriculum vitae for both Bill Caversham and Ridley MacPherson, a copy of a graduation certificate in Business Administration from the University of Manitoba for Caversham, and a copy of a marriage certificate for Margaret Anne Taylor and William David Caversham, dated twenty years earlier. A note from Rosemary, Mike's secretary, said that annual work histories and evaluations for both men had been requested, but would take more time as their release had to be approved by someone higher up in the company.

It was a start, Dan thought as he placed the paperwork into stacks, but there was a long way to go and it was quite possible he was duplicating work that the Prince Rupert detectives had already done, but that couldn't be helped.

The last pile he looked at were the photos of the crime scenes, including close-up shots of the wounds. All of them, with the exception of the female reporter, looked remarkably similar. He spread the gruesome portraits across the table, and then placed the relevant police file and coroner's report beside each one. The files listed the exact location of the murder, any other people known to be in the area at the time, the position of the body, and any evidence found at the crime scene. The reports listed not only the name and age of each victim together with the time and cause of their death, but also detailed their physical characteristics including height, weight, and general health.

Dan shuffled and re-shuffled the piles until he had it organized the way he wanted, then leaned back against the cushions and picked up the first page on the first pile. With luck, the steady rumble of the big diesel under the floorboards would have the same effect on him as did the music of John Coltrane or Charlie Parker or any of the other jazz musicians he loved: it would fire up the synapses in his subconscious brain and allow it to absorb and analyze the information in front of him.

Three hours later he placed the last page of the paperwork in its appropriate pile, and closed the folder. A yellow legal pad lay in front of him, filled with notes and questions that still needed answers, but now Dan had a much clearer picture of things. The locations had become three-dimensional. The days and times had taken on reality. The victims had become people.

He stood up and stretched muscles cramped by hours of sitting, then made his way forward to the wheelhouse. Claire was sitting at the wheel, pointing out the distant islands that appeared on the edge of the radar screen while Walker peered out through the windshield and tried to locate them.

"Which one is that?" Walker pointed to a dark smudge ahead and to the right of their course.

"Porcher, I think, although Stephens and Prescott are both in front of it. They're both low, so you can't really make them out from this angle."

Walker shook his head. "Amazing. That thing sure makes navigation easy."

"Thinking of getting a radar for your canoe?" Dan interrupted the conversation.

"Nah. Weighs too much. I'm just gonna rely on the ravens."

"Yeah, right. You guys want a coffee? I'm going to make a pot and then I can take over, if you like."

They drank their coffee in the wheelhouse, watching the islands grow larger as they approached, talking about boats and navigation and technology. When they had finished, Claire headed to the galley to make lunch, and Dan turned the conversation back to Joel.

"How tall would you say he is?"

"Joel? Hell, I don't know. Shorter than me before the accident."

Dan glanced over at Walker's bent legs. "So, five foot eight? Five foot seven?"

"Maybe. Probably less. I'm no good at figuring height, but he's a pretty small guy. Doesn't weigh much either, but he's strong. Why are you asking?"

Dan took his time answering, staring out the windshield as he let his mind run over the mental images of the victims he had formed from the information he had read.

"I think I might have figured out a way to eliminate him from suspicion."

He could feel Walker's eyes boring into the back of his head.

"That a fancy way of saying you think he didn't do it?"

Dan nodded. "Yeah, I guess it is. But it's more than that. If I'm right, it means I'll be able to prove he couldn't have done it, and that means he'll be completely off the hook. He'll be cleared, and everyone will know he's innocent."

"So how do you get to find out if you're right?"

"I need to talk to the coroner. I'm going to see if Mike can set it up for tomorrow."

▶ By six o'clock, *Dreamspeaker* was once again tied up on the outside float of Rushbrook Marina in Prince Rupert and Walker's canoe was already barely visible against the shoreline of Digby Island. Dan hadn't heard back from Mike about getting an appointment to meet with the coroner, although he had received more information on schedules and more reports documenting daily locations for the staff staying at Kitsault. He had glanced at them, but hadn't printed them out. He needed a clear mind and an uninterrupted stretch of time to sort the details out, and right now he had neither. He had an entirely different problem that he needed to deal with.

"Want to go up into town for dinner?" he asked Claire.

"Sure. Sounds great."

Cooking was not a strongpoint for either one of them, and unless they had caught some prawns, or come across a fish boat with fresh fish for sale, they mostly lived off canned or frozen food when they were out on the water. That meant that restaurant dining was always their preferred choice when they were at a dock.

The tide was rising, and the ramp leading from the floats up to the wharf was much less steep than the last time they had used it, when it had been almost vertical as it adjusted to the twenty-six-foot tidal range. With luck—and a good meal to linger over—it would be almost level by the time they returned. They walked to the parking lot, climbed into the car, and drove into town.

"You're awfully quiet. Is the case getting to you?"

Dan looked across the table to where Claire was sitting, her face illuminated by the slanting rays of a low sun that poured through the windows like liquid gold.

"No, it's not that. It's what I'm going to have to do next that's bothering me." He reached his hand out across the table and grasped her much smaller one, stroking the smooth skin of her palm with his thumb. "If what I think is right, I'm going to have to go back to Kitsault, and you can't come with me."

She stared at him. "Why on earth not? I don't have to be back for another ten days. I would love to see Kitsault!"

"I know you would. It's beautiful. But it would be much too dangerous. I can't let you come."

Her eyes narrowed and she leaned toward him. "You can't *let* me come?"

"Claire, it's just too dangerous. Whatever is going on, it's centered in Kitsault. It has to be. There are already six people dead, and I think whoever is killing them is traveling by water. You know the second we got there you would have that damned kayak out exploring every nook and cranny and creek around—exactly where there would be the most risk."

She leaned back, the mutinous set of her jaw relaxing just a little.

"Are you going to take Walker with you?"

"I don't know. He might not want to come."

"But you're going to ask him, right?"

Dan heaved a sigh of frustration. She was not going to let him win this without a fight.

"Yes. I'm going to ask him. It would really help to have him around. To be able to see things through his eyes."

"And it's not too dangerous for him?" Her tone was dangerously sweet.

He shook his head, not so much in answer to her question as to clear the headache he could feel coming on.

"It's not the same. You know that. Walker is . . ."

"A man?"

"No! Yes! Ah, hell. Of course he's a man, but that's not it. It's just that he's so at home on the water. So aware. The chances of anyone even getting near him are almost nil." Dan wracked his brain for more ways to buttress his argument. "And he's Native. He will look like he belongs there. The killer's not going to be interested in a Native man paddling a canoe."

Claire sat back and stared at him. "Dan Connor, that's both sexist and racist—not to mention the most pathetic argument I've ever heard. No one has been killed on the water. They've all been killed up on the road. You told me that yourself. And all the victims were working for the pipeline companies, although how the murderer would know that I don't know, unless they were wearing some kind of uniform. Anyway, if it's safe for Walker, it's safe for me."

"Claire—"

"I'm going." She looked over and beckoned to a passing waitress. "I would like the halibut, please."

NINETEEN

► Walker arrived soon after they returned to the boat. Dan and Claire were sitting in the wheelhouse looking at a chart of Alice Arm when they heard his slow progress across the deck, and they both went back to the salon to greet him.

"Keeping white man's hours now?" Dan asked with a smile of welcome.

"Thought I'd give it a try," Walker answered. "But it might be a long night for all of us."

Dan stared at him, his expression suddenly serious. "And why is that?"

Walker shrugged. "You been checking your email?"

"No. We just got back from dinner. Why?"

Walker eased himself down onto the settee.

"Saw a couple of police boats out there. They had a dive boat with them. Couple of divers in the water. They were pulling something up. Looked like a body. I figured maybe they'd found the guy you were talking about."

"McGilvery? Shit. How long ago was this?" Dan was already halfway back to the wheelhouse.

"Don't know exactly. About an hour, I'd guess."

"Where were they?" Dan's voice floated back to where Claire and Walker sat in the salon.

"Out in the channel off Digby Island."

115

Minutes later, Dan returned to the salon and slouched onto the settee beside Claire.

"Was it him?"

"There's nothing there yet. It's too soon anyway. They're not going to release anything until they have a positive ID."

"Wouldn't they tell you if you went and talked to them?"

"Yeah, probably, but I can't do that. The media will be swarming all over this. They haven't had anything to talk about for three days. If I show up and walk into the station, they'll have my face plastered all over the place in no time. I've kept off their radar so far. I would hate to screw that up now."

"Speaking of the media, I'm going to turn the TV on," Claire said. "It's almost eleven. They might say something on the news."

It was close to midnight and the local news was almost over when the announcer said there was an update on the earlier report. A body had been recovered from Digby Channel. It had been found by a shrimper pulling his trap. Police had identified it as the missing kayaker, Kent McGilvery.

Dan rubbed his hands over his face. He was tired, and he felt as if his brain was spinning uselessly, its gears refusing to engage and mesh the individual cogs that would bring all the random pieces together. Images of Claire and Walker out on the water merged into a picture of the man he had seen bringing his kayak into the dock just a few days ago. He had only met Kent McGilvery a couple of times, but he had liked the man, and the fact that he had died so soon after their last conversation was too coincidental to ignore. The sense of urgency that drove his desire to talk to the coroner moved up several notches. He debated whether or not to phone Mike at home and drag him out of bed, but decided against it. The coroner would not be in his office until the morning anyway, so there was nothing to be gained. Better to get a good night's sleep. Tomorrow promised to be another busy day.

▶ Gray light seeping into the stateroom woke him the next morning. Claire was still sleeping, only the top of her head visible above the down duvet. Dan eased out of the bed, pulled on jeans and a sweater, slid his feet into deck shoes, and made his way to the galley. Walker was already out on deck, and as soon as coffee was ready, Dan filled two cups and carried them outside.

"Any chance you might like to take a trip up to Kitsault?"

"What's at Kitsault that you need me to go?"

Dan looked out across the floats of the marina. Here at Rushbrook most of the boats lining the floats were work or fish boats, unlike Cow Bay where Kent McGilvery had kept his little cabin cruiser and where Bill Caversham and Ridley MacPherson and probably other pipeline managers were moored.

"I don't know. I guess that's why I need you." As usual, Walker had seen straight to the heart of his request. "As you're so fond of pointing out, I'm not as good an observer as you are—plus you can get up those little creeks and inlets without an outboard engine announcing your presence. If something's out of place, you'll see it."

"You figure there'll be anything to see?"

"Gotta start somewhere. If Joel didn't kill those people, then someone from Kitsault did. It's the only place where there are people who would know the schedules of the victims, and it's the only settlement close enough to launch a canoe or kayak that could get up those little creeks."

"You given up on the idea of those environmentalist crazies now?" Walker's eyes peered at Dan over the rim of his cup.

"It just doesn't fit—and if Kent McGilvery's death wasn't an accident, then there's something else going on here."

"Claire going with you?" The sudden change of subject caught Dan off guard.

"I guess."

"You don't sound too happy about that."

Dan shrugged. "I'm not, but trying to stop Claire doing something she's decided to do is like standing in front of a freight train and waving at it to stop. It's just not going to happen." He drained the last of his coffee, then stared down into the empty cup. "I don't think you would be in any danger out there, but this thing with McGilvery bothers me. It's so out of sync with the others. And after the journalist . . ."

He fell silent as he thought about the implications, not only of the sequence of murders, but about what he was asking Walker to do. It had been almost three years now since his wife had been murdered, and although no one had ever been charged, he was certain it was an act committed by a man he had been tracking at the time as a personal message to him. He still felt not only the loss, but also the guilt. For the first months after her death he had tried to drown the memory in a bottle. Even after Mike and the guys in his division had tried to rescue him by finding a boat that he could pour his hours and his minutes and his muscles into, he had simply switched his focus from losing himself in an alcoholic haze to losing himself in the lonely, scattered islands that clung to the long western shore of Canada. He had quit the force, no longer able to deal with its demands, and no longer able to summon the energy and dedication it required, although pure chance had put him in the way of a couple of criminal events and he had become involved without any real decision on his part. Even his reinstatement was something he had taken no active role in. He had simply allowed it to happen; it had been the passive acceptance of someone else's plan.

He shook his head. The fact was he *had* accepted it, and he was here, now, as a member of the RCMP, and that meant he had no right to involve civilians in this case. Hell, he wouldn't have the right to ask them even if he *wasn't* in the RCMP. Who the hell asked friends to put themselves at risk when six people—probably seven—had been murdered?

He looked at Walker. "I'm sorry. I think I must be losing it. I'm way out of line. I shouldn't be asking you to go out there. Forget it."

Walker grinned. "I figured that's what you were thinking about. Too late now. You've got me hooked."

"Walker—"

"No." Walker's smile disappeared and his voice was serious. "You're not losing it, and you're not out of line. I was the one who asked you to come, remember? Why do you think I did that?"

Dan didn't answer, thrown by the intensity in Walker's voice.

"You're a good cop, that's why. You do your job differently than the other cops I've known—and yes, some of them were good cops too, even if I have a hard time admitting it. But your way of doing things is a good thing for me, and for Joel, and for others like us—and there's a lot of 'others like us' out there. You might not understand our culture, but you respect it. You're open to it. You don't dismiss it—and you're good at figuring stuff out. At putting all the pieces together." He turned away and stared out over the water, then turned back. "Of course you're still a lousy observer, and someone has to keep an eye on Claire." The grin was back in place.

Claire's arrival on deck made Dan bite back the retort that had risen to his lips.

"Are you guys talking about me?" Claire was still flushed from sleep, and the oversized raw wool sweater she was wearing enveloped her from neck to knee.

"Walker was just saying it would be good to explore Alice Arm with you." Dan's eyes met Walker's across the top of Claire's head.

"You're coming with us?" Claire's pleasure was apparent in her voice. Walker nodded. "Never been there before. Be good to see it."

"It's supposed to be beautiful," she answered. "I was just reading up on it in the *Sailing Directions*."

Dan left them talking and made his way up to the wheelhouse. It was time to roust Mike out of bed.

▶ "You going to make a habit of this?" Mike's voice was thick with sleep.

"Hey, you're the one who set this crazy scheme up. If I have to be up all hours waiting for information to find it's way up here from Victoria, you can at least give up half an hour's sleep."

"Half an hour? It's only five o'clock!"

"Don't whine. I've been up since four. Anyway, you talked to the coroner yet?"

"Yeah, I talked to the coroner. He said he'll see you at eight thirty at some coffee shop. Hang on and I'll find the notes I took." There was a click as Mike laid the phone down, and a few seconds later he returned. "Here it is. He said it's a couple of blocks from his office. If you'd checked your email you would already know that."

Dan ignored the jibe. "You heard about them finding Kent McGilvery?"

"Who the hell is Kent McGilvery? Don't tell me there's another one."

"Kent McGilvery is—or, more accurately, was—one of the pipeline guys. Worked as some kind of environmental manager out of Kitsault like the rest of them. I met him up there, and then Claire and I ran into him again down here at the marina where he kept his boat. Seemed like a nice guy. Liked to kayak. They found his body out by Digby Island yesterday. It appears he tipped his boat over."

There was silence while Mike digested this news.

"So it was an accident?"

"That's one of the things I need the coroner to tell me. Seems kind of suspicious that it happened right after I'd talked to him."

"Hell. This keeps getting weirder and weirder. You got any ideas yet?"

"Nothing definite, but it's not Joel."

"You sure of that? The Rupert guys still think he might be good for it."

"I can't prove it yet, but I don't think it was him. I'll know more after I talk with the coroner, but if McGilvery was murdered, then it's tied into the others somehow, and Joel wasn't anywhere near Rupert that day. He was over in Haida Gwaii. I talked to him there."

"Shit! Well, keep me posted. I should be in the office all day. You staying in Rupert?"

"Nope. I'm going to head up to Kitsault as soon as I've finished talking to the coroner. Should be there in time for dinner—maybe earlier if we're lucky."

"We? You're taking Claire up there?"

Dan cursed himself for the slip. He hadn't meant to bring that particular issue up.

"Yeah. Claire and Walker are both with me."

"You sure that's a good idea?"

Dan sighed. "No, I'm not sure it's a good idea, but it does support my cover story, and there haven't been any problems at the town site. Besides, I really don't have any other option unless I put them in a hotel or fly them back down, and neither of them seem too keen on that idea."

"I don't know Dan . . ."

"If you want to explain your reasoning to them in person I'd be glad to put them on the phone. Maybe you'll have more luck than me."

"Okay, okay. We'll leave it for now. Take them up there, but be careful."

Dan ended the call with Mike's warning ringing in his ears. He just hoped that being careful would be enough.

▶ TWENTY ◀

▶ The coroner turned out to be a heavyset man with a florid face and thick, black eyebrows that almost met above a pair of startling blue eyes. He slid onto the seat across from Dan at exactly eight thirty, and beckoned to the waitress.

"Good morning, Lucy. I'll have a coffee, black, two sugars, and one of those damn cinnamon rolls." He looked at Dan. "I try to stay away from this place because those cinnamon rolls are so good I just can't resist them. You should try one."

Dan shrugged and nodded to the waitress. "Sounds like a good combo. I'll have the same. Just hold the sugar."

"You won't regret it." The man smiled and reached out a beefy hand. "Adam Lancaster—and I believe you must be Dan Connor. Your boss gave me a pretty good description. So what can I do for you?"

"Did Mike explain what I'm doing here?"

Lancaster nodded. "He did. Interesting arrangement—and one I've never heard of before, although I can certainly see why you've decided to try it. This town is bursting at the seams with media types. Every time some poor bastard is brought into the morgue there are so many of them outside the doors we can hardly get in and out of the building ourselves!"

He stopped talking as the waitress returned with two mugs of coffee and a dinner plate loaded with two of the largest cinnamon rolls Dan had ever seen.

"See why I try not to eat too many of these?" Lancaster asked as he picked one up and took a bite. "They have to be a thousand calories apiece, but dammit, they're worth every one of them."

"Guess I should have jogged up here instead of driven," Dan said as he bit into his own hot, sweet, yeasty roll. "I think I had better take one of these back to the boat for Claire."

"You've got your lady with you?" asked Lancaster. "Seems a bit risky given the numbers. Aren't you worried?"

"That kinda depends on what you can tell me about McGilvery," Dan answered. "Have you done an autopsy on him?"

"McGilvery? That's the kayaker they brought in last night, right?"

Dan nodded.

"You think he might be tied to the other stuff?"

"He works for the same company, and he stays up at the same place as the others when he's working. If it wasn't an accident, then it's one hell of a coincidence."

Lancaster stared at him for several seconds, then nodded. "Well, I haven't done the report up yet because there are still some test results that have to come in, but I can tell you he didn't drown. No water in his lungs."

"So what killed him?"

"Well, that's what the tests are for, so I can't really answer that, but I will say it was almost certainly not natural causes."

Dan sat back, his cinnamon roll forgotten. "Are you saying he was murdered?"

"Off the record?"

Dan nodded.

"That would be my guess. He's got a cracked skull and a broken wrist. I'm waiting on the results from some tissue samples so that I can rule out drugs or alcohol, but he seemed healthy—heart was in good shape, lungs and liver were fine. Considering the shape of the head wound, and the fact that the water was calm yesterday, and adding in the direction of the current and the geography of the area and all those other related factors, I think he was hit on the head with something heavy, maybe the end of a baseball bat, or even a paddle or a fish bonker—you know what those are? Lot of folks around here have one of those for killing fish."

"Shit." Dan pushed his plate away. "Any chance it was the same weapon that was used up there near Kitsault? The one you got the yew wood sample from?"

"You mean the pipeline murders?" Lancaster asked. "No. Totally different kind of wound. No trace of any cut. This was something heavy and blunt, not sharp." He eyed Dan's plate. "Are you actually going to leave that? You should ask Tracy to pack it up for you."

"What? Oh, sure. I'll do that, but listen. Getting back to the pipeline murders. You did all those autopsies, right?"

"I signed off on them, but I didn't do them all. I have two very capable assistants. Between them, they did three. Why?"

"So you wouldn't know if there was any correlation between the angle of the cuts and the height of the victims? Or about what kind of force would be needed to inflict them?"

Lancaster stared at him for a long moment. "Ah," he said. "I see where you're going, but that's not usually my job unless forensics makes a request—and so far, they haven't."

"You got any thoughts on it—off the record?" Dan asked.

"Not without going back over each one. As I said, I only conducted two of the autopsies—three if you count the journalist, but that one won't help you with this. I'd have to go back and look at the reports, study the photographs. Check heights and weights of the victims. It would take a lot of time and I'm not sure I can spare it without an official request to justify it."

"And I'm not sure I can get you that. It would mean going over the heads of the guys who have the case, and that's something I don't want to do. They'll probably come up with it on their own, but it might take more time than I have. If you can just give me an off-the-record opinion, I'd really appreciate it."

Lancaster nodded slowly, then gestured to the waitress. "I've got to get going. I'm due in a meeting. I'll try and take a look, but I can't promise I'll get to it today—or even tomorrow. You going to be around for a while?"

Dan shook his head. "I'm heading up to Kitsault, but you can send anything you come up with to Mike. He'll make sure I get it—and breakfast's on me."

"Thanks." Lancaster took a business card out of his wallet and wrote a number on the back of it. "This is my home number. The media have my office number, although I don't know that they can—or would—go so far as to tap into it. Still, better safe than sorry, I suppose. If you need to get hold of me, try me at home after about six-thirty at night. I'm usually there—unless there's another autopsy required."

▶ "You get what you needed?"

Walker was still onboard *Dreamspeaker* when Dan returned.

"Yes and no," Dan answered. "I found out McGilvery was murdered; that in itself tends to let Joel off the hook. He was over in Haida Gwaii when that happened, and he has witnesses to back him up."

"You figure it was the same guy?"

"I figure it was linked somehow. Might not have been the same guy, although it could have been."

"That going to help you figure out who it is?"

"No, not really. They sent everyone who was staying at Kitsault into town to give them a break. There might have been a few that took off out of town for a few days, but most of them would have been here in Rupert."

Walker looked at him. "So you've got nothing."

Dan grimaced. "Yeah. I've got nothing—although if the coroner comes through it might give me enough to clear Joel. Problem is, without him, Rupert has nothing either."

▶ By five that afternoon, *Dreamspeaker* had made her way up Portland Inlet, then into Observatory Inlet, and finally into Alice Arm, and was tied up at the wharf at Kitsault. Marjorie Wakeshaw saw them come in and drove down to the dock to greet them, saying she had been on her way over to the pub where the crew were holding some kind of makeshift memorial to Kent McGilvery. She invited Dan and Claire to join her.

Walker wasn't with them. He had spent most of the trip up in the wheelhouse, watching the chart scroll by on the screen, getting Dan to point out the creeks that led up into the area where the murders had taken place. About an hour before they reached Kitsault he asked Dan to stop and help him unload the canoe.

"You don't want to wait until morning?" Dan asked. "It's pretty steep shoreline here. I could bring you back in the dinghy tomorrow. We could tow the canoe."

"Thought you wanted me to be your secret weapon," Walker said, his face twisting into his trademark grin. "Pretty hard to be secret if everyone in Kitsault knows I'm out here."

Several different replies flashed through Dan's mind, but he dismissed all of them. Even if Walker was offered ten perfectly logical choices, any one of which would provide the option of a good night's sleep and a hot breakfast, he would ignore all of them. Comfort and convenience had never been a consideration in any circumstance Dan had ever seen him in, and leaving *Dreamspeaker* now, before anyone in Kitsault had a chance to see either him or his canoe, was undeniably the best and the safest course of action.

"Be careful," Dan said as he released the line on the canoe and let it drift off the stern. "And stay in touch." He pointed to the handheld VHF he had given to Walker.

Walker grinned and raised his paddle in the air before slicing it down into the water, turning the tiny vessel and sending it gliding toward the shore.

► Unlike the previous time Dan had been there, the Kitsault pub was full, and while the buzz of conversation could be heard from out in the now-crowded parking lot, there was something subdued about it. The workers had returned, but it sounded as if McGilvery's death was casting a pall over everybody.

"I think you met Kent when you were here, didn't you?" Marjorie asked Dan as they walked toward the entrance doors.

"Yes," Dan answered. "And Claire and I both met him at the marina in Prince Rupert. He seemed like a nice guy."

She nodded. "He was. Got along with everyone here, that's for sure. He taught a lot of people how to kayak, including Jim—that's my husband—and me." She reached for the door, pulling it wide to usher them in. "I think that's why we were all so shocked by his death. He was such a stickler for safety."

▶ "So they don't know it wasn't an accident yet."

Claire and Dan were sitting in the salon, enjoying a glass of wine. They had eaten dinner up at the pub, but then excused themselves from the gathering, saying they planned on taking the dinghy out to explore the area the next day, and wanted an early start.

"Do you think the police are keeping that quiet?" Claire asked.

"I doubt it. More likely Lancaster hasn't released his report yet. He knows the media will swarm on this like bees at a honeypot, so he's probably playing it cautious."

"Will the companies send everyone back to Rupert once the news is released?"

Dan had been wondering that himself, but he thought it unlikely. This was the best time of the year for pipeline construction. June and July were relatively warm and dry, but come October there would be nearly fifteen inches of rain to contend with and the roads would turn into bogs. This far north the nights would quickly grow cold, and the length of day would shorten rapidly. No company could afford to have their operations sitting idle while they paid their staff to do nothing, and certainly for these companies, working in this area, it would be critical to get as much done as possible before the weather changed.

"I don't think so," he replied. "I think they'll probably concentrate on the fact that it happened in Prince Rupert, not here. They might say the killer has moved, or even push the idea that it's not linked to the previous murders. Wouldn't be too hard to sell. The way Kent was killed is certainly different to those other ones."

Claire looked at him. "Do you still think they're linked?" she asked.

"Yes, I do. I just can't figure out what the link is. If I could do that, then maybe I could figure out the motive, and that might lead me to the killer."

"So what are you going to do?"

He reached out and picked up her empty glass, leering at her over its rim. "Right now I think I am going to haul you off to the stateroom where we can indulge in a lascivious workout of exhausting proportions that will stimulate both my circulation and my brain cells."

She smiled and held out her hand. "My, my, my. What big words you have! Are you sure it's only your circulation you want to stimulate?"

He laughed. "Oh I'm sure. Everything else is already stimulated enough."

TWENTY-ONE

▶ Dawn arrived in Alice Arm with the slow creep of daylight lifting up the hem of night just after four in the morning, but the sun would not make its appearance over the tall peaks of the Coast Range until after seven. By then, Dan and Claire were winding their way up yet another of the many creeks that emptied into the inlet. A couple of them had been blocked with waterfalls or the narrow slots in the rocks were too small to allow them access, but most had led deep into the forested shore. Only two had approached the road anywhere near the murder sites, and neither one showed any trace of human passage, let alone a place where a small boat could be tied.

"There should be a turn to the right up ahead, and then another, smaller creek joins up." Claire held a sheet of the topographical map of the area, folded into a clear plastic sleeve. They had highlighted all the waterways they wanted to explore. "The smaller one goes back the way we came, so stay on this one. It's going to turn again, but it's heading in the right direction."

They were working their way slowly south-southwest, checking the banks for signs of disturbance, looking for anything that would indicate that someone had attempted to climb up. Walker would be doing the same thing, but from the opposite direction, and they planned to meet up around noon.

By ten thirty they were hungry, thirsty, and tired, their ears ringing from the constant sound of the engine. They had already been on the water for almost six hours and they had seen nothing except a deer trail that led nowhere. Dan cut the engine and let the boat drift in to shore. The banks were too steep to climb out and stretch their legs, so they sprawled back on the tubes of the inflatable as they ate the sandwiches they had packed, and drank cold juice from the cooler.

"Where are we exactly?" Dan asked, nodding toward the map that lay on the seat in front of him.

"There." Claire put her finger on one of the highlighted lines. "We've only got a few more possibilities before we get to that little beach where you told Walker to meet us."

"Yeah, well, at least our timing's good. We should be able to cover most of those before we join up with him, and we can do anything we miss on the way back."

"You think he might have found something?" she asked. "We haven't heard anything from him." She gestured at the radio that lay silent on the seat beside her.

Dan laughed. "He hates that thing. Even if he found something, he probably wouldn't use it. He knows he's going to be seeing us in a couple of hours, so he'll just tell us then."

Twenty minutes later, he started the engine again, and they continued their slow passage along the narrow stream, reversing their course when it reached a narrow culvert that ran under the road high above them. They tried three more, with the same result, and then entered a larger waterway that, according to their map, was joined by a second, smaller creek that ran almost parallel to the road for some distance after crossing it. It was a creek that Dan had identified as one of the most promising, and he wanted to take his time exploring it. The banks were steep here, cut into the rock by centuries of rainwater rushing down to the ocean, and graceful branches arched high above them, forming a leafy tunnel filled with green light. Several times they brushed against outcroppings of rock where every crack and hollow was filled with intricate fronds of ferns and lush mounds of moss. They saw occasional birds flitting overhead, and salmon swam below them, but there was no sign of any disturbance on the shores.

"It's almost one," Claire said, pointing to her watch. "We need to go. Walker will be waiting for us."

Dan nodded. "We're nearly at the road, five minutes at the most. We may as well finish this one. It'll be faster going back out."

Five minutes later he manoeuvred the dinghy back and forth between the narrow banks and headed back toward the ocean, having seen no sign of anyone ever having come there before. They were only a few hundred yards from re-entering Alice Arm when Claire saw it. She leaned forward and pointed ahead and to the left, where one of the larger rock faces jutted out into the water. Coming from the other side it had been just another outcrop, its dark surface shiny with moisture and dotted with greenery, but from this side there was a deep cleft that angled back and formed an almost-invisible vee. Hanging down at the point of the vee was a rope.

Dan turned the dinghy and tried to push it into the deepest part of the notch, but the wide bow and curving tubes of the inflatable kept it too far back to reach the rope.

"Can you see what it's anchored to?" he asked Claire.

She shook her head. "I can't see much of anything. Did you bring a flashlight?"

Dan muttered a curse. A flashlight. The one thing he had not thought of. Why would he? They had almost eighteen hours of daylight at this time of the year and they were out on the water at noon, with the sun high overhead.

"No. We'll have to come back. We'll go meet Walker and see if he's found anything—there has to be more than one place this guy comes ashore—and then we can head straight back to *Dreamspeaker* and pick up what we need. It won't take long now we know where to go."

He eased the dinghy out of the cleft and turned it toward the open water of the inlet. Fifteen minutes of running at full speed would get them to the rendezvous.

▶ Three hours later they were standing on a small curve of shingle where one of the bigger creeks swept in a wide arc on its way to the ocean. It was one of the few flat shoreline areas Dan had found on the topographical map, and it was the place where he and Walker had agreed to meet, but it was more than two hours since the time they had chosen and Walker had still not put in an appearance.

"Do you think we should we go looking for him?" Claire was standing at the edge of the water, staring down the creek as if willing Walker to appear.

"Let's give him another half-hour," Dan answered. "He doesn't have a watch and he might have got held up somewhere." He hoped he sounded more convincing than he felt. Walker had an innate sense of time, and could read not only the angle of the sun, but also the weather and all the other signs nature provided better than anyone he had ever known. It wouldn't have been the lack of a watch that delayed him.

The half-hour came and went and still there was no sign of a canoe.

"We have to do something. We can't just wait around here all day." Dan went down to the water, to where Claire was still keeping her vigil, and slid an arm around her shoulders. "Let's go look for him."

"But where do we look?" She leaned against him. "He might have figured we would go back to Kitsault when he missed the rendezvous and head straight there. If we aren't there . . ."

"If we aren't there, he'll wait for us. We need to use the daylight to check where we know he was headed. Maybe he lost his paddle. Maybe he fell asleep under a tree—he doesn't get nearly enough sleep anyway, so maybe it crept up on him." As he spoke, Dan ushered her toward the inflatable. "He's probably going to give us a hard time because we took so long to come and get him." His words sounded hollow in his own ears.

An hour later the first raven arrived. It landed on a branch that hung over the small creek they were navigating. Shortly after that, they saw a second, then a third. An hour after that they found Walker's canoe. Walker wasn't in it.

TWENTY-TWO

► Three o'clock in the morning found Dan standing at the stern rail, staring blindly out into the night. Sleep was impossible. The image of that empty canoe was much too vivid for that. If it had belonged to someone other than Walker it would still be a cause for concern, but it wouldn't have meant nearly as much. Without his canoe Walker was basically helpless, and the steep shoreline only exacerbated that fact. Climbing up would be difficult for an able-bodied man. For Walker, whose legs could barely carry him on flat ground, it would be impossible. Even if he tried to swim—and Dan knew how powerful a swimmer Walker was—that steep bank would provide no escape from the cold water.

Dan and Claire had searched the creek banks and the surrounding waters for hours after their discovery, only heading back to Kitsault when darkness made continuing their efforts both dangerous and useless. They had left the canoe where they found it, partly in the hope that Walker would come back for it, and partly because they didn't want to explain where an empty canoe had come from if they towed it back. *Dreamspeaker* was dark and empty when they returned, and the village was quiet. Dan went straight to the wheelhouse and spent hours trying to reach Charles Eden on his boat, but there was no response. The man was probably still over in Haida Gwaii and out of radio range or else he had his radio turned off—maybe both. He then called Mike and got him out of bed, only to be told what he already knew: there was nothing to be done until the next day, and even then, there wasn't much. Prince Rupert didn't have the resources to search for a man who had probably fallen out of his canoe, Search and Rescue would not consider this an emergency until Walker had been missing for at least twenty-four hours, and the Coast Guard didn't have the ability to search small creeks. Mike also told him he was an idiot for involving a civilian—not that he needed to be told—but once the harangue was over, Mike's tone changed.

"So are you thinking of this as simply an accident or do you figure it's linked to the other stuff?"

"Hell, I don't know," Dan answered as he ran a hand through his hair for probably the twentieth time. "Out on the water he's the most capable man I've ever known. I can't believe he would just fall out of his canoe, and he would never let it just drift away, even if there was some place he found to go ashore, which is pretty well impossible. But to think this could be linked—why would he be targeted? He was just a Native guy out in his canoe."

Even as he said the words Dan heard himself talking in the past tense.

"Maybe he saw something he shouldn't have seen. Maybe he came across the guy we're looking for."

"Where? Claire and I found that rock cleft with the rope, but there was no one there, and we didn't see anyone the whole time we were out there—and it's not as if there are a lot of places to hide."

Mike broke the silence that fell as the two men considered the possibilities.

"Well, keep me posted—and look after Claire."

"Oh, I will. She's not going to be out of my sight."

▶ Dan shivered in the night air and headed back inside to the salon where Claire was hunched over the Tide and Current Tables, the pages of her notebook covered with scrawled calculations and notes.

"I'm going to load up some rope and blankets," he said. "We should probably think about heading out. It'll be starting to get light in about half an hour."

She nodded and closed the book.

"I'll pack up some food. Have you got the radio and flashlight?"

Neither one of them could bring themselves to mention Walker's name.

They left just after four, with the sky still dark and only the faintest gleam of light limning the peaks of the mountains. The fear that gnawed in both their bellies increased the chill of the morning as they headed back toward the black void that Walker's empty canoe had created. Neither one of them spoke. What could they possibly say that would not evoke the specter they were both trying to deny?

By the time they reached the mouth of the creek, the light of the new day was reflecting off the tops of the waves, patterning the ocean with movement and life, but in keeping with their mood, they returned to darkness as they moved inland. They traveled slowly now, gripped by both natural caution and a growing apprehension. What would they find? Would the canoe still be there? Would Walker be there? Would they find a killer? If they did, what then?

There were no answers, and as their speed slowed even more, Dan patted the gun he had cleaned, oiled, and loaded before leaving *Dreamspeaker* that morning and that he was wearing for the second time since his arrival in Prince Rupert. As he did so, he felt a corresponding twinge in his shoulder, a reminder of the bullet that had sent him to hospital the previous year. Walker had played a major part in that case too, as he had in one Dan had been involved in the year before that; it was largely due to Walker's knowledge and skills that both cases had been successfully resolved. Dan owed him a debt of gratitude that he could only hope he would have the chance to repay.

They rounded the last curve and peered into the shadows. Their arrival disturbed two gulls, which lifted off the beach to land on an overhanging branch where they screeched their protest. The canoe was still there, its bow resting on the narrow curve of shingle, and it was still empty. Even the small woven cedar basket that Walker kept his fishing line and other gear in was gone, and there were two or three inches of water in the bottom. Dan studied the creek banks carefully, and then ran the inflatable up beside the canoe. Reaching over, he dipped his finger into the water and tasted it.

"What on earth are you doing?" Claire asked.

He didn't answer her directly. "Let's move up the creek a little."

Using an oar, he pushed the dinghy back into the water and faced it upstream before starting the motor again. When they had passed the next couple of bends and the canoe was completely out of sight, he put the engine into neutral and let them drift back down. The creek was a little wider here, already anticipating its rendezvous with the sea, and at this time of year, with the heavy rains more than a month behind them, it was shallow, and the current was slow. They spun slowly as the water pushed against the vee of the hull, then straightened as they slid past the beach where the canoe rested, the current holding them to the opposite bank.

"Dan?"

He had engaged the engine again and returned to the tiny beach.

"It doesn't make sense," he said. "That water is fresh."

She stared at him, frowning. "Why wouldn't it be? This is a creek."

"Yeah. But think about it. If he'd tipped over further up, he could have grabbed the canoe. The creek's not deep. He could have hung on, even climbed back in. You know how strong he is. Even if he couldn't, if he was injured or something, and the canoe got away and drifted down by itself, it wouldn't have ended up here. You saw what just happened to us. We went right on by."

She looked from him to the canoe and back. "So how did it get here?"

▶ They left the canoe and continued up the creek, as they had done the day before, but it was just as Dan remembered it. Shortly after the second bend it narrowed and the banks grew steeper. A few stunted trees clung to life in the crevices of the rock and there were the soft green clusters of ferns and mosses, but the possibility of anyone climbing up or down without a great deal of assistance was non-existent. Long before they reached the place where it crossed under the road, they had to give up as the sheer walls closed in on them.

They returned to the narrow alcove in the rock where they had seen the rope, hoping they would find something there—a kayak, a canoe, a dinghy, anything that would lead them to an answer, however indirectly—but it was exactly as they had seen it the day before: a length of rope hanging down from an overhang, presumably tied to something above but perhaps just caught on a snag of some kind, abandoned by a work crew or dropped from a truck. With nothing to go on, they moved on to the creeks where Walker would have likely been exploring after they dropped him off. Like the ones they had checked out the day before, most were too small or too shallow to allow access, but four were deep and wide enough to allow entry. One split around a huge boulder a short distance inland creating a series of shallow, rocky passages that were impossible to pass, while two others led to narrow culverts leading under the road. The fourth was bigger, but they didn't need to go far to see it ended in a waterfall. A wide ribbon of white water tumbled twenty feet down the rock face below a bridge where three ravens lined up along the edge and mocked them as they turned around. Nowhere was there any sign of Walker, or of anyone else for that matter.

"Should we head further down Observatory? The current only changed an hour or so ago." Claire's voice sounded loud above the idling motor, echoing off the steep rock faces and startling both of them.

Dan shook his head. "There's no point. We already know where the canoe is." He left unsaid the impossibility of Walker either walking or swimming any distance, and he refused to think about the logistics of searching for a body.

"Let's go back to where we started yesterday and work our way down. There has to be something."

Even as he said the words, a flash of lightning split the sky above them and a loud peal of thunder rumbled overhead. Dan looked up to see the branches of the trees tossing in the wind. He had been so involved with searching the creek banks that he had failed to notice the approaching storm.

He turned the inflatable toward open water and opened up the throttle as far as he dared. He had been so consumed with the need to find Walker that he had failed to check the forecast before leaving *Dreamspeaker* that morning and they were not prepared for any serious bad weather, but even as they rounded the last bend of the creek, they could see whitecaps dancing on the waves out on the inlet.

He slowed the engine and leaned forward toward Claire. "I'm going to head back to that alcove where we found the rope." He had to shout to make himself heard. "It will give us some shelter. We're not going to be able to make it back against this wind."

He saw her nod of agreement, and then felt the first drops of rain sting his face. By the time he turned into the inlet the visibility was so poor that he barely saw the dark hull of the fish boat sitting just off the point.

TWENTY-THREE

► The pontoon of the inflatable had barely touched the hull before Charles Eden appeared and tossed down a ladder. Dan held them steady while Claire climbed up, and then he passed her the tie-up line before following her up onto the deck.

The cabin of the fish boat was warm and dry with the heat from the cast iron Dickenson stove radiating into the cozy space. They shrugged out of their jackets, hung them on hooks beside the door, and slid onto the banquette behind the table.

"I'm sure glad to see you," Dan said as he accepted a cup of tea. "I was trying to reach you for hours last night. I thought you must still be over in Haida Gwaii."

"I was—at least during the day. I came back across last night." Eden answered. "Why were you trying to call me?"

Dan turned his head and stared out into the rain. Even saying the words was difficult. "Walker's missing. He was supposed to meet us yesterday but he didn't show up. We went looking for him and found his canoe, but there was no sign of him. We searched until it was too dark to see anything, and we've been out since dawn today, but there's just no trace."

He turned back, his face haggard with worry and lack of sleep drawn in the furrows beside his mouth. "It's my fault. I should never have let him go out there."

Eden poured himself a cup and sat down across from them. "Did he ask you for permission?"

"Walker? Are you kidding? Walker does what Walker wants to do."

"So how could you have stopped him?"

Dan stared at him, surprised by the question and unable to come up with an adequate response.

Eden smiled and sipped his tea. "Walker may be in trouble, yes, but I do not think it is as you fear. I do not think he is dead."

Dan heard the breath catch in Claire's throat as she heard the words. "How can you know that?" she demanded.

"I don't," Eden answered. "It's what Joel told me, and I believe him."

"Joel?" Dan and Claire chorused. "How would Joel know? How would Joel even know Walker was in trouble in the first place?"

Eden shrugged. "He said the ravens told him."

They could only stare at him in confusion. They didn't have the words to answer a statement like that.

Eden smiled again and reached for their cups to refill them.

"It sounds strange to you, I know that, but to us it is the natural way of things—and if you think about it, you will realize the truth of what I say. How else could Joel have known to come here?"

Dan searched Eden's face. "Are you saying Joel is here? That he's gone looking for Walker?" He pushed himself up, bracing himself on the table. "We have to stop him!"

Eden stayed seated, the quiet smile still in place. "You can't stop him. He knows what he's doing. He'll bring Walker back here when he finds him."

Somewhere in the recesses of his memory, Dan heard an echo of Walker saying the same words two years previously when Dan had tried to stop Percy and his young charges from disabling the black ship, but he pushed it away.

"You don't understand! It's too dangerous. Walker didn't have an accident. He was attacked."

Eden shrugged. "Yaahl will look after him."

"Ravens can't protect him from a maniac! This has to be the man Joel thinks is trying to frame him. The murderer. A man who has already killed seven people—maybe eight if Walker is dead. Killing Joel will be less trouble for this guy than swatting a fly." He turned to Claire. "Come on. We need to get back out there."

"You may put him in danger if you try to follow him."

Eden's voice was still quiet, but his words stopped Dan in his tracks. "What? How the hell could *I* put him in danger?"

"You have a motor. The sound could alert this man you are talking about. Or it could distract Joel when he should be concentrating on other things." Eden gestured out the window. "And you could get into trouble yourselves in this weather. If you went missing, then Walker and Joel would have to search for you when they get back."

"Walker and Joel are not going to get back!" Dan could hear his voice rising as his fear and frustration grew. "That's what I keep trying to tell you. That's why we . . ."

He felt Claire's hand on his arm and her touch helped him regain some measure of control.

"I think Charles might be right," she said, looking up into his face.

"What?"

"Think about it. How *did* Joel know? He was over on Haida Gwaii. There has to be something going on here that we don't know about—that we don't understand. We were out there. We couldn't find Walker. Maybe Joel can."

He looked down at her. "And what if Joel goes missing too?"

Her fingers dug deeper into his arm, but her voice remained steady. "You can't stop people doing what they want to do. I guess if that happens, we'll just have to figure something out."

As he heard her words, Dan felt the knot in his gut loosen just a little, and the surging panic that raced through his bloodstream subsided to a steady hum. Impatience, a driving need to act, to control, had always been the cornerstone of his personality. It had served him well when he had been a member of an anti-terrorist squad in the city, his impetuous urges directed by the needs of the team, but out here he needed to employ other attributes. His time with Walker had showed him the value of quiet observation, of careful thought, of respect for those around him. The least he could do now was to honor the man by following the path he had been shown.

He sank back down on the banquette and accepted the fresh cup of tea that Charles Eden slid toward him.

"So we just wait?" Accepting the advice being offered didn't necessarily make it easy, and Dan could still feel the doubt and fear churning in his gut.

Eden nodded. "For now that is all we can do."

The rain eased two hours later, although the sky remained dark and mist curled between the trees. Eden moved outside and started to work on one of the winches at the stern. Dan joined him.

"Any idea what the forecast is?"

Eden looked up at the sky. "Should be okay for a while," he said. "But there's another storm coming. Why?"

"I was thinking maybe I should go and get Walker's canoe. If Joel does find him, he's going to need it."

Eden nodded slowly. "Joel will find him," he said. "There will be plenty of time to get the canoe then."

Dan looked out over the water. "You seem so sure."

"I am sure," Eden replied and turned back to the winch.

▶ Almost three miles away, Joel steered his canoe around yet another bend in the stream he was exploring. The woven cedar hat he was wearing had done a good job of protecting him from the worst of the rain, but he was damp from the effort of paddling upstream against a rain-spawned current fed by the torrents of water cascading from the surrounding mountains.

He had been guided into this particular creek by the presence of two ravens sitting on a low branch that jutted out over the narrow waterway's confluence with the larger stream he had been on and he had been working his way up it for almost an hour now, but the steep banks were starting to draw closer and from somewhere up ahead he could hear the sound of rushing water. It sounded like rapids, and if it was, their presence might make further progress impossible. Already his shoulders and arms were protesting from the relentless push through the racing water, but Joel was oblivious to the pain. Walker was out there, and he would not stop until he found him.

He drove his paddle in again, forcing his way forward around yet another curve and suddenly the source of the sound he was hearing was right in front of him. It wasn't rapids and it didn't completely block his passage, although it may as well have done. The waterfall cascaded down from under a bridge that spanned a road that in turn clung to the side of the mountain some twenty feet above him. The storm had turned what might have been a steady spout into a foaming torrent. It covered the rock face behind it with a curtain of white and churned the surface of the pool below into a seething mass of waves and eddies.

Joel reached out and let his hand slide along the rock as his fingers searched for a crevice to hold him steady against the flow. Why would the ravens have brought him here if it were just a dead end? They had never steered him wrong before, and they had made no protest when he turned into this creek. True, he hadn't seen one of the huge birds since he turned, but then he hadn't expected to. They knew where he was. They knew where he was going. He let his eyes drift up the flume of water to its source, watching the mist dance and coil over the rocks and wrap itself round the edges of the bridge. As his gaze reached the top, his felt his fingers dig into the rock beside him. A single white raven was perched on the mid-point of the railing. It was watching him.

"Xuuya," he breathed, and dug his paddle into the water to send the tiny canoe surging forward into the thunder of the waterfall.

▶ Charles Eden straightened up from his examination of the winch and scanned the inlet as if looking for something, and then he turned back to Dan. "Have you seen any waterfalls while you were searching those creeks?"

"What? What have waterfalls got to do with anything?" Dan asked. He had sometimes found it hard to follow Walker's rapid change of subjects, but this was crazy.

Eden shook his head, his expression showing his puzzlement. "I don't know. I just thought about one, that's all. Seemed odd. Might mean something, but maybe not."

Dan stared at him. "What do you think it might it mean?"

"I don't know." Eden's gaze sharpened. "Did you see a waterfall?"

"Yeah. There's one that comes out from under one of the bridges along the road. It's pretty high but not that big, at least it wasn't when I saw it yesterday, although it's probably much bigger now with all this rain."

Eden's gaze turned inward and he was quiet for several moments, then he looked up at the sky. "Think you could find it again pretty quickly?"

"Find it? Yeah, sure. It's not that far from here. Why?"

"I think Joel may need your help."

TWENTY-FOUR

▶ The creek was too narrow and the channel too twisting to run flat out, but Dan pushed the speed as high as he could, his fingers gripping the controls so hard they looked like claws, his body tense and his eyes locked on the water ahead. Only an hour or so ago he had wanted to do exactly this, but he had let himself be talked out of it. Now, somewhere in the back of his brain—the rational part he had cultivated for most of his adult life—he was aware of a voice telling him to slow down, to think about what he was doing, to ask himself why he would respond to something so completely illogical. He ignored it. This was not the time to rely on logic. This was Walker and Joel and Charles Eden. This was their world, and if he had learned anything at all from Walker, it was that this world operated in a different way, under different rules. It was a world where everything was fluid. Where spirits could transform themselves, and communication relied less on speech and more on acceptance and understanding. Where the heart ruled the head. It was a world Dan had never been completely comfortable in, but now he found himself wanting to embrace it.

The sound of the engine masked the roar of the waterfall, and even though Dan slammed the controls into neutral as he rounded the last bend, momentum carried him almost into the wall of water rushing down from below the bridge before the current caught him and pushed him back. Jockeying the control lever he crept forward again, scanning the rock walls and the road above the culvert. There was no sign of human life. Behind the road the dark trees climbed up the steep mountain slopes, their moisture-laden branches drooping down toward the ground with a heavy, brooding menace, while the wet rocky banks of the stream gave off a dull gleam. Moisture was condensing in the air itself, forming a thick mist that coiled and twisted as it rose, and the roar of the falls rose above the mutter of the engine and pounded on Dan's ears, creating a pressure that threatened to overwhelm his sanity.

If Charles Eden was correct in believing his vision, this had to be the right place. It was the only waterfall Dan and Claire had found yesterday, and they had searched every creek that Walker would have traveled, as well as revisiting those they themselves had searched the day before. There had been a couple of thin trickles, and those would certainly be running a little harder after the rains, but there was no way they would qualify as a waterfall—and Charles was adamant that he had seen a large cascade of white water dropping into a narrow stream.

Dan manoeuvred the dinghy from side to side, trying to see past the churning water to the bank on the other side, but it was blocked by mist and spume. It probably didn't matter anyway, because there was no way a canoe could get there: not only was the bank in front of the falls almost sheer rock with no handholds or places to tie up, the current was far too strong and the volume of falling water far too great to get past it. Even with the motor he was having trouble keeping the boat steady. It was useless. Another wasted effort and more time lost. He should have listened to the voice of reason and dismissed Eden's vision for what it was—a flight of fancy created by imagination and based on hope. Well, at least he could say he had tried, but it was time to do what he should have done long before this: go back to the beginning and conduct a methodical search of each creek. Let Charles and Joel talk to their damn ravens. He shook his head as he thought of it. What was it with those crazy birds? Charles had even said that in his vision he had seen a raven sitting over the waterfall, but Dan hadn't seen a single raven since he had left the fish boat. Even as the thought came to him, Dan felt his eyes lift to roam over the face of the waterfall and up to the narrow vee that funneled it out over the bank, looking for what had now become a familiar black shape. He didn't find it, but he thought there was something there, and it did look like a bird. He squinted his eyes to bring it into focus, but it was mostly hidden by the mist that swirled over the water. All he could see was that it looked large and appeared to be white, which made it even more difficult to see clearly. What bird would sit right above a waterfall? All he could think of was some kind of eagle or hawk, but none of them were white. A gull perhaps, but that seemed unlikely.

He shook his head, annoyed with himself for allowing something as trivial as a bird to distract him from the urgent task ahead of him. He turned the dinghy away from the waterfall, feeling it start to pick up speed as the current caught it. He was already twenty feet downstream when the bird swooped in front of him. It was huge and it was white, but it was unmistakably a raven. It passed close to the bow then wheeled and soared back up the bank where it resumed its perch. Its piercing shriek was audible even over the roar of the torrent.

Adrenalin surging, Dan wrenched the dinghy back around and battled the current yet again. He had never seen a white raven before, although he had heard rumors that they existed. Still, the fact that there *was* a raven there added weight to Charles Eden's theory . . . belief . . . fantasy . . . whatever it was. But then again there was no sign of Joel, or his canoe, or Walker, and there was no place they could hide, unless . . .

Dan stared at the waterfall. The water arched out for about four or five feet where it exited the vee of the creek bed, then it hit a rock ledge and arched out again. There was no way of telling for sure what shape the rock wall behind it was, but from the little he could see from this side, it either dropped straight down or perhaps sloped inward a little. Given the outward curve of the falls, it might be that there was a space—and perhaps a relatively still pool of water—behind it. But how could he get in to check? The volume of water was huge and it would fill the dinghy in seconds. Worse, if it hit one pontoon before the other it could flip it, and would certainly stall the motor, which meant he would be at the mercy of the current and would be carried back downstream with no way to slow his progress.

But Joel had a canoe. It was narrower, and if it were lined up properly it would possibly be less vulnerable to tipping. If Joel had somehow found a way to outpace the current, he might have been able to get in there. Perhaps he could have slid the narrow craft along the rock face immediately downstream of the falls and then pushed off to help develop enough speed to clear that solid sheet of water, but there was no way of checking if he was there or not. No way of contacting him. Shouting was useless and no one would be able to hear the motor over the noise of the falls.

The air horn! If he were there, Joel would certainly hear the air horn. Dan braced himself against the pontoon and dug under the seat for the emergency pack. He had tested the horn before he left Campbell River, and he had checked and replaced the canister of air. Quickly he pulled it from the bag and pressed the button. The blaring shriek seemed to penetrate the rock itself as Dan pressed it again and again.

The fog that swirled around him had no edges, and this close to the falls the trees that climbed the slopes above the banks took on a ghostly shimmer. Even the rock itself seemed to move in time with the thunderous percussion, and it took Dan several seconds to realize that the darker shape he was seeing within the foaming curtain of water was a canoe. He angled the dinghy so it would provide a barrier to catch the tiny vessel as it emerged, and fought the current to hold the bow steady. Seconds later the curtain parted and the canoe surged out. It slammed into the side of the inflatable, pushing it downstream for several yards before Dan could slow its progress. Once he had things under some degree of control, he took the rope that Joel was holding out and he wrapped it around the tie-up cleat on the inflatable before passing the loose end back. With the two boats firmly tied together, he let them drift downstream far enough to allow for shouted conversation.

"Did you find Walker?"

Joel nodded. He was shivering, his clothing soaked. "He's back at the waterfall."

Dan looked back at the cascading falls in disbelief. "He's at the waterfall? How the hell did he get there?"

Joel shrugged. "Swam."

Dan would have laughed had the situation not been so serious. No wonder Joel and Walker were friends. In addition to their love of being on the water, they shared the same disdain for long explanations.

"Is he okay? Why didn't he come with you?"

"He hurt his shoulder climbing up the rock. He can't get down."

But he was alive. Of all the thoughts racing through Dan's mind, that one was paramount. Walker was alive. The dread he had been feeling drained out of him to be replaced by the adrenaline he had once enjoyed so much.

"I've got rope. We can get him down with that. Can you get me back in there?"

It took nearly half an hour and a great deal of ingenuity and perseverance, but between them, they managed it. Dan used one of the ropes he had brought with him to tie the inflatable to the stern of Joel's canoe in such a way that it would hang back about thirty feet when he released it. He passed his first aid kit and emergency paddle across and then joined Joel in the canoe. With the two of them paddling, they managed to push the tiny vessel around the face of the falls and then to maneuver it close to the bank where the arching water left a narrow gap that allowed them to slide inside.

Once in, they found themselves in a different world, a world of eerie green light and dripping rock. The steep wall behind the cascade had been eroded into a concave curve by the relentless pounding of the stream, leaving a series of protuberances where harder rock had resisted the endless cascade. A single longer horizontal ledge was visible about ten feet above the water. Walker was perched on the edge of it, one arm hanging at an odd angle by his side.

"Took you long enough." His teeth were clenched against the pain and the cold, but in spite of his obvious discomfort, his grin was still in place.

"Yeah, well I didn't figure you'd take up climbing." Dan kept his tone light as he searched the rocks above the ledge for a place to anchor the second rope he had brought with him.

He found one, but even with Joel's assistance, it took much longer to get it up there than he liked. Walker's shivering was starting to abate, and he was less alert than he had been when they first arrived. Hypothermia was setting in. It was Joel who finally got the rope properly secured and Dan's inflatable PFD wrapped securely around Walker's chest to cushion the crude harness Dan fashioned. With Dan feeding out the rope from below, and Joel guiding from the ledge, they finally managed to get an almost incoherent Walker into the bottom of the canoe.

Pushing off from the rock wall, they shot through the falling water and out into the stream. The current caught them and with Dan supporting Walker with one hand and bailing with the other, it took all Joel's skill to steady the overloaded vessel as it raced toward the inlet and Charles Eden's waiting boat. There was no way that Dan could climb back into the inflatable, but he did manage to pull it up close enough to reach the emergency pack he had left on the seat. He carefully removed his own jacket, took off the zipped fleece he wore underneath, draped it around Walker's shoulders and then wrapped him in a space blanket from the pack. It was the best he could do for now.

By the time they reached the fish boat, Walker was barely conscious and there was no way he could climb aboard, or even participate in his own rescue. Charles finally solved the problem by running ropes through the power blocks on one of the trolling poles and lowering them down together with a safety harness. Dan snapped the harness on and with Charles operating the winch controls and Claire guiding the ropes and calling instructions, they slowly hauled the inert form up and swung him onto the deck.

It took three of them to carry Walker into the cabin and lay him on the bunk, by which time he had lost consciousness completely. Dan stripped him of his wet clothes and dried him, then wrapped him in the blankets that Charles provided. Claire lit the stove, boiled a kettle and filled two large juice bottles with hot water. Wrapped in towels and placed on either side of Walker's chest, the bottles were the only way she could think of to heat the man up, but as she was placing the second one, she noticed the awkward angle of his shoulder.

"It's dislocated," she said as she tucked the blanket in again. "He must have been in agony."

Dan nodded his head in agreement. "It's amazing he survived at all. He had to have been there for hours." He looked down at the motionless form. "Do you think we could get it back in place while he's still out? It would be a lot easier on him than waiting till he wakes up."

They both had basic first aid training and between the two of them they managed to lift and pull on the arm until they felt the ball snap back into its socket. They then strapped the arm to Walker's chest by wrapping it with strips that Charles tore from an old sheet. Joel had taken over the job of heating water, and Claire refilled the bottles and gently replaced them under the blankets.

"Do you think we should we call the Coast Guard?" Claire asked. They had moved back into the galley where there was room for them all to sit, but they had left the door to the sleeping cabin open so they could keep an eye and ear on Walker. The stove was still lit and the boat felt oppressively hot, but no one was complaining.

"No!" There was both concern and fear in Joel's quick answer. "Walker would not want that."

"Charles, what do you think?" Dan asked. "He's still unconscious. Maybe he needs more help than we can give him."

Charles didn't reply. He looked from Joel to Dan and then stood up and walked back to where Walker lay unmoving on the bunk. After several minutes he returned and resumed his seat.

"I think we should wait a little longer. His breathing seems a little better." He looked at Joel. "But if he doesn't wake up soon, we will need to get help."

Joel nodded reluctantly. "He would not like to be in a hospital, but if it is necessary . . ." His voice trailed off.

"Maybe we should start heading back to Rupert," Dan said. "There's no clinic or hospital at Kitsault—in fact, it's probably dangerous for Walker to be there when there's a crazy man who just tried to kill him still on the loose. It's almost certainly where the guy is based, and he wouldn't be happy to know Walker has survived. If you went to Rupert, Joel could leave before you tied up, and you could just say that you found Walker on the shore somewhere."

Even as he said it, Dan realized it wouldn't work. The hospital would call in the RCMP and they would want to know exactly where Walker had been found and what he had been doing out there. They would also question why Charles Eden had taken his boat so close to the area where the murders had taken place—murders his nephew was suspected of committing.

"Shit. There's got to be something we can do." It seemed every idea he came up with turned into a dead end.

"I'm going to change the water in the bottles."

Three pairs of eyes followed Claire as she stood up and went in to the bunk. She started to slide her hand under the blankets, then straightened up and stood looking down at Walker's face.

"Is he okay?" Dan asked.

"You should ask him yourself," she replied, a tremulous smile on her face. "He's awake."

TWENTY-FIVE

▶ "I never saw the guy close up."

Walker was sitting up in the bunk, leaning against the bulkhead. He had drunk two cups of sweetened tea and eaten three slices of toast. Claire was out in the galley making him more.

Dan grimaced. He had been hoping that Walker would be able to identify his attacker, or at least provide a good description.

"Where did he get you?"

"Right at the waterfall. I figured maybe there was a pool behind it. Some place someone could hide. I thought I might be able to get around to the other side of it and use the current to get through the fall so I went in real close to the opposite bank. One minute I thought I'd made it and the next this damn long branch or pole or something comes down and bangs onto the side of the canoe. I think it was aiming for me, but the water's rough and the current kept swinging me around."

"Any chance it was a paddle?"

"No. Too long and too heavy, and it felt rough, not sanded smooth like a paddle would be." He thought for a minute and then added, "It wasn't a branch either. No bark or twigs. I guess it felt most like a fence pole, but it was way too long for that."

"So he tipped you over with this pole?"

"No. I grabbed the pole to stop him and he yanked it up the same time as the current caught the canoe and spun it sideways."

The two men fell silent as Claire returned with another plate of toast, which Walker ate as she looked on with a maternal gaze.

"Thanks." Walker passed the plate back to her with a smile. "Are my clothes around? I seem to have lost them."

"They're still wet," Dan answered. "Charles doesn't have a clothes dryer aboard and we were too busy worrying about you to hang them up."

"Yeah, well Charles probably has something he can lend me."

"Charles took the skiff out. Said he wanted to catch something for dinner."

"So he won't mind if you dug something out."

"I'd rather wait for Charles," Dan said. "And you need to stay where you are for a while." Walker seemed to have recovered completely from his ordeal and his appetite was an encouraging sign, but Dan was still worried about possible after-effects from the hypothermia.

"Hey, it was just the cold and the shoulder that knocked me out. I feel fine."

"You didn't look fine when we brought you here. You looked whiter than me and your lips were blue."

"If I was any whiter than you I'd be dead," Walker retorted.

"You damn near were," Dan replied. "And speaking of your shoulder, did that happen when the guy attacked you?"

"No. I had to pull myself up onto that ledge. Got the wrong angle, I guess, and it popped."

Just thinking about the pain and the determination that comment implied made Dan wince.

"Is there anything at all you saw of the guy?"

Walker shrugged. "It happened too quick. He was just an outline, really, sort of a silhouette against the sky." He was quiet for a couple of minutes and Dan could see him reliving the event, searching for any memory that might help them identify who it had been. "He was big, that's one thing. Kinda solid. Wide shoulders, thick body."

"Was he tall?"

"Hard to say. I didn't have anything to compare him with, but I'd say he was around your height, but heavier. Not fat. Just . . . big."

"You see what he was wearing?"

"No. Jeans maybe. Something dark. Same with the jacket."

"You sure it was a jacket?"

Walker frowned. "Yeah," he answered thoughtfully. "I am, but I don't know why . . . wait a minute! Yes, I do. It came open when he pulled the pole up. He kinda twisted his body and I saw the bottom edge of the jacket. It was long—covered his hips. I think it had buttons too. They must have caught the light as he turned. I remember seeing a row of them, maybe three or four." He looked at Dan. "Weird thing to remember, huh?"

Dan shook his head, remembering all the times he had questioned witnesses the same way and had unearthed similar revelations. "Not really. You remember anything else? Boots? A belt buckle? Shirt collar? Glasses?"

"No." Walker's gaze turned inward as he struggled to recapture the moment. "I think that's it." His head suddenly snapped up. "Except he had red hair!"

"What? You sure?" For the first time since he had taken on this case, Dan felt the electricity of the hunt start to tingle through his veins. Joel had also mentioned seeing a man with red hair.

"Yeah. I am. It was when he turned. He lifted his head somehow and I saw his hair. It was just a quick look, but it was red. I don't know why I didn't remember it right away, but it wasn't that real bright red—you know, kinda like a carrot or something. It was dark red. I guess I thought it was just the sun catching it, but there wasn't any sun. It was red hair."

Walker had a bemused expression on his face as he spoke, as if he couldn't believe either his lapse of memory or his sudden volubility. Dan had seen the same look on the faces of many people who had suffered some traumatic event, and then recalled small, previously forgotten details during questioning.

"Long or short?"

"Huh? Oh, short I think. Yeah. Short."

There was nothing more after that. Charles returned a half hour later with a fat Chinook salmon, several fronds of kelp, and a handful of sea asparagus. Not long after that they had dinner seated around the scarred wooden table in the galley. Walker was wearing an old pair of coveralls that Charles had lent him, with a heavy knit sweater he had somehow managed to get his arm into underneath. He had complained so loudly about the heat in the cabin that Dan had finally relented and opened the door out onto the deck, and a light breeze wafted through the crowded space.

"So what do we do now?" It was Claire who asked the question they had all been thinking about.

"Good question," Dan replied. "I need to get back to Kitsault—see if I can find any big guys with red hair wandering around—but I'm not sure you should come with me."

"Oh, for goodness sake!" Claire sighed in exasperation. "We've been through this before. Nobody is going to attack me on board *Dreamspeaker*, and if it makes you feel any better, I promise I won't take the kayak out by myself."

"It does make me feel better," Dan answered. "Although I still think you should have stayed in Rupert."

"Staying in Rupert didn't help Kent McGilvery," Claire pointed out, her voice tart. "Besides, how on earth could you explain to Marjorie and all the other people in Kitsault where I had disappeared to if I didn't come back with you?"

Dan threw his hands up. "Fine. You win. And yes, it would be difficult to explain—but that doesn't mean it's safe for you there, and it doesn't mean I'm happy about it."

He turned to Walker. "What about you? Are you staying with Charles and Joel?"

"Guess I have to. I don't have a canoe any more."

"Shit! I forgot to tell you. Claire and I found it yesterday. It's beached way up one of the creeks. I can pick it up in a couple of days when I've finished here and bring it down to Rupert. It should be fine where it is, and none of you should be out there on your own."

"How about we go now?" Walker pointedly ignored Dan's words. "It wouldn't take long and there's still plenty of light."

"How about we don't. You need to get at least one night's sleep and I need to get up to Kitsault. I'll show Charles where it is on the chart in case I'm longer than I think I'll be. It's easy to find."

Charles went up to the wheelhouse to retrieve the chart, which he brought back and spread on the table.

"Where are we?" Walker asked, his eyes roaming the lines and contours drawn on the paper.

"There." Charles pointed to a spot on the blue representation of Observatory Inlet.

Walker stared at the chart for several minutes and then looked out the window toward the shore where the creek pushed into the ocean with a dancing pattern of white wavelets.

"So that creek is this line here?" He traced a thin black line on the chart.

"Yes." Dan had watched as Walker oriented himself. "And your canoe is here." He indicated another line that joined the inlet further up toward Alice Arm. "It's about half a mile up, just below that curve."

Walker frowned as his eyes shifted from one line to the other.

"And where's the waterfall?"

"Here." Dan finger moved to yet another line. "It comes out under a bridge that crosses the road."

The three men all stared at the chart and Dan knew that all of them were calculating distance and figuring in currents and water flow.

"Doesn't make sense." It was Walker who voiced the conclusion Dan had come to the day before.

"No, it doesn't. It had to be either towed or paddled there," Dan answered.

"But why?"

Dan shrugged. "I don't know. Maybe so you couldn't get to it again. Maybe to make sure nobody looked too closely around the waterfall. Probably both, which means I need to go take a closer look around that bridge." He looked at the chart again. "But the big question is, how did he do it? We didn't see any sign of another boat, and you said the guy was up on the top of the bank when he attacked you?"

"Yeah."

"So maybe there are two guys." It was Charles who spoke.

"Still would have had to have a boat to tow the canoe," Walker said.

"No." Dan bent over the chart again. "No, maybe they didn't. Not if there are two of them and they have a dirt bike or an ATV or something. See?" He ran his finger across the area between the two creeks. "I need to check the topo map back on the boat, but if they can move around on land, then one of them could have paddled your canoe and the other one could have met him where they abandoned it." A note of excitement had crept into his voice. "Maybe I've been wrong all along! Maybe the guy's not traveling by water. Maybe he's on some kind of all-terrain machine. He could get to the site early, stash the bike, and just wait for the victim to show up." He looked at Walker. "I don't suppose you heard anything before he jumped you?"

Walker shook his head. "Nope. Doesn't mean there wasn't anything, though. That waterfall makes enough racket to drown out everything else."

"Yeah." Dan's disappointment was obvious. "Well, it gives me something else to think about. I didn't see any bikes or ATVs when I was at Kitsault, but that doesn't mean there weren't any. Either one would be a handy thing to have in a place like that." He looked at Claire. "We should head back. We don't want Marjorie sending out a search party to look for us."

▶ Back aboard and with *Dreamspeaker* safely tied up at the Kitsault wharf, Dan pulled out the topo map of the area and spread it out on the table. He had already marked the murder sites, but now he added the locations of the waterfall, the rock crevice with the hanging rope, and the shingle beach where he had found Walker's canoe. One by one he revisited each site, letting his finger trace across the paper as he followed the roads and the creeks, trying to imagine possible scenarios. An hour and a half later, when Claire interrupted him to say she was going to bed, he was no closer to figuring out who or why, but he was sure that both a vehicle and a boat had been involved.

He stood up and flexed his shoulders. It had been a long day and the next one promised to be even longer, but if he was right it might bring him the information he needed to break the case. The murder of the journalist was the key. It had been so completely out of pattern with the others. Why? And why had it occurred within a few yards of the bridge and the waterfall? Tomorrow morning he would head up to the pub and see if he could borrow a vehicle for the day. If he couldn't, he would have to find another way to get there, but one way or another, he was going to check out that bridge.

TWENTY-SIX

► Dew sparkled on the grass like shards of glass and the sound of voices hung in the air as Dan and Claire walked through the town of Kitsault the following morning. It was no longer the ghost town Dan had seen on his first visit. The harsh rattle of engines starting and the slam of car doors directed them toward the pub, which appeared to serve as the control center for all activity. There was no sign of either Bill Caversham or Ridley MacPherson, but Dan would have been surprised if they had been there. Neither MacPherson's cherished Bertram nor Caversham's old Chris-Craft were at the dock, and while Caversham might have to put in an occasional appearance in his role as personnel manager, media relations officer MacPherson would have no need to spend much time out of the city. Even as he thought of it, Dan made a mental note to check when the man had last been on site. If he was in any way involved with the murders, he either had to have been here at the time or driven in from Rupert.

A heavyset gray-haired man was standing in the middle of the parking lot holding a clipboard and handing out keys. Dan waited until the crowd cleared and then approached him.

"Hi. Dan Connor," he said, introducing himself. "I've got that boat down at the wharf."

"Oh yes. I saw that yesterday. Nice boat." He held out his hand. "Marcus Zubrinski. Anything I can help you with?"

"Well, maybe. I was talking to Bill Caversham when I was down at the marina in Rupert and he said I might be able to borrow a vehicle for a few hours. Show my partner Claire around a bit."

"That sounds like Bill. Sure. I don't see why not." Zubrinski glanced down at the clipboard. "Looks like everyone who needs one has already checked out." He nodded toward a mud-splattered Jeep and two equally grubby pickups. "Take your pick. The Jeep's probably the most comfortable."

"That's great. Thanks. We probably won't be long."

"Doesn't matter. If I'm not around just throw the keys in the box on the bar."

▶ They saw only one other vehicle on the road as they made their way to the bridge. It was a pickup that was parked in a pull-out and there were two men working a few feet into the forest, apparently taking some kind of soil sample.

"Looks like they're not going out alone anymore," Claire said.

"Could be," Dan said. "It's not a bad idea, and it might be working too. It's been almost two weeks since the last murder."

"Except that someone tried to kill Walker just a couple of days ago. You don't think that was the same guy?"

"Yeah, I do, but I don't think it was planned, and the only way I can make any sense of it is if Walker was getting too close to something the guy—or maybe the guys—didn't want seen."

They reached the bridge a couple of hours later, and Dan drove past and continued on for another ten minutes to check the road was empty before he turned around. When he finally stopped the Jeep, they rolled the windows down and sat quietly for another ten minutes, watching the trees and the creek and listening to the sounds that signaled that the forest residents were returning to their normal daily routines. It was something he had learned from Walker, and as he heard the birds resume their chatter, and saw a mink scamper across the road, he offered up a prayer of gratitude for the shared wisdom.

Dan patted the loaded gun he wore in a shoulder holster for reassurance as he reached for the door handle. He was pretty sure they were alone—the mink had told him that—but it didn't hurt to be cautious.

"We'll stay together," he told Claire, his voice quiet and intense. "Wait there and I'll come around to your door and help you out. Bring the camera with you. It will look good, and if we see anything we can take a photo of it."

She nodded, her tense muscles and erect posture expressing her nervousness far better than her words ever could as she took in his serious demeanor and stern voice, and she waited until he swung her door wide.

"We can probably see it best from over here." He inclined his head to indicate the far side of the bridge, making no effort to keep his voice quiet, hoping that if anyone happened to be listening they would think it was just two tourists checking out the waterfall.

He wished Claire wasn't there with him, although leaving her on the boat had not been an option. Once he had agreed that she could come with him to Kitsault, keeping her close was a foregone conclusion. If he had left her back on board *Dreamspeaker*—something he could never have brought himself to do—he would have been able to concentrate on his surroundings even less than he could now with her here beside him.

Even as the thought came to him, an unbidden image of Susan flashed through his brain. He had left her alone that day . . . His sharply inhaled breath caused Claire to glance at him.

"What?" She asked.

"Nothing." Dan cursed himself for allowing his memories to interfere with his job. "I think we're fine, but keep your eyes and ears open." Now was not the time, but when this was over, he had some hard thinking to do. It was not the first time he had told himself that, but this time he was going to follow through.

They walked across the bridge together, shoulders touching, their eyes constantly scanning their surroundings. The noise of the falls made hearing anything highly unlikely, but Dan tried to listen for any sound that was discordant with the pounding drumbeat of the water. There was nothing.

Gravel crunched under their feet as they stepped off the old timbers, and Dan leaned over to peer at the rushing water. It hadn't rained since Walker's rescue, and the volume seemed a little less, the force of the stream not quite as powerful, so that the arching curve as it left its bed and tumbled to the pool below was flatter and closer to the rock. It prevented any possibility of seeing what was behind the falls, even from this oblique angle, and the bank dropped off so steeply there was no way anyone could climb down.

The two of them walked back along the bridge and checked from the other end, but the land had almost the same contours; not only was the bank steep, it was undercut, and a descent there was completely impossible. That left the opposite side of the pool, where the bank curved around in a wide arc and where the attack on Walker had taken place. They wouldn't be able to get there unless they hiked through some very rough terrain, and there was no indication that they would be able to see anything more than a sheet of water. Dan had been there yesterday, and had not been able to see through it even though he had been looking. True, he had been down low at the foot of the falls and not up on the land, but still, there was no way that the extra height would change things.

They returned to the truck and Dan locked the doors and sat there, fingers drumming on the steering wheel as he stared out through the windshield. There had to be something. Why else would Walker have been attacked? Why else would the attacker be there in the first place? There was something he was missing, but what?

Heaving a sigh, he started the engine and put the Jeep in gear, letting it idle across the bridge as he scanned the surrounding forest. After fifty feet the road curved gently inland and started to rise while the bridge disappeared from view behind them. Dan drove far enough to give himself a good margin of visibility, then wrestled the Jeep around and pointed it back down.

The forest was thicker here, the trees shorter, and their thin trunks let in more light so that the ground was covered with undergrowth. Down toward the creek, the old-growth spruce and cedar towered up into the sky, the dense canopy forming a roof that only an occasional ray of daylight could pierce. In the gloom underneath there was only stunted grass patterned with dappled shadow, and the faint line of a trail . . .

Dan slammed on the brakes, put the transmission into low and then edged it forward again. There! He hadn't imagined it. The light hit the forest floor differently as it followed the flattened blades of grass. It was too wide for a deer trail. It had to have been formed by footsteps, and maybe by something being dragged. A boat?

"What are you doing?" Claire asked as he jockeyed the Jeep back and forth, trying to see where the trail led.

He glanced across at her. "There's a trail there. You can only see it when you have the right angle, but it's there."

She peered past him, a dubious look on her face. "Are you sure? I can't see anything. It just looks like forest to me."

Dan chuckled. He felt oddly elated. "That's what it would have looked like to me too if Walker hadn't shown me how to read that trail on Nootka last year. Maybe his powers of observation are actually starting to rub off on me!"

He slapped the steering wheel. "Good thing too. I should have figured it out as soon as we arrived here. Of course the access is on the other side of the bridge. It would have to be."

Rolling down his window, he nodded for Claire to do the same. "We're far enough away from the waterfall to hear what's going on. Let's listen for a while, and then if everything seems okay, I'll go take a look."

She looked reluctant, but did as he asked. The two of them sat there without speaking, breathing in the fresh scent of cedar and spruce, feeling the air move over their skin, watching the mist rise above the falls, until a trilling whistle signaled the first darting flight of a bird. Dan smiled.

He started the Jeep again and drove to the bridge, then reached for the pack he had brought and removed the flashlight. He was pretty confident that they were alone, but he wasn't about to take any unnecessary risks. He patted his weapon again for reassurance. As he released the door locks, he waved Claire closer to him.

"Slide over here when I get out, and lock the doors. If you see anything, honk the horn. I'm just going to take a quick look."

He ignored her quick glance of concern and stepped out onto the road, waiting until he heard the click of the door lock before he stepped into the trees. The trail had led off some distance away, but he picked it up easily now he knew what to look for, and he followed it almost to the edge of the creek where it turned and disappeared under the bridge. Bending down low, he shone the flashlight into the dark space, watching as the beam of light caught the fast-moving ripples on the surface of the water, glinted off the wet rocks, caught on the rough timbers overhead, and was finally swallowed by daylight and mist on the far side.

Moving slowly, he edged deeper into the blackness, bracing his hand against the wood above him until he could no longer reach it and then, crouching down to work his way forward until he could peer over the curve of the rock, his eyes slid downward with the arching, tumbling flow of water. Watching its movement was disorienting—the flow was fast, but somehow the individual molecules seemed to move in slow motion and there were no reference points to anchor his gaze. Vertigo grabbed him, pulling him forward, and he put his hands out to stop himself from falling, feeling as if the earth was moving beneath his palm as he thrust himself back. Heart pounding, he waited until his breathing slowed and his head steadied, and then he lay down on his belly and eased himself forward again.

He kept his eyes on the rock this time, following the beam of the flashlight as he shone it down the glistening surface, moving it over the contours and studying the shadows as they danced away from the light. He was so mesmerized by the movement that when it stopped, blocked by a solid, horizontal rock ledge, he felt a moment of shock and jerked his head back.

Chiding himself for being overly cautious, he pushed forward yet again and peered down. It was hard to discern exactly what he was seeing. The beam of light simply stopped, the focus suddenly spread across a wet, black surface that shimmered with the movement of water and glinted with reflections from the falls themselves. It was impossible to accurately gauge how far down it was, but by swinging his flashlight up and back along the rock face, Dan figured it couldn't be much more than six or seven feet, and maybe less right below him. He tried to get a grasp on the substance and contours of the ledge itself, but it eluded him. He thought it was fairly flat, but there was some kind of bulge where the light seemed to bend around a series of folds, scattering shadows along different planes, then seeping into a blacker blackness in others.

He bent his wrist and shone the light immediately below him, feeling excitement spark as two rock protuberances appeared, one above the other. They could serve as steps, although it would take a very brave and agile man to try negotiating them on his own. A rope would help. If it was tied to a something and fed out . . .

He sat up and peered at the bridge foundations. They were solid cement set into the rock, but heavy wooden beams ran from one to the other, each one spanning the length of the bridge. They in turn supported the decking, and Dan could see narrow gaps between the boards, probably deliberately placed to prevent the rain from pooling and perfectly spaced to allow a rope to drop through. He twisted to his knees and pushed himself up into a crouch. No sign of any rope there now, but there was something resting on the beam below one of the gaps. Whatever it was, it was tiny. Probably garbage that had either been dropped or washed through the decking. As he reached a cautious finger it to poke at it, Dan heard the blare of the Jeep's horn.

TWENTY-SEVEN

▶ Dan scrambled out from under the bridge and raced up to the road, his heart pounding. The Jeep was still where he had left it, with Claire sitting at the wheel. As he ran up, she leaned out the window and pointed up the road.

"Someone's coming."

He followed her finger and saw a green pickup coming over the rise. Claire must have seen it as it rounded the curve another couple of hundred yards away.

"Pass me the camera," he said, leaning into the Jeep. "And just follow my lead."

The truck slowed to a stop beside them, and a heavily bearded face looked out the lowered window.

"You guys okay? Need any help?"

Dan smiled and let himself relax a little. He could see hardhats and lunch boxes on the seat between the two men, and there was no hint of threat or suspicion in the words.

"We're fine, thanks. We stopped to look at the falls. They're pretty spectacular."

The man glanced over at the bridge and nodded. "Yeah, the rain really kicks it up. You should see it in a month or two. It's really something then."

The second man leaned forward to peer at them from the passenger seat. "You the people from that boat down at the wharf?" he asked.

"Yeah," Dan nodded. "Bill Caversham let us borrow the Jeep so we could look around."

"That sounds like Bill. Well, we'd better get going then. Gotta unload this lot before we finish for the day." The man used his thumb to indicate the back of the pickup.

"You building a fence?" Dan asked as he took in the load of thin logs protruding from the pickup bed.

"Hell no!" The bearded man laughed. "Would be a mighty tall fence if we were. These are for the roads. The logging companies pay us to thin these out from the areas where they've replanted. Trees grow real quick up here, and after a few years they gotta be spaced to let the light in. We cut them, clean them up a bit, and then lay them in the road in the dips where it turns into a mud bog when the heavy rains set it. Stops the trucks from getting stuck. We call it corduroy."

Dan shook his head. "Learn something new every day," he said. "I've never heard of that before. You going to do that now? I wouldn't mind seeing how it works."

"Nah. Need to have a good thick bed of mud to work them in. We just stack them for now. There's a storage area right there at the town site just before you turn in."

"Huh. Well thanks for stopping," Dan said, and watched as the truck moved past them heading back toward Kitsault.

▶ "What was all that about?" Claire asked as he climbed back in the Jeep. "Surely you didn't really want to see them put those logs on the road."

"No, I didn't. But I did want to know where they got them and what they used them for. They looked a lot like what Walker described when he said the guy tipped the canoe over with a pole. He said it looked like a fence post, but it was longer, remember?"

"Yes, of course! And those ones would be long enough to reach down from the top of the bank too. They stuck way out past the end of the truck bed."

"Yeah. So. Kitsault again. Everything keeps coming back to there. Now if I could just figure out who and why."

"Did you find anything under the bridge?"

Dan took his time answering. "Well, there's a second ledge there for sure. It's higher than the one Walker was on, and there may even be something on it, although I can't be sure. It's not so far down that it couldn't be reached by someone who had a little help, or maybe just with a good rope if he was fit and knew what he was doing. There's even a couple of rock projections that could be used as foot or hand guides. The question is why anyone would climb down there. It's still another ten to fifteen feet or so down to the creek."

"Maybe you can get down to the other ledge—the one Walker was on."

"Could be. No way of checking that unless I went down, and I don't think I want to do that without backup, which would mean calling in the Rupert guys, and it still doesn't answer the question."

They drove in silence with the windows open, breathing in the fresh scent of the forest as Dan thought about what he had seen and what it might mean and how it might help him figure this whole thing out. It was more than ten days since they had arrived in Rupert and he was not much further ahead than when he'd started.

They left the Jeep in the parking lot and dropped the keys in the box. The pub was empty, although they could hear the sounds of voices coming from the kitchen where the catering staff was preparing an evening meal. Dan walked over and pushed open the door.

"You got enough for a couple more for dinner?" he shouted over the clatter of pots and dishes.

"Got enough for whoever shows up." The answer came from a young man who looked barely old enough to be out of school. "We serve it at six. Just grab a plate and help yourself."

Dan gave him a thumbs up and left him to continue his chopping and stirring.

"So what now?" Claire asked as they headed back down to the wharf.

"Well, we've got three hours until dinner, so I think I'll check my messages, put on some good music, and see if that will help me make any sense of all this."

▶ The computer screen showed only two new messages. One was from Rosemary with more background information and schedules for the Kitsault workers, and the other was from Mike with a preliminary report from the coroner. Adam Lancaster had obviously found the time to follow up on Dan's request, and although there was more work to be done, his initial finding was that all of the victims who had been beheaded had been attacked from behind, and that the blows had probably been delivered by the same person, almost certainly male, very strong, right-handed and above six feet in height. Mike had added a note to say that in his conversation with the coroner, the man had told him that he had asked the police to let him have Joel's paddle back so he could recheck its dimensions, but that after revisiting all of the cases, he doubted it could have made such clean wounds. Dan gave a whoop of delight when he read it.

"Joel's clear!" he called to Claire as he reached for the VHF. "Lancaster came through."

He depressed the button on the microphone.

"Blackbird, Blackbird, Blackbird," he said, using the call sign they had decided on when Charles Eden had agreed to turn his VHF on.

"Yeah?" Charles answered.

"You still got your two passengers on board?" Dan asked. VHF radio was public; anyone who was familiar with the channels could listen in, and he was not about to broadcast any names.

"Got one. Dropped the other one off a while ago, but he'll be back."

"Well, next time you see him, tell him he's clear. It's not official yet, but it will be soon. I'll try and get his . . . carving . . . back to him before I leave."

There was a pause, and then Eden spoke again. "Thank you. We are both grateful."

"No problem. Please give him my best wishes."

There was another pause, and then another question.

"My other passenger asks if it is now finished. He says he would like to go home."

"Not yet. Might figure out something tonight, but I should be back at the marina late tomorrow if you want to drop by."

Dan switched the radio back to channel 16 and headed back to the salon where he turned on his stereo and once again spread out his charts and topographical maps. As he let his eyes wander over the roads and creeks, he thought about the bridge again, and the waterfall with its hidden ledges. Had there been something on the higher one? It would certainly be ironic if Walker had been saved by the existence of one ledge while the other one was used to somehow assist in the murders they were both trying to solve. He wished he could have gotten closer, but it would have been impossible without help. He made a note to ask the guys in Rupert to check it out. For now, all he could do was to try and shake loose the feeling that he was missing something, that someone had said something important. Leaning back, he closed his eyes and let his mind wander.

Just minutes later, he sat up with a jolt. How could he have forgotten? Claire. It had been Claire who had mentioned uniforms—something about not understanding how the murderer could tell he had the right person unless they were wearing a uniform. Dan should have picked up on that himself. It meant that the murderer had to know his victim personally, had to be able to recognize him and not simply know where he was going to be working, which meant that he was certainly one of the people at Kitsault. That in itself wasn't any great revelation—he was already looking at that as a probability—but it did confirm that he was on the right track. All the victims—at least the first five—had been Kitsault-based, but in three instances there had been other people with them who had been spared. There was still the slim possibility that those others had simply been lucky, and that if they had been the one who wandered away alone for whatever time it took for the killer to strike, they would have been the one now lying on that cold slab in Adam Lancaster's mortuary. But if you added in the fact that other people would sometimes be out on the same roads—people like him and Claire, locals from the Nisga'a villages, hikers, hunters, tourists—then the possibility of it being anything other than targeted was almost non-existent. That meant that the killer knew his victims well.

What else did he now know? The killer, or killers, had access to a land-based vehicle of some kind, and it had to be either an ATV or a bike. Probably an ATV if there were two of them. Dan opened his eyes and let them drift down to the topo map again. An ATV and a boat, he thought. Two of the murder sites had been so open it would have been almost impossible to approach them unseen in anything but a very small boat.

He went out onto the deck. There had been no other boats at the wharf since they arrived, and as far as he knew, the two Kevlar kayaks that Kent McGilvery had thought so highly of had not moved from their resting place on the float. So not those. Another boat. Almost certainly a canoe or kayak, and probably not kept here.

Another elusive memory tickled across the synapses of his brain; he tried to catch it, but it danced away. Something about a boat. He shook his head and made a quick note, reminding himself to come back to it.

What else? The weapon. If it hadn't been a paddle, then what was it? Something made with yew wood—or could that have been a red herring? An effort to throw the blame on Joel? That would mean that the murderer had seen Joel in the area, had known that he spent time paddling his kayak up the creeks—and that thought brought Dan back to Ridley MacPherson. Not only did Ridley MacPherson have red hair—although it was more sandy than real red, but Bill Caversham had mentioned that MacPherson hated Native people and MacPherson himself had called them "savages" when Dan and Claire had run into him at the protest. He had even announced that the police suspected a Haida when Dan had first met him that day in the pub. At the time Dan had wondered how he could have had that information, and whether he had some kind of inside access to the investigation, but if he had been the one who provided it, it might all make sense.

TWENTY-EIGHT

▶ "Aren't we supposed to be up at the pub for dinner at six?" The sound of Claire's voice snapped Dan out of his reverie.

"Yes. Why? What time is it?"

"We have exactly ten minutes, so let's get going. I'm starving."

Dan grabbed his jacket and they stepped out onto the wharf and started up the path toward the town. Once they reached the road, Dan nudged Claire into a cross street that seemed to angle in the right direction.

"Let's go this way. I think it might be quicker."

They found themselves walking between two rows of townhomes, each with a carport in front and a paved path leading to the front door. Further up the townhomes gave way to single-family houses, all with attached garages and some with vehicles parked in the driveway. One of them was a bright red Porsche Cayenne.

"Isn't that the same car that man was driving?" Claire asked. "The one who nearly ran me down at the protest rally?"

"Ridley MacPherson." Dan replied. "It certainly looks like it, and it doesn't seem likely there would be two red Porsche Cayennes up here."

It was odd to think that anyone would bring a car like that over those incredibly rough roads from Prince Rupert, and Bill Caversham had said that both he and MacPherson went up and down by boat. Had something happened that would cause MacPherson to change his routine?

They were just turning the corner when the front door of the house opened and a woman came out carrying a sheaf of papers. It was Marjorie Wakeshaw, and she seemed to be in a hurry. She didn't look up as she strode past the car and turned down the road toward the water. Dan watched her go. Why on earth would Ridley MacPherson need to visit Marjorie Wakeshaw?

▶ The pub was almost full by the time Dan and Claire arrived. They loaded their plates with food and found two empty chairs at a table right at the back of the room where three men they hadn't met before were eating.

"You the folks from the boat?"

Dan smiled. It wasn't likely that there would be anyone in the village who didn't know about their presence.

"Yes," he answered. "I found this place by accident when I was driving around exploring the area. Bill Caversham and Ridley MacPherson were in here having a beer with Marjorie, and they invited me to bring the boat up."

One of the men snickered. "Yeah. Bill does like his beer. He pretty well lives in here when he's up. Guess that's why MacPherson likes to travel with him. Once Bill's got a load on, MacPherson can spend all the time he likes with Marjorie."

"Ah, come on, Neville." Another of the men spoke up. "Bill's not a bad guy."

"Never said he was," Neville answered. "It's MacPherson I can't stand. Arrogant bastard!"

The second man turned to Dan and Claire. "Don't listen to Neville. Neville thinks MacPherson blocked a promotion he was going after, and he's had it in for him ever since—isn't that right, Neville?"

"I don't think it, I know it." Neville snapped the words out, his voice betraying his anger. "Larry heard him talking to Bill Caversham about it. The bastard waited until Bill had a few, and then he told him that he 'just happened' to have some real solid info about me being unreliable. Said it wasn't too surprising considering my background, but I probably wasn't a great candidate."

"Your background?" Dan had been listening to the conversation with growing interest. "What did he mean by that?"

"Ah, hell." Neville's resentment was mixed with resignation. "I guess it's no secret. I don't look it, but I'm half Native. My dad was Ojibway. Came over this way to find work and met my mom. I take after her in looks, so I don't know how MacPherson figured it out. He probably just saw my name on the application—it's Debassige—but he has a real hard on for all Natives. Calls us savages to our face—if he talks to us at all—but then he's the first to boast about 'proactive hiring' and 'providing jobs for the indigenous people' when he's talking to the press! Makes himself out to be a real hero. Asshole! The only thing he's proactive about is jumping on Marjorie's bones whenever Jim's away."

He suddenly remembered Claire was there and his face flushed. "Sorry. I get a little carried away when I'm talking about Ridley MacPherson."

"I can understand that. I would be upset too if someone talked about me that way." Claire leaned over and put her hand on Neville's arm, and Dan watched as the anger drained out of the man's face.

"Ah no, it's okay. I'm used to it now. Shouldn't be bending your ear about it anyway." He collected the plates he had emptied. "Good to meet you both, but we gotta run. You guys ready?" he asked his two other table companions.

As they stood up one of the others nodded across the crowded room to where the door was just swinging open to allow Ridley MacPherson to enter. "Pretty good timing, Neville," he said and they all laughed. "You must have known he was coming."

▶ Ridley MacPherson made his way straight to the buffet table, loaded his plate with food and then looked around the room for a place to sit. As soon as he saw Dan and Claire, he made his way over to their table.

"Hi there. Good to see you again. Sorry I missed you back there at the marina." He pulled out one of the three now-empty chairs and sat down. "Okay if I join you?"

175

"Sure," Dan said. "I've got to say I'm a bit surprised to see you here. I thought you'd be back in Rupert dealing with the media after that fiasco in the park."

"Tempest in a teapot," MacPherson said dismissively. "Those things happen every time there's one of those bloody protests. They probably plan it themselves just so they can get some attention. I don't know why the government allows them to continue. If it was me, I'd throw the whole damn lot of them in jail."

"I didn't see your boat down at the wharf," Dan said. "Did you just arrive?"

"No. I drove up this morning. Don't often do that—it's hard as hell on the car—but Bill's out of action and my boat's in getting a fuel pump replaced."

"Is Bill sick?" Claire asked.

"No more than usual, but the people here needed the work schedules for next week, and they're already a day late. I try to cover for him, but it's getting harder."

"Bill does the work schedules?" Dan asked.

"Yeah. He's the personnel manager, or at least that's his official title, so that's one of his jobs. He's supposed to get them here by Thursday every week. The guys that are already here pretty well know what they're doing—at least until the snow arrives—but Marjorie needs to know how many others are coming in so that she can have the rooms ready."

Dan thought of the sheaf of papers he had seen Marjorie carrying.

"Never thought of that," he said. "Does she do all the housekeeping herself? Sounds like quite a workload."

"She does some of it but not all. There's a couple of the s . . . the Nisga'a women . . . come in on the weekend. Marjorie's got her hands full keeping track of what Jim needs for maintenance and doing the book-keeping."

"So Jim does all the maintenance? That must be a helluva big job too."

MacPherson laughed. "Well Jim would certainly agree with you, and if he hadn't talked the company into giving him three maintenance guys to help him out it probably would be, but the truth is Jim does dick all except play supervisor and go hunting." He looked from Dan to Claire. "You guys ever seen him?"

They both shook their heads.

"Not that I know of," Dan said. "What does he look like?"

"Shit, if he's around you can't miss him. He's about six five and built like a tank, but you're not likely to run into him. The crazy bastard's out there on that goddam ATV of his playing at being the Great White Hunter. He'll be out there for days. Might even bring in a deer if he's lucky—although it'll probably be gut-shot." He leaned back in his chair and stared off into the distance. "I don't know what Marjorie sees in him. He's completely nuts."

He caught himself, perhaps realizing that he was revealing too much, and gave an embarrassed laugh. "Stay out of his way if you do see him. He's got a temper to match that red hair of his. Doesn't lose it often, but when he does he's meaner than a rattlesnake."

"Why on earth do they keep him on?" Claire asked. "He sounds like someone you wouldn't want to have around—and if he's out there with a gun . . ."

"Oh, I'd love to fire him," MacPherson answered. "So would most of the people out here, but Marjorie won't let me. And it isn't the gun we worry about—he's probably the lousiest shot out here—it's that damn knife he always carries."

▶ If he hadn't been concerned about drawing attention to himself, Dan would have run back to the boat. As it was, he walked so fast Claire had to jog to keep up with him, which was why she ran into his back when he came to an abrupt stop at the top of the wharf.

"What is it?" she asked, grabbing at his arm to balance herself as she tried to follow his gaze along the wharf.

"One of the kayaks is gone," he said, nodding his head toward the empty space.

"Do you think Jim Wakeshaw took it?" she asked.

"No. MacPherson said he was out on his ATV. I think Marjorie took it to go and meet him. If Wakeshaw is the one committing these murders, then Marjorie is probably involved too. I think she's taking the schedules out to him. That was what she had in her hand when we saw her at the house."

"But why?" Claire asked. "It doesn't make sense."

"Might not have to if he's as crazy as MacPherson says, but I can't see Marjorie helping him if there's not something driving this."

Back on board, Dan used the satellite phone to call Mike in Victoria.

"Jim Wakeshaw," he said, as soon as Mike answered. "I need everything you can dig up on him. On his wife too."

"Wakeshaw? Isn't that the caretaker? I thought we already checked him out."

"You checked his work history and you checked for a record—which he apparently doesn't have. What I need to know is why he left those jobs. Did he quit or was he fired? Get that fancy research department you've got down there to check and see if anything odd happened around his previous work. Maybe take a look at the newspaper archives for the same time period. Anything they can think of. And check his financial stuff too."

"You figure he's involved in this?"

"I think he's more than involved. I think he might be the guy—and I think he might be planning another one."

"Shit! Do you need some help out there? I can have Rupert send in a team. No point keeping you under wraps if we don't need to."

"Too soon. I don't have any proof, and we would have to find him first. He's out there in a few hundred square miles of forest on an ATV, but he's going to have to meet up with his wife at some point—or at least pick up the papers she's carrying—and she's in a kayak. That means he has to come down to the water, and I think I know where he might do that. What I need are a couple guys who know the outdoors and maybe do a bit of climbing. I'll give you some GPS coordinates and you can have them come out and meet me there with an ATV. I'll be in the dinghy."

"You want them there tonight? It's already pretty late. They're not going to be able to make it before dark."

"No. It will have to be first thing in the morning. As early as possible. Oh, and Mike? Make sure they bring a weapon."

▶ "You're going after Wakeshaw in the dinghy?" Claire's face reflected her distress.

Dan wrapped his arm around her shoulders and pulled her to his side. "No. I'm going to use the dinghy to check out that rope we saw. I think I've figured out what it's for. They use it to pass information. Marjorie would have no problem getting her kayak into that rock cleft, and she could simply tie the papers onto the end of the rope. That way she wouldn't have to hang around for him to show up. He arrives on his ATV when he's ready and pulls up the rope. Easy."

"But he could be there when you arrive!"

"Not likely, and even if he is, he can't get down to the water. He can only pull the rope up. You saw it. There's no way to get down there."

"What if he shoots you? That man said he had a gun."

"That man also said that he's a lousy shot—and even if he wasn't, how's he going to see me? There can't be more than a narrow slot up at the top. We didn't even see daylight."

"But . . ."

He kissed the top of her head. "I'll be fine, and you need to stop worrying. I'm not even going out there tonight. How about we both go out and sit on the float for a while? I'd like to be there when Marjorie gets back."

She stared at him I confusion. "So you're not going out to check the rope?"

"First thing tomorrow morning. I'll check it on my way to the bridge and my rendezvous with the guys the Rupert detachment sends up. Tonight, I would like to have a chat with Marjorie."

"You think she'll be back tonight?"

"Yes, I do. There's nowhere out there she can stay. She's got a fast kayak—it's long and it's light—and she looks like she's in really good shape. She should be able to make five knots through the water, and if I remember yesterday's tides and currents correctly, she left on the last of the ebb. That means she'll get a bit of a boost both ways. I figure she'll be back soon after dark."

They took two deck chairs out onto the float and sat watching the water darken, first to indigo and then to sapphire and finally to black as the sun slipped behind the mountains, leaving only the reflected blue of the sky overhead. Dan smiled as he leaned forward to peer over the water. He was close. He could feel it. There was that hum that sang through his bloodstream when things started to come together, a vibration that resonated through his brain, made him feel more alive. In the past it had fed the pounding, high-test energy of the team he worked with, but here, sharing the quietness of the evening with Claire, it melded into something different. Something more real. More grounded. Here his response was no less intense but certainly more reasoned. He couldn't chase Jim Wakeshaw tonight. He didn't have a vehicle, let alone an ATV, and he had no way of tracking the man. Even if he did, he had no proof, nothing that would allow him to make an arrest. What he could do, though, was question Marjorie Wakeshaw—see if he could get some kind of confirmation of his suspicions and then try to find those papers in the morning before her husband had a chance to commit another murder. After that, with an ATV and another officer to help him, maybe they could find the murderer himself. It was back to real detective work—work he had been doing when he and Walker had first crossed paths all those years ago, but it was work he had enjoyed.

His one concern was Claire. He would have to leave her alone, and if he screwed up his talk with Marjorie and somehow alerted her that he was on to them, then Claire could be vulnerable. He didn't know if the Wakeshaws had an easy way of communicating with each other. It didn't seem likely, but it was a risk he didn't want to take.

"How do you feel about handling *Dreamspeaker* on your own for a while tomorrow?" he asked. He knew very well she could handle a boat of that size. Not only had her father been a fisherman, her work as a marine biologist demanded that she spend most of her time out on her own boat. Truth be known, she was probably a better mariner than he was.

She looked at him for a long minute. "Should be fine," she answered. "Why?"

"I was thinking that if we left early, I could take the dinghy and go and check that rope, then meet up with the guys from Rupert. Once I've checked that ledge under the bridge I should have a better idea of what's going on. If the guys and I think it's necessary, we could get all the workers called back in to Kitsault and then I could come back to the boat."

"Sounds like you could be gone a long time."

"Not likely. Once I've passed on the information I'll leave things with them. I'll probably only be out there for a couple of hours. You okay with that?"

She shrugged. "Sure. All I would have to do is circle and drift. As long as the weather's good there shouldn't be a problem. Are you taking a radio?"

He nodded. "Yeah. I won't be far away. The VHF should be good." He smiled. One less problem he had to worry about.

▶ They chatted quietly as the last light drained out of the sky, both of them letting their minds run over the events of the past couple of weeks. It had not been the holiday they been planning, but they had seen a lot of the coast, crossed Hecate Strait, gotten a glimpse of Haida Gwaii, and explored Alice Arm and Observatory Inlet, much of it together with Walker. The memories of all that, and of the people they had met, would give them months if not years of stories, and if Dan could wrap up the murders they still had time to cruise back down together, although it would have to be a pretty quick trip.

"How are you going to get the inflatable into that crevice?"

Claire's question snapped Dan back from his reminiscences. "What?" For a second his mind segued to another conversation about an inflatable, but it flickered out of reach. "Oh, I'm going to take the boat hook. Should be able to reach the rope with that."

He searched for the elusive thought—something to do with Kent?—but couldn't grasp it.

"What?" Claire asked, watching him try to puzzle it out.

He shook his head. "Just trying to remember something. One of those things you can almost remember but not quite. It's been there for a few days but I just can't get to it. What you said about the inflatable seemed to trigger it, but damned if I can pin it down."

Claire peered at him through the gloom of twilight. "Didn't Kent McGilvery say something about an inflatable kayak when we were talking on Bill Caversham's boat?"

Dan stared at her. "By God," he said. "I think you're right."

"I think he said that Ridley MacPherson had one, or something like that," Claire said.

"No. I don't think that was it. I can't remember the exact words, but I think he said it was Jim Wakeshaw. Something about him taking one with him when he went out hunting." Dan's voice grew louder as excitement gripped him, and he forced it back to a whisper. "You know, I've been trying to think what Kent said that might have got him killed. Maybe that's it."

"But Jim Wakeshaw wasn't there!"

"No, but if Kent mentioned to MacPherson that we had been talking about kayaks, and somehow it got back to Wakeshaw . . ."

The faint splash of a paddle and the luminescence as it carved a path through the water ended the conversation and they watched as a kayak nudged against the float and Marjorie Wakeshaw stepped out.

▶ "You're out late tonight." Dan's voice cut through the still night air, and Marjorie let out a small scream of fright.

"Oh my God! You scared me. What on earth are you doing here?"

"Just enjoying the evening. I can bring you a chair if you'd like to join us."

"Oh, no. No. But thanks. I need to get back to the office. We have some new people coming in and I have to get things ready for them."

She sounded nervous. She was almost babbling, her words tumbling over each other. Certainly not the calm, confident woman who had greeted them earlier.

"Oh yes. Ridley was saying he had to bring the work schedules up because Bill Caversham was indisposed," Dan said. "Must be tough on him carrying that extra load."

Her quick intake of breath was audible. "Ridley? You were talking to Ridley?"

"Yeah. We had dinner with him up at the pub." Dan let her worry about that for a few seconds and then added, "We actually saw you on our way up. You were just coming out of your house. We were going to invite you to join us, but you didn't see us. You had a bunch of papers you were carrying and you were sure in a hurry. We figured they were something important so we let you go." He softened his words with a laugh. "Must be tough on you carrying that load too. Don't see your husband around much."

"Jim?" Her voice had risen almost to a squeak. "Oh, Jim's here.

He's been out hunting, but I just talked to him—I went to his camp. I needed to tell him about the new people coming in. There are rooms to fix, maintenance stuff. He has to figure it all out. He should be here tomorrow. You can meet him then." The flood of words trailed off.

"Ah, that would be good, but it's not going to work." Dan tried to project the right amount of warmth and regret. "We have to leave early tomorrow. Got to get back down south."

"Oh," she said, "Well . . . that's too bad. He'll be sorry to have missed you." She was back on more solid ground and her voice was almost back to normal. "I had better go and get my stuff done."

They watched her walk away, and as soon as she was out of sight they carried their chairs back aboard the boat.

► THIRTY ◄

► "That was sneaky!"

Dan and Claire were back aboard *Dreamspeaker*, the chairs stowed, the kayak strapped securely onto the transom, and the equipment Dan needed to take with him ready for an early departure in the morning.

"Worked, though, didn't it?" Dan was too revved up to even consider trying to sleep. He was checking the email that had come in to see if Mike had come up with anything new.

"But you still have no proof she's involved in anything. Maybe she was telling the truth. Maybe she did have to tell him about some new people arriving."

"Possible—but I don't think so. If there really was maintenance to be done, he would have done it before he went hunting. And she was nervous. Besides, why would she need to take the schedules out if she just wanted to tell him she needed him back here to do some work?"

"I guess." Claire sounded dubious. "It just seems so—odd? Weird? Something like that. I mean, I like her! She seems so . . . normal."

"Yeah, I like her too. But you would be surprised at how many likeable people do really bad things. The jails are full of them."

► Dan woke in the thin light of moonrise. The land lay quiet under the dark sky, the black water silvered with the luminescent glow of a narrow slice of moon. It was a time when lines were blurred and the earth took on a different dimension, a time when thoughts drifted, and sometimes found new paths. It was too late to try getting back to sleep and too early to start down the inlet so he made himself a cup of coffee and carried it out to the deck. He knew what had woken him. It wasn't the excitement of the chase; that was a just a hum in the background—and besides, he wasn't planning on chasing anyone, he was just going to look under a bridge. No, this was guilt—the same guilt that had haunted him since Susan's death. He was putting the people he loved at risk. He had done it with Susan by neglecting the warning signs; he had done it with Walker by deliberately putting him into danger and now he was doing the same thing with Claire. It didn't matter that last night he had managed to convince himself that it was okay. It wasn't. It would never be okay to involve someone else. It seemed as if the job that had once demanded he be part of a team was now demanding that he be alone.

He leaned against the railing, his coffee forgotten. In just a few hours he would be meeting up with other cops and they would be checking one of the haunts of an armed man who, if his suspicions were right, had killed at least six people and perhaps seven. He couldn't afford to worry about Claire's safety while that was happening, wondering if she would be okay alone on the inlet . . .

A hand brushed his shoulder and he straightened in surprise.

"Are you okay?"

He looked down into Claire's sleep-flushed face. "Yeah. I was just thinking about you alone out here on the boat."

"You mean you were just *worrying* about me being alone out here on the boat."

"Yes, I guess so."

"Dan Connor, what was I doing when you met me?"

"What?"

"You heard me."

"Running away from some bad guys?"

She punched him on the shoulder. "Not that. What was I *doing*?"

He stared at her, seeing the serious look she was giving him. "Studying sea otters?"

186

"Yes. And what was I doing last year while you were chasing that guy all over Nootka Island?"

He fought to keep a smile off his face. "Studying sea otters?"

"Right. And where was I living while I was doing that?"

Ah. Now he knew where this was going. "You were on your boat, but that's not the point. You—"

"That is exactly the point. I work and live on my boat. I have worked and lived on my boat for years. I grew up on a boat—and before you say that there weren't any bad guys out there then, you need to think harder about how we met."

"Claire—"

"Don't you 'Claire' me. You are not responsible for every situation that crops up—and I can handle a boat as well as you can, and you know it."

Dan sighed and turned to face her. "So do I get a chance to say my piece?"

She shrugged. "As long as it's not some chauvinistic nonsense, yes you do."

"It's not chauvinistic to worry about your safety."

"How on earth can my safety be a problem if all I'm doing is making slow circles in the middle of the inlet? Do you think this guy is going to swim out with a knife between his teeth and swing a grappling hook over the rail?"

Dan had no answer for that. She was right—at least in this particular instance, although he still had those hard thoughts to think about in terms of future events.

"I'm going back to bed," Claire said. "You should do the same. We have to leave in a few hours."

He did as she suggested, although neither of them got any sleep.

▶ They left Kitsault a little after four in the morning, the sky still dark and a building cloudbank blanketing the stars to the west. By the time they reached the mouth of the creek, dawn was staining the edge of the sky, painting the jagged peaks of the mountains with a pale gold.

Dan lowered the inflatable off the transom and stepped aboard. He loaded the two coils of rope and the bosun's chair he had dug out of the storage locker the night before and then reached up to grasp the telescoping boat hook that Claire passed down.

"I shouldn't be that long," he said as he untied the line. "Probably be back for breakfast—well, brunch anyway."

"Just make sure it's no later than lunch," she answered as she disappeared back into the wheelhouse. "I don't want to drift around out here all day with nothing to do but wait."

▶ Without the need to search the banks for places to get ashore, the trip to the rock cleft should have been faster than his earlier one, but night lingered in the narrow confines of the creek, which made navigating difficult, and it took him longer than he had planned. Even so, it was barely full daylight out on the inlet by the time he arrived, and the darkness of the cleft was so deep that the thin beam of the flashlight was almost swallowed by the blackness. Almost, but not quite. It found the rope and wavered down its length until it reached the end, where it reflected off a heavy plastic bag. The bag was empty.

"Damn!"

Dan had hoped that Jim Wakeshaw would wait until later in the morning to check the drop site, but obviously that had not been the case. Still, in the end it probably didn't matter—it was clear a drop had been made as the plastic bag had not been there when he and Claire discovered the place—and they already knew what had been in the bag. Not only had Marjorie acknowledged that she had received the schedules, but she had also stated that she had gone to meet up with Jim. By itself, the statement might not amount to much in a courtroom, but with luck, both of them would have left their fingerprints behind.

Dan extended the boat hook and pulled the rope toward him, careful not to snag the bag itself or damage it in any way. It had been attached with a metal spring clip and he carefully placed both the clip and the bag in a plastic box he had brought for exactly that purpose. It was only as he swung the flashlight back up that he saw the single sheet of paper pasted to the rock above his head. It was held there only by water adhesion, and even from this angle he could see that whatever information was printed on it was dissolving, but there were still marks and smudges that the RCMP forensic sciences people might be able to decipher.

He revved the motor up to push the inflatable more firmly into the crevice, and reached up with the boat hook to gently peel the paper loose. It fell onto the bow and lay draped over the curve of the pontoon, sodden and dripping. He knew if he tried to pick it up it would fall apart, but if he moved the dinghy at anything faster than a snail's pace the thin paper would be thrown off. Reaching under the seat he released the first aid kit and extracted a gauze bandage. He used his teeth to tear it into strips and then gently pressed each strip onto the paper. It was far from a perfect solution, but it was the only one he could come up with; at least it allowed him to lift the paper and sandwich it between other strips of bandage. With luck the forensics people would be able to restore enough of it that it could be identified.

He placed the paper in its gauze wrapper on top of the plastic bag in the makeshift evidence box, closed the lid and eased the inflatable out of the niche. He had spent more time than he had planned and the Prince Rupert guys would be waiting for him, wondering where he was. The GPS coordinates he had given them were close to the road and only a short distance away from the bridge, but it would take him another ten or fifteen minutes navigating the waterways to get there. It was getting late. Although the sun still hadn't lifted above the mountain peaks it was almost full light. Dan knew the workers from Kitsault liked to get an early start. They would be out on the road soon if they weren't already there and he didn't want to be seen climbing up the bank.

By the time he arrived at the rendezvous the two men from Prince Rupert were standing anxiously on the edge of the bank, watching him approach. They lowered two ropes and he tied the dinghy to the one they had tied to a metal peg driven into the ground; he used the other, which had a harness attached, to pull himself up. There were quick handshakes and introductions, and then they all piled into the big crew-cab pickup truck that was sitting on the road a short distance away, a sturdy ATV filling up the box and two rifles clamped into a rack on the back window.

"So where are we heading?" The speaker was Burnell, the younger of the two men, both of whom were dressed in rugged outdoor gear.

"Just keep following this road," Dan answered. "There's a bridge a couple of miles ahead. We're going to take a look under it."

The only response was a nod from the driver.

▶ "We're supposed to climb down that? I thought we were going to be rock climbing." The two Prince Rupert guys were peering over the bridge railing at the waterfall. They had parked the truck in a wide clearing a couple of hundred yards away and carried their gear back.

"No, we're not going to climb down that. At least not from here." Dan answered. "We're going in from the other side. There's a ledge I need to get a good look at."

Burnell stood watch while his partner Sean Jones accompanied Dan as he scrambled down the creek bank and crawled under the bridge. The lights they had brought from Prince Rupert were considerably brighter than the flashlight Dan had used on his previous visit, but even using those they could not be sure of what they were seeing; the rock was too black and too wet. Dan relieved Burnell up on the road and watched as the two climbers anchored their rope to the beams that supported the bridge and attached carabiners and belay devices. Jones then returned and Dan joined Burnell, who strapped him into a harness and eased him over the lip of the creek.

It was an easy descent, but standing on the ledge was disorienting. The thunder of the falls, the darkness of the rock, and the movement of the water gave him vertigo, and he had to cling to the rope to keep himself oriented. Grasping the light in his free hand, he shone it along the rock. It rippled and folded but there was nothing there that didn't belong there. Twisting himself around by pushing against the vertical wall, he shone the light in the opposite direction. Again it picked out the contours of the rock and danced over its surface as the movement of the water caught the reflections. He stared at it for a few minutes, thinking that it looked somehow different than when he had seen it from above the last time he was there, but there was no way of being sure. The different angle of view alone could be enough to account for the feeling that something had changed, that something was missing. He tugged on the rope to indicate he wanted to ascend, but as he turned his eye caught a dark tube-like object and he stopped and picked it up. It was small and flexible and he thought it was probably just a piece of junk that had fallen through the gaps in the bridge decking, but it still needed to be checked out. At this point, except for one piece of sodden paper that may or may not be legible, it was all he had.

"So is there anything down there?"

The three of them were gathered around the truck, the climbing gear stowed once again.

"Not really. Certainly nothing major." Disappointment and frustration colored Dan's voice. "All I found was this, and I think it's probably just some kind of trash." He dug in his pocket for the thing he had picked up, and as he did so he felt something else small and hard that had sunk deep into the seam. He pulled both items out at the same time and put them on his palm where he pushed at them with his finger. "Looks like this was some kind of hose. It probably fell off a vehicle," he said as he poked at the tube. He rolled the other item around. "Don't know what this is, though. I picked it up last time I was here. Just junk too, I guess."

Even as he said the words, some of the random pieces that had been bothering him for the last few days suddenly clicked into place. The items he held in his hand were a tube and a plastic nozzle—the kind used to inflate things such as inflatable boats—and Kent McGilvery had said Jim Wakeshaw took an inflatable kayak with him when he went out hunting. Dan would be willing to bet that it was a kayak that had been on the ledge when he and Claire had checked it out. A black rubber inflatable kayak. That would account for the odd folds and curves his flashlight had picked out, and its absence was why he thought something was different now.

He stared at the two RCMP officers standing beside him, his mind racing.

"Shit! He's out there. He's hunting for his next victim. He's going to kill again."

THIRTY-ONE

▶ "Can you guys get hold of the detachment?" he asked as he checked his watch

"Yes. We've got a satellite phone in the truck. Why?"

"Call them. Tell them what's happening. We need them to shut down Kitsault and get any of the workers who are out on the roads already to come back in. Tell them to phone . . ."

He paused. Who the hell could they phone? They certainly couldn't phone the office at Kitsault because that would alert Marjorie Wakeshaw, and while he was beginning to think Ridley MacPherson might just be a pawn in all this, he still wasn't sure and that meant they couldn't call him either. Bill Caversham was a possibility, but that man was down in Prince Rupert and was probably already well on his way to inebriation, so there was no use talking to him. There would be kitchen staff in the pub organizing breakfast, but they would have no way to contact the men out in the field, so that left Zubrinski, the man who had let them use the Jeep yesterday and the only other person Dan had spoken with.

"Tell them to call Marcus Zubrinski. I don't know what his official title is—maybe dispatcher or transportation manager or something—but he looks after assigning the vehicles. He'll know who's out already and he'll know how to get hold of them. And make sure Prince Rupert talks to him directly and tells him not to say anything to Marjorie Wakeshaw; in fact, they need to send someone out to pick her up. I have to call Claire and give her a heads up, and then we need to go look for Wakeshaw's ATV."

He fumbled in his jacket for the handheld VHF and pressed the transmit button as he watched the men head for the truck.

"Claire? Where are you?"

Her response was almost immediate. "About a mile from where you left me, why?"

"It's Wakeshaw, and he's out on the water. He's got an inflatable kayak, almost certainly black. I don't think he'll be out in the main channel, but make sure you keep an eye out and call me if you see him. If he looks like coming anywhere near you, leave."

"Okay, I can do that, but what about you? Are you coming back here in the dinghy?"

"I'm going to help the guys look for Wakeshaw's ATV first. I shouldn't be long. I'll call you."

"But then you'll be out on the water alone when you come!" There was worry in her voice.

"I'll be fine. We'll either have caught him or know where he is by then, and even if we haven't, a kayak can't compete with a motorized dinghy. You just look after yourself. I hate the idea of you being out there alone."

Her laughter carried clearly across the airwaves. "Nothing to worry about there. I'm not alone. In fact, it's been positively crowded. Walker and Joel are here."

"What!"

"Walker and Joel. They're both here. Charles dropped them off about half an hour ago. He's gone fishing for a few hours but he said he'd be back . . ."

The sound of the ATV being driven off the pickup drowned out the last of her words.

"Claire, listen. Don't let them leave, okay? Keep them there on *Dreamspeaker*." The signal had started to fade in and out, and any reply she might have made was lost.

▶ The ATV could only carry two people. Dan told Burnell to take the truck and drive the road looking for anyone who might be out there and to send everyone he came across back to Kitsault, while he and Jones searched the immediate area. He figured if Wakeshaw hadn't left the ATV close by it meant he had a helper, and that helper was out there wherever the murder was going to take place, ready to play his part.

A dense canopy of branches overhead created a deep shade that had prevented much in the way of undergrowth between the ancient trees. That should have made their progress easier, but the rotting trunks of fallen cedars and spruce made any foray off the road both treacherous and slow. The crumbling wood was often hidden in moss and the risk of overturning or becoming stuck was constant.

After more than an hour of working their way around and over and across a minefield of decaying logs, Dan realized that they probably weren't going to find anything, even if there was something to find, which he now thought was doubtful. After all, if the ground was difficult for him to maneuver on an ATV, it would be equally difficult for anyone else, so unless Wakeshaw had found an easy way in and they happened to stumble upon it, continuing their search was useless.

Back on the side of the road, the two men turned off the engine, climbed down, and stretched muscles bruised during their tortuous ride.

"There's gotta be another guy." Dan's voice sounded loud in the sudden silence.

"Burnell will find him if he's heading west," Jones answered.

Dan nodded, but the fact that none of the people who had been out in the area at the time of the murders had mentioned seeing an ATV—or any other vehicle for that matter—bothered him. He was still missing something. He had to be.

"Let's head the other way," he said. "We'll stay on the road. Maybe there's a trail or something."

They turned back to the ATV and clambered on, trying to ignore the discomfort of wet jeans that clung to their legs as they settled onto the seats. It was Dan's turn to drive, but as he reached forward to start the motor, his fingers froze on the key.

"You hear that?" he asked.

"Yeah. Sounds like there might be an ATV out there."

They were both looking off into the trees in the direction the sound was coming from, but there was no sign of movement even though the noise of a motor continued to rise and fall.

"There's got to be a way in, and it has to be close," Dan said as he started the engine. "We need to find it."

Find it they did, only five minutes later. It wasn't a road, or even a trail, but simply an opening in the forest where an old streambed had left behind a narrow line of gravel and rock. As it was mostly hidden by thin grass and ferns, Dan might never have noticed it except for a single tire track on the road, created as a vehicle made a sharp turn. They followed the trail for perhaps half a mile as it meandered through the trees before Dan stopped once again. The sound was louder now, and it was no longer fluctuating.

"Can you see him?" Jones asked.

"No, but there's a clearing up ahead. I don't want him to see us, so let's walk from here."

The day seemed to grow brighter as they approached the limit of the trees, the sky appearing through the canopy above them and light pouring through the spaces between the trunks. Beyond those there was simply nothing but empty space. It was as if the Earth dropped away where the forest ended. Dan found his feet slowing as his eyes told his brain he was approaching the edge of a precipice, and without conscious direction his hand moved to rest on the handle of the gun that rode in his shoulder holster.

The apprehension proved unnecessary. The precipice turned out to be no more than a steep bank dropping down a few feet to a wide stretch of clear-cut land. It was obvious the logging companies had been and gone. Little was left except stumps, and twisting its way between them on an apparently random path was a single ATV.

Dan and Jones stood in the shadows of the trees and watched as it traced an aimless passage back and forth, sometimes circling a particular stump two or three times before weaving a figure eight and then circling back to where it had started. At one point it approached so close to where they were standing that Dan was sure they would be seen, but the rider never looked up, intent on whatever private obstacle course he had laid out.

Whoever it was, he was dressed in heavy, dark clothing and he was wearing a black knitted cap, but other than that it was impossible to tell what he looked like. All Dan could tell from this distance and angle was that it was a man, and that he was big—very big. MacPherson had said James Wakeshaw was big. Could this be him? If it was, everything Dan had been thinking about Wakeshaw being the one was wrong, and he was back to square one. *Goddamn this case! It's going to drive me nuts!*

Pointing down the slope to get Jones to take a different route, Dan waited until the ATV was close, then moved out of the trees and half ran, half slid down in front of it. The vehicle came to an abrupt halt, scattering gravel and detritus in a wide arc. The rider sat motionless, hands frozen on the handlebars, staring at the man in front of him with wide, frightened eyes.

"Jim?" Dan asked.

There was no answer, but Dan could see panic and fear written in the tense muscles and trembling lips.

He injected a friendlier tone into his voice. "Are you James Wakeshaw?"

It took a while, but finally there was a jerky head shake.

"You're not James Wakeshaw?"

This close, Dan could see that this man was much younger than Jim Wakeshaw could possibly be, but he could also see strands of dark red hair curling out from under the cap. A son? If it was, the boy looked like he had both physical and mental challenges: he was big, but not in proportion. His hands and feet were massive, finger and wrist joints thick and heavy, but his neck and head were small and out of proportion, and his expression was that of a ten- or twelve-year-old. Dan decided to take a chance.

"Is James your dad?"

Again the delay before an abrupt nod.

"He know you're out here?"

The nod came more quickly this time.

"You know where I can find him? I'm a friend of his." Dan held out his hand. "Dan Connor. I'm supposed to meet him."

The young man stared at Dan's hand for a minute, and then thrust his own out in an awkward show of reluctance.

"I'm sorry," Dan continued. "I don't remember your name."

Another delay, another nod, and then finally there was speech.

"I'm Stevie." The voice was curiously high pitched and childlike.

"Hi, Stevie. Nice to meet you. Your dad around here somewhere?"

Again the delay before the exaggerated head shake. Dan was starting to get used to it.

"Not here."

"You know where he is?"

"Gone hunting."

Stevie was starting to relax a little and the responses were coming faster.

"Gone hunting in a boat?"

This time the nod was accompanied with a smile.

"Did he say when he would be back? I really need to talk to him."

Another head shake and then Stevie thrust his hand in his pocket and pulled out a handheld VHF very similar to the one Dan had in his jacket. "He call me."

Dan looked at the radio lying innocuously in the huge palm. It was such a simple system. One quick call when James arrived back at the bridge and Stevie would go to pick him up.

Dan reached into his jacket and pulled out his own VHF. "Hey, we've got the same radios!" He held it out to the young man. "Guess I must have the wrong channel set up. Mind if I take a look at yours?"

Stevie looked at him in confusion for a moment or two and then looked down at the radio he was holding. After staring at it for a moment longer, he suddenly thrust out his hand and gave it to Dan.

"Channel 72," Dan said as he looked at the screen. "That's the problem. I had 73." He passed it back. "Thanks," he said. "I'll give him a call."

► THIRTY-TWO ◄

► The ATV, with Jones driving, bounced over a berm and surged out onto the road, spraying rocks and dirt as its wheels fought for grip on the loose surface. Dan clung onto the seat, willing the tiny machine to stay upright as it lurched down the embankment on the other side and headed for his dinghy.

They no longer had the extra ropes and harness he had used just an hour ago to climb up, but retrieving them from the truck was out of the question, so Dan simply looped the line that was holding the dinghy around his waist and with Jones bracing him, carefully lowered himself down, scraping the skin off fingers as he dug them into the rock.

"Call the truck," he shouted at Jones as he freed the dinghy from its tether. "Ask Burnell if he's seen anyone on the road; if he has, make sure he's sent them back to Kitsault."

Jones nodded and waved as he pulled the rope up and headed back to the ATV and Dan lost any reply the man might have made in the roar of the outboard as he raced downstream toward the inlet. Twice he almost overturned as he threw the little boat around tight curves, but he needed all the speed he could get. Wakeshaw was out there preparing to kill again; Dan could sense him, almost smell him. If Burnell had gotten everyone off the road, there might be no new victim today, but unless Wakeshaw was caught, there would surely be one tomorrow, or the next day. The man was crazy—he had to be—and the police could not keep the workers off the roads indefinitely; their employers would be in an uproar. Even if they did, there would be other potential targets: loggers, hikers, tourists, environmentalists. Even the people whose territory this was, the Nisga'a, might be at risk.

That thought made Dan think of Joel. Joel could be the most vulnerable target of all. It was Joel, with his preference for solitude and his habit of wandering the waterways, on whom Wakeshaw had deliberately directed the blame. If the man learned that his ruse was no longer working, then who better to vent his frustration on than that same gentle soul. He might even set it up as a double murder—kill another worker, then make it look as if that worker had been attacked by Joel, and then had killed Joel in self-defense.

But Dan was getting ahead of himself. There was already enough complication and threat without adding imaginary plots to the mix. Joel wasn't even out on the water right now. He was safely onboard *Dreamspeaker* with Walker and Claire—or was he? Dan had asked Claire to make sure Joel and Walker stayed aboard, but he wasn't even sure she had heard him. Even if she had, Dan knew Walker was seldom swayed from his own plans by someone else's requests. There was no reason to think Joel would be any different, especially given the fact that he barely knew Claire and would probably feel uncomfortable on an unfamiliar boat with a woman he barely knew. Dan slowed the motor and pulled out his VHF.

"They left over half an hour ago, just after you called," Claire said. "I told them you had said they should stay on board, but Walker said you worried too much and they would be fine."

Dan grimaced. He could almost hear Walker saying the words. He would have had that aggravating grin on his face as he said them.

"Did he give you any idea of where they were going?"

He knew even as he asked what the answer would be. In Walker's world, and he suspected in Joel's as well, the coves and inlets and creeks had no names. They were simply there, a part of all that surrounded them. Perhaps they might refer to a location as "the place where the otters live" or "the place of falling water," but to someone like Dan, who lived in a world delineated by charts and maps, the references would be useless.

"No, but he did say they wouldn't go anywhere near the waterfall."

Great, thought Dan. *Right now that was probably the safest place they could possibly be.*

"Okay. Did you happen to see what direction they went?"

"They headed south, down the inlet, but I really don't think they'll go far. Walker still can't use his arm, so Joel's doing all the paddling, and Charles said he would be back to pick them up this afternoon."

South. The direction that led to all of the murder sites. Two unarmed and unprepared men, one of whom couldn't use one of his arms and who could barely use his legs, and the other with no ability to deal with regular society, let alone its most severely troubled members. Dan shook his head and pointed the bow of the dinghy south. While he couldn't afford to focus all his efforts on finding Walker and Joel first, he would be a much happier man if he came across the pair before he found Wakeshaw.

▶ From out in the inlet, all the creeks looked remarkably similar and all were equally attractive as possible destinations for a man intent on murder. Assuming Wakeshaw was in good physical condition—and everything Dan had heard so far indicated that he was—then it would be possible for him to scramble up a bank from almost all of them. If he had equipment—a rope or something that would serve as a handhold—then the ascent would be relatively easy.

Dan slowed the boat and let it drift. There was no way of knowing which of the pipeline workers Wakeshaw was targeting, and equally impossible to know exactly where the attack was planned, but logic told him that it would be from a place that was very close to the road. He had the feeling Wakeshaw was in a hurry. The way Marjorie had almost run from the house after receiving the schedules supported that belief, which meant that this was something that had not been carefully planned. Would that make a difference as to the location? It might. Wakeshaw might not have had time to establish exactly where a given man would be at a particular time, and that meant he might simply have to wait until his target arrived. That in turn meant that where he was waiting would have to be really close to the road so that he could remain unseen until he heard a vehicle arrive. Which of the creeks Dan and Claire had explored on their search for Walker fit the description best?

Closing his eyes, Dan struggled to create a mental image of the chart they had used and match it up with his memory of the trips they had made. The first creek they had entered after they came out of the one leading to the falls had been wide and shallow at the mouth, but had narrowed so much they could barely get through, and the bank near the road was more like a cliff. Not a likely choice for someone who wanted to wait close by, unseen and unheard, and then appear and disappear quickly and silently.

The second one had been shallower. Where it crossed under the road it was contained in a narrow culvert, and the road itself dipped so low there was almost no bank. Anyone waiting there would easily be seen. Not a likely choice either.

He thought the third and fourth were both good candidates. The third was the narrower of the two, but would be no problem for a kayak, while the fourth was wider, with a slower current. Easier and faster to paddle. Both had steep banks, not steep enough to prevent someone from climbing them if they were determined, but enough to hide that someone from view if he was waiting at the base. Also, Dan thought he remembered both creeks curving sharply just before they reached the road, which would provide even more cover for a man laying in wait for the truck bearing his victim to arrive. The fourth was also where they had found Walker's kayak.

He had to choose. Sitting around out here in the inlet certainly allowed him time to think, and he would see anyone coming out of either the second or third creek, or returning from the fourth for that matter, but it did nothing to protect the intended victim who, unless Jones and Burnell had managed to stop all traffic, might already be out there on the road. And if Dan didn't catch Wakeshaw with a weapon in his hand, he still had only circumstantial evidence. Hell, he had even less than that. He had nothing but his own suspicions. Certainly nothing that would hold up in court.

On the other hand, if he chose wrong, then Wakeshaw might very well get away completely and be long gone, maybe even back in Kitsault, by the time Dan found him. Even if he chose right, the sound of his engine was going to alert the man that someone was coming, and give him a chance to get rid of whatever paddle or knife he planned to use.

Taking a deep breath, Dan made his choice. He cranked up the motor and headed for the fourth creek.

THIRTY-THREE

The weasel led her kits along the shore, totally oblivious of the two men sitting motionless and silent in their canoe. There were five young, each a miniature replica of its mother, with their long, thin bodies clad in their brown summer coat, white bellies so low to the ground as to be almost invisible. They were learning to hunt and they copied every move their mother made, sniffing the same smells, examining the same holes, checking the same cavities as they followed her along some invisible trail. Soon they would be on their own, prowling the land for mice and voles, taking unwary rabbits or ducks, efficient and deadly killers who could find their own prey.

Walker and Joel had paddled south before turning toward the shore of the inlet and letting themselves drift in the ebb current. Even though they had not had the chance to spend any time together for several years, they had no need for talk. It was enough to be out on the water together, watching the rhythms of life flow around them, hearing the sigh of the wind as it moved through the trees, listening to the birds chatter in the branches, seeing the diamond sparkle of herring rising to the surface, feeling the gentle movement of the waves as they washed along the land. The harsh scream, when it came, shattered it all into a million pieces. They reacted instinctively, both driving their paddles into the water to push the canoe deep into a jumble of rocks.

"What the hell was that?" Walker was holding onto the rock with his good arm, his knuckles white as his fingers gripped the rough surface. Both men had crouched low, their bodies tense. Joel slowly held up his hand and pointed to the right. Walker nodded.

"Yeah," he whispered. "Sounds like someone is really pissed."

The scream came again, rough and angry, followed by a series of heavy thuds. Whoever or whatever was causing it was close, very close, perhaps just beyond a rise of land. The thuds continued, followed by a sharp snapping sound and the clang of metal against rock.

Silence returned, and after a couple of minutes the two men cautiously backed the canoe far enough out of the rocks so that Walker, who was sitting on the rear seat, could see a little way up the inlet. If it hadn't been for the faint rhythmic splash of a paddle as it dipped into the water, he wouldn't have noticed the man in the kayak: both his clothing and the tiny craft he was paddling were black, and the kayak was so low in the water it was almost invisible. Walker watched its progress as it moved steadily away, and then he slowly eased the canoe further out so that Joel could see what was happening.

"It's him." Joel's voice was low but certain and his eyes were riveted on the receding figure.

"It's who?" Walker asked.

"The man who is killing the people."

"How do you know that? Have you seen him before?"

"I think so, but it doesn't matter. I am sure it's him. I can feel him. He's crazy." There was no doubt on Joel's face or in his words.

Walker stared at his friend for several seconds then turned to watch the small black dot that was diminishing into the distance as it moved over the water.

"We should get back to the boat," he said. "Claire can call Dan and warn him."

▶ The journey back to the boat was going to be longer and harder than their journey out. The current was still ebbing and would reach maximum flow in less than an hour. They would be fighting it all the way, and in order to avoid being seen by the man they were following, they needed to stay close to the shore where they would blend in with the background—and that would increase the distance. On the other hand, there were two of them to do the work of paddling, even though Walker's arm meant he couldn't switch sides or contribute the power he would have liked.

Several times they lost sight of the kayak completely, but each time they found it again when they rounded some outcropping or skirted some point, both vessels still moving steadily north. Finally, after nearly an hour of steady paddling, they emerged from behind a scattering of rocks that ran out from the shore and discovered that the kayak and its passenger had completely disappeared.

"You think he saw us?" Joel asked.

"No. He was still heading up last we saw, and even if he looked back he wouldn't have been able to see us against the shoreline. He must have gone into one of the creeks."

They moved further out toward the center of the channel, watching the shore for any sign of movement, but they saw nothing. Then the mouth of a creek appeared, the outflow of fresh water dancing over the tops of the waves, droplets catching the light like a school of flying fish.

"That's where he must have gone," Walker said. "There's something about that creek he likes. It's where he took my canoe."

He stopped paddling and stared across the water.

"I wonder if he knew you had gone back to Haida Gwaii. Dan and I were trying to figure out why he took my canoe there. If he knew you were gone, he might have thought he could shift the blame from you to me by letting it be found near where he was planning a murder."

Joel turned in his seat. "Why would he do that?"

"Guess one Indian is as good as another to guys like him. I was just handy." Anger mixed with the cynicism in his voice.

Joel's answering smile was brief and it suddenly gave way to a look of horror. "Does that mean someone else is dead?"

Walker thought back to the noises they had heard. Was it possible that what they had heard was a murder taking place? Had the screams they heard come from a victim? The thought sent a cold shiver through his blood, and he knew Joel was feeling the same way, but the idea didn't really make sense.

"I don't think so—at least I don't think that's what we heard." He hoped that was true. "It's not likely anyone else would be out there, and that was only a one-man kayak. It didn't sound like someone in trouble or hurt, either. I think that was just the guy himself. He sounded angry. Maybe he was mad because he hadn't been able to do what he wanted to do and he was taking out his rage on his weapon."

Joel was still looking across at the creek. "So what should we do?"

"Good question." Walker was seldom indecisive, and he felt annoyed with himself that he couldn't make a clear choice now, but he had never been in a position like this before. This was Dan's territory. Dan was the cop. He was trained to handle this kind of situation.

"We should probably go back to the boat and tell Claire. She can call Dan and let him know."

"Maybe we should follow him. Keep track of where he goes."

"We're not going to be able to do much by following him and he would see us right away. There's no place to hide out here and the last time I ran into him he damn near killed me—and that was when I had two good arms. Now I've only got one." Walker didn't add that Joel would be completely unprepared to take part in any confrontation, and would be not only vulnerable, but also traumatized by even coming close to this evil man. Joel nodded reluctantly and pushed his paddle in the water.

The canoe had only moved a few feet when a black shadow passed across it and a raucous call split the air. The raven swept low over their heads then wheeled and headed back toward the shore.

"Yaahl says we should go to the creek," Joel said as he spun the canoe back toward the show. "There is something happening there."

"Like what? It's you Yaahl looks after, not some stranger who might be murdering people."

Joel had a look on his face that indicated both puzzlement and wonder.

"Yaahl helps who he will. He is the trickster, and this is not some stranger who needs help. It's your friend. The policeman."

"Dan? Yaahl told you Dan needs help?"

Walker's eyes went from Joel's bemused face to the empty shore and back again, and then he drove his paddle deep into the water to send the canoe surging toward the mouth of the creek.

THIRTY-FOUR

▶ Dan kept his speed low as he moved up the creek. There was no need to hurry. Wakeshaw was either there or he was not. If he was not, then slow or fast made no difference. If the man himself was not there but his kayak was, then Dan could simply wait until he returned. And if he was there, then a slow speed was less likely to panic him. It was a psychological thing all cops learned. Arrive on the scene fast, and whoever was there reacted as if you were a threat and their brain instructed their body to produce adrenaline. Go slow, and that fight or flight instinct was not activated. It was instinctive. It happened even with witnesses and bystanders. Of course, the problem was that it applied only when the person you were approaching was sane and could be expected to react normally and Dan figured that was probably not the case here. Everything he had heard about Wakeshaw led him to believe the man was at best unbalanced and quite possibly insane, and if he had just murdered yet another victim, then he would be so wired and jumpy he would be completely unpredictable.

The sandbar where he and Claire had found Walker's canoe came into view, the flat gravel area empty and quiet. Dan took a wide path around the bend just above it, knowing from his previous visit that it was the best course to get a view of what was ahead, but as before there was nothing except the steep rock banks studded with occasional low growth. The creek only made a few more curves before it reached the point where it ran out through a narrow culvert under the road and any further passage was blocked. All of them were clear. He had obviously chosen wrong. Dan looked up at the wet black face of the rock wall where the stream poured from the culvert, spreading and dividing into myriad small rivulets as it found ridges and fissures in its path down. The harsh finality of that sheer massif only served to emphasize the futility of his search. A dead end. Shaking his head, he turned the bow of the dinghy back down toward the ocean. Wakeshaw had to have gone up a different waterway, probably the one he had dismissed, the third one on his list of candidates. This trip had been a waste of time. He only hoped that Burnell had been successful in clearing the road and that Wakeshaw was still out there, waiting in vain for his next victim to arrive.

The current caught the inflatable, and Dan increased the speed of the motor, no longer caring about psychological advantage or stealth or anything other than the need to get to the one creek he had chosen not to search. He felt the inflatable heel slightly as he threw it round the first curve, then level out. A couple of easy bends and another sharp turn in the opposite direction as he approached the sandbar again and then it would be easier. He was concentrating so hard on keeping the boat in control around the sharp turn that the presence of a small, black kayak in the water ahead of him didn't immediately register, and when it did it was too late to stop his forward progress. Belatedly he saw the kayaker raise his arm high above his head, caught the glint of metal catching the light as it descended, and then the two vessels collided.

It all happened so fast Dan wasn't sure of how it happened, but he was suddenly immersed in water so cold the shock of it forced all the air out of his lungs. His muscles contracted and went into spasm, frozen in place, but his nervous system felt as if it were on fire with a thousand knives stabbing into his skin. Momentum forced him deep, and his legs scraped along the gravel bottom as the current dragged him along. Panic seized him. He was going to drown. Water filled his nose, his ears, pressed against his eyes and mouth. His feet, clad in hiking boots, weighed a hundred pounds. His jacket and sweater, heavy with water, pulled his arms down.

He was helpless. Drowning had always been his worst nightmare, even as a kid on his father's fish boat. He had loved the boat and loved the sea, but feared the water. He remembered dreaming of seaweed wrapping around him, caressing him as it pulled him down deeper, deeper, ever deeper. He could feel it now, even thought he knew there was none. How crazy was that?

He forced his brain away from the memory. Goddamn it, he wanted to live. He needed to live. He was not ready to die. He could not leave Claire alone. Frantically he fought to right himself, to get his feet down onto something solid so that he could push himself up to the air he so desperately needed. His body twisted and his hands clawed at the water, pulling, reaching, stretching toward the dim light he could see above him. He clamped his lips shut, fighting the urge to inhale as his lungs screamed for air, and finally his head broke the surface and he heaved in huge gulps of needed oxygen. He blinked the water out of his eyes and tried to look around, but it was dark and he couldn't see anything. Fear grabbed him harder, panic vibrating through the neurons and pathways in his brain. The darkness was wrong. It was still morning. It had to be. He couldn't have been under more than forty or fifty seconds, a minute at the most. It couldn't be dark. He reached up a hand and felt something solid above him. That wasn't right either. Was he trapped somewhere? Forced into some underwater cave? He searched with his fingers, feeling a smooth curve that rose out of the water. It had a slightly rough texture. He moved his hand higher and touched something hard and flat and suddenly he knew what had happened. He had come up underneath the overturned inflatable. He slid his hand along the flatness of the seat to the other pontoon, some part of his brain already figuring out how to flip the boat back, but there was something wrong. On that side it was no longer a smooth curve and the jagged remnants of its fabric trailed in the water. The whole floor of the boat floated at an odd angle and he realized that one pontoon was partially deflated, split open. He turned his face upward to inhale the air trapped in what had now become a small triangular pocket, and as he did so another section of the pontoon exploded, the concussion caused by its sudden decompression rippling through the water as the fabric folded him into an even closer embrace.

Instinctively he reached up and grasped the seat, wanting to anchor himself on something solid while he tried to force his brain to function. He knew he didn't have long. The only remaining air would be trapped above the seat and that was now sitting on the surface of the water.

He started to push the seat up, and then stopped. The black kayak. The flash of metal. It was Wakeshaw, and he had to be still out there, waiting. The man was using something metal—maybe even the murder weapon, although from the glimpse Dan had gotten he thought it had been more like a hunting knife—to systematically shred Dan's inflatable, ensuring Dan would not, could not, survive. The man had not been able to find his intended victim and Dan was the substitute. Or maybe he had found him and Dan was just a follow up, another target to vent his rage on. Either way, if Dan couldn't figure out a way to get out of the water very soon, Wakeshaw would succeed in his plan. The cold was already numbing Dan's hands and feet and was moving up his arms and legs.

His shoes dragged along a rocky bottom and he felt it shelving toward the shore. Using every ounce of his fading control, he dug the toe of his shoe into the gravel and used the purchase he gained to inch himself and the overturned inflatable toward the shore, trying to make the movement smooth and steady as if it was simply the current working. It was his only chance. His strength was fading fast. There was no way he could tackle an armed man. He needed to get himself out of the water.

▶ **THIRTY-FIVE** ◀

▶ Joel and Walker had almost reached the mouth of the creek when the man in the black kayak appeared ahead of them, traveling fast, his shoulders hunched as he pushed the vessel through the water. They both raised their paddles in the air in a half-threatening, half-protective gesture, knowing instinctively that this was the danger the raven had warned them about. Although Walker had not seen him well at the time, he was sure this was the man who had attacked him just a day ago in this very same creek. It was possible, in fact almost certain, that he was also the man who had attempted to frame Joel, and who was more than capable of attacking them now, but after an initial glance, the man ignored them. He turned up into the inlet, heading north toward Alice Arm and Kitsault, and Joel and Walker lowered their paddles and continued on into the creek, paddling with renewed vigor as Walker's imagination painted ever more graphic and macabre problems for Dan.

Walker's apprehension grew as they approached the shingle bar where his canoe had been abandoned. If Dan was in trouble, this is where he was likely to be—unless of course he had been killed— murdered by the same man who had tried to murder Walker and who had murdered all those other people. The man they had just seen paddling away. In that case they might not find Dan at all; they might already have paddled over his body.

The thought brought with it a shudder of revulsion. Dan had become a friend, and he was here largely because Walker had asked him to come. If something had happened to him, Walker would carry the guilt for the rest of his life. But it was even more than that. Walker had spent many long, hard years working to achieve balance in his life. Ever since he had returned from the city many years ago, injured in both body and spirit, he had acknowledged and embraced the legend of his people, the legend of Sisiutl, the double-headed sea serpent. He knew how carefully the two heads, the good and the evil, had to be balanced, and he had struggled to attain harmony in every aspect of his life. But he also knew only too well that many of his own people had forgotten the legends and the teachings, had forgotten to pay the proper tribute and respect to the most powerful of all the spirits, and the same was certainly true for the white man, even though they knew their spirits by different names. The balance had been broken here in these waters. The evil head had succeeded in dominating his twin and this was the result. A powerful shape-shifter, Sisiutl was one of the few spirits who could take human form. Now it seemed that he had become the man in the black kayak.

They rounded the curve and the shingle bar came into view. Where Walker's canoe had rested just a day ago, there was now an odd pile of shapeless gray fabric. One trailing end stretched out into the water and bobbed in the current while the remainder was heaped up in a mound that almost reached the bank. It was only when they were almost close enough to touch it that Walker realized what it was: the overturned remains of an inflatable dinghy, almost certainly the one that Dan had been using.

They cautiously drove the canoe up onto the edge of the shingle, not knowing what to expect when they got there. Both pontoons had been shredded, and only one airtight chamber remained inflated, which tilted what remained of the dinghy at an odd angle. Even the floor had been slashed and through the slit Walker could see what he thought was more loose fabric trapped below the seats.

He reached out to lift one of the deflated pontoons up; as he did so, the whole dinghy—or what had once been a dinghy—moved, and the tip of a boot appeared in front of him.

"Dan?"

The fabric heaved and another boot appeared, followed by two legs clad in sodden jeans. Walker leaned over, lifted up a piece of the thick Hypalon fabric that was covering the rest of the emerging body, and peered under it.

"You okay?"

"Hell no, I'm not okay. I'm cold, wet and completely pissed. That bastard damn near killed me and he wrecked my dinghy—what the hell are you grinning at?"

Walker leaned back in the canoe and rested on his paddle.

"Good to see you too." Amusement and relief mingled in his voice.

Dan glared at him for a moment, and then his face relaxed into a smile.

"Shit. I'm sorry—and I'm very glad to see you. You too, Joel." He nodded at the other man. "How the hell did you find me?"

Walker's grin widened.

"Would you believe me if I said a raven told us?"

Dan snorted. "Hell yes. Why not? After this I'll believe anything you say."

He zipped open his jacket and extracted his arms from the sleeves.

"Glad I decided to wear my floatation jacket. I think I would have been a goner without it. I could feel my legs and hands going numb."

"I know the feeling." Walker's face was suddenly serious. "Whoever that guy is, he almost added two more to his list—you and me—and that's not counting what he tried to do to Joel. If that had worked, it would have been even worse than death. He needs to be stopped."

"He's damn well going to be stopped, believe me." Dan pushed himself to his feet and stepped over to the canoe. "Is there any way you can take me back to *Dreamspeaker*? I need to call Prince Rupert."

Walker glanced at Joel then down at the canoe. "You figure it can carry all of us?"

Joel nodded. "Yes, but he will have to sit down low, in the bottom, so it doesn't overturn."

"You okay with that?" Walker asked, turning back to Dan. "It won't be comfortable but it will keep you out of the wind so you'll be warmer. Better put that jacket back on."

Dan laughed. "Talk about turning the tables. It's only been a couple of days since I dragged your sorry half-dead ass back to the boat. Now here you are doing the same for me. Guess we're even—not that I'm keeping score."

"Good thing too," Walker retorted. "Otherwise you would owe Joel and me a salmon dinner."

"You can have whatever dinner you like if you get me back to *Dreamspeaker*," Dan said. "Jim and Marjorie Wakeshaw need to be behind bars, and their son needs to be picked up too."

Joel and Walker pushed the canoe off the shingle and held it steady with their paddles as Dan climbed in and settled himself on the floor. He had offered to paddle, thinking that not only would it warm him up, but that it would give Walker a rest, but both Joel and Walker had refused.

"Better balance this way," Walker had replied. "And Joel and I know each other. We know how we work. Makes it easy. You would probably tip us over."

That was the end of the conversation.

By the time they got back to *Dreamspeaker*, Dan was cramped, cold and impatient. He clambered up onto the stern deck as soon as they reached it, tied the bowline around a cleat, and started up the ladder to the aft deck. Claire heard him coming and met him halfway across.

"Dan? What on earth happened to you? Are you okay?" Her gaze took in his wet hair and dripping clothing.

"I'm fine—I'll explain in a minute. I've got to call Rupert and get them up here. Joel and Walker are back there."

He nodded toward the stern, gave her arm a reassuring squeeze, then pushed past her and ran up to the wheelhouse before she could ask any more questions.

THIRTY-SIX

▶ Twenty minutes later Dan replaced the microphone in its holder, grabbed the towel Claire had brought him, and headed for the shower. He could hear her talking with Walker and Joel in the salon, and knew they were going to demand a detailed explanation of everything that had happened once he joined them there, but first he needed to get rid of his wet clothing and get into something more comfortable.

It didn't take him long, and as he stepped into the warmth of the galley, silence fell in the salon just beyond.

"So, what happened?" Walker broke the silence first.

"Let's talk about what's going to happen before we get to that," Dan answered. "There are going to be a couple of police boats here in a few hours—small ones, not the big catamarans, although the *Inkster* is on its way too. It won't get here as quickly because it was out on patrol, but they're sending one of their big inflatables to come and pick me up." He looked at Joel and smiled. "They aren't interested in you any more. They know you didn't do it."

Joel looked at him for a moment, and then he gave a slight nod of his head.

"Thank you. Will they give me my paddle back?"

"Yes. In fact, they already have. It's at the coroner's office in Prince Rupert right now, but he's finished with it. I'll pick it up as soon as we get back to the marina."

"That going to be today?" Walker was making no bones about the fact he wanted to go home.

"Yeah. Might even be there in time for dinner if we're lucky."

"What if you're not?"

"Lucky? We will be. There's nowhere for this guy to run."

"Seems like he did a pretty good job of not being seen when he was killing all those people. I think he's pretty familiar with this area. Lot of places around here to hide if you know where to look and don't mind a little rough living."

"You said he was heading north when you saw him. Probably going back to the bridge so his son, Stevie, could come and get him. My guess is they'll head back to Kitsault. They don't know for sure we're onto them, and that's home base for all of them. Those two guys from Rupert that I was with this morning have got all the workers back into town and they've shut it down. They're going to stay out of sight and let anybody who arrives there come in, but they're not going to let anyone out."

"They shut down that thing too?" Walker nodded toward the handheld VHF that was lying on the table. "You said that's how he was going to call his son. His wife probably has one too."

"Yeah, you're right. She probably does. But I don't think she can reach him until he's pretty close to home, and Prince Rupert said they dispatched another bunch of guys over three hours ago—they should be there soon if they're not there already—and a couple of them are going to stay with her and make sure she doesn't do anything we don't want her to do."

Walker nodded slowly. "Sounds like you figure it's all wrapped up," he said. "Maybe you should leave now and let Prince Rupert handle the rest."

Dan shook his head. "I figure we have enough to pick him up. Marjorie too. The problem is I don't know if we've got enough to nail him—or even to charge him. Without the weapon everything is circumstantial. The son might talk, but there's no way he's going to be considered a reliable witness. He's probably only got the IQ of a ten-year-old, if that. I was hoping to get some fingerprints off the papers Marjorie left for him, but all that got lost when he wrecked my dinghy."

"But you can identify him!" Claire had been following the conversation closely. "Surely that's enough."

Dan shook his head. "I didn't see much more than Walker saw when the guy almost killed him. I came around the bend and saw a guy in a black kayak with a knife in his hand and next thing I knew I was in the water. I know it was him, but I can't prove it. We need the weapon he used for the murders. Unless we catch him with that, or find where he's hidden it, we really don't have much. And if he ditches the kayak, we've got nothing."

"So why are you going? It sounds as if there's nothing you can do."

"I know Marjorie, and I know MacPherson. I might be able to get one of them to talk—and I know more than any of the Prince Rupert guys about how they've been operating, so I can maybe trip them up if they decide to try and bluff their way out."

"Yes, but . . ."

Claire would have said more, but the roar of a fast boat approaching drew them all out onto the deck. The big inflatable curved up to the stern, the rooster-tail of water arching up behind its propeller slowly diminishing as it neared the swim grid and bumped alongside. One man, clad in a yellow rain jacket, stood at the control console. He looked up at the group of them as they lined up along the stern rail.

"One of you Dan Connor?" he asked.

"I'm Connor," Dan answered as he stepped down onto the grid. He turned and waved a hand at the rest of the group. "I won't be long. I just want to see this part of things wrapped up."

"Seems to me I've heard that before," Claire said. "I think your definition of 'long' is a bit different to mine. I'm tired of waiting, I have to be back in Campbell River soon, and it looks like the weather may be changing." She nodded out the window. "How about I take *Dreamspeaker* back to Rupert and you catch a ride with one of your RCMP buddies. That way you can do what you need to do without hurrying and I can get the boat fueled up and ready to head back down south."

Dan tried to gauge whether she was angry or simply being practical.

"You comfortable doing that by yourself? She's pretty big and heavy and she can be tough to berth if there's a wind and current running."

Claire didn't answer but simply stood with raised eyebrows and stared down at him. After a couple of seconds, Dan grinned, climbed aboard the inflatable, and nodded to the pilot to crank the throttle. If Claire said anything more as she turned away—and he thought she might have—her words were lost in the roar of the engine.

▶ "Do you two want to come back to Rupert with me?" Claire was tidying up the deck and getting the boat ready to leave. "We can try to radio Charles, but we'll probably meet up with him on the way."

Walker glanced at Joel before he answered. "Thanks, but no," he answered. "There are still a couple of places we want to explore, and my kayak is still on Charles' boat. We'll wait for him to come get us, but I'll come over as soon as we get back."

Claire nodded. "So what exactly happened out there?" she asked as she swung the empty davit back inboard and clamped it down.

Walker shrugged. "I don't know. That's something we'll have to get from Dan. By the time Joel and I arrived, he was lying on that shingle where you guys found my canoe, with the dinghy upside down on top of him."

"So had he just flipped it somehow?"

"Nope. It was all cut up. Slashed with a knife from the looks of it."

She stared at him in horror. "Was it that same guy? The one who's killing all those people? Marjorie's husband? My God! He must have been trying to kill Dan."

She looked so upset that Walker tried to reassure her.

"Well, if it was, he did a lousy job of it—and he won't get another chance. He was heading north last we saw him. Back to Kitsault and a police welcome."

"You saw him?" Walker's attempt at reassurance had obviously failed. Claire's expression was even more upset than before. "He could have tried to kill you too."

"He wasn't interested in us. I think he was running away."

▶ Claire watched the two men climb into their canoe and paddle toward the shore, and then she went up to the wheelhouse and turned *Dreamspeaker* south. The breeze was definitely freshening, and the clouds that were building far in the west had a purplish hue that hinted at major storm approaching. The idea of a comfortable berth at the marina, a hot shower, and a good book to read until Dan arrived back from Kitsault seemed more attractive by the minute.

THIRTY-SEVEN

▶ "We're not going to get anything out of her."

Paul Johnson, the detective who had been grilling Marjorie Wakeshaw, sipped on a cup of stale coffee that he had poured himself from the big coffee urn that sat on the counter in the bar.

"She sticking to the same story?" Dan asked.

"Yeah. He's been out hunting. She took him the schedules because he needed to figure out the maintenance. Yadda, yadda, yadda."

"She know you've picked up the son?"

"Not yet. I want to talk to him first. If he's as challenged as you say he is, maybe you should be in on that. You've already met him, so it might relax him a little. The guys that picked him up said he's pretty upset. He keeps saying he has to wait for his dad to call him."

"They get his radio?" Dan had told them about the way Stevie and his father communicated.

"Yeah. The guys are listening for a call. Nothing yet."

Dan thought that probably meant Wakeshaw had figured out what had happened—or at least some of it—and was hiding out somewhere. There were certainly places where he could scramble up the bank and he obviously knew the area well. If he still had the knife he had used to slash Dan's inflatable, and could get to the gun MacPherson said he had taken out with him, he might be able to survive for a good long time.

"You got people out on the road?" Dan asked.

"Yeah. Two trucks on the road plus the ATV, and the *Inkster* is parked down in Observatory with two of her fast boats out. We've put a man on the bridge, and we've got two of our own boats patrolling Alice Arm. If he sticks his nose out, we'll get him."

Paul's radio crackled and he lifted it up and pressed the switch. "Yeah?"

"Where do you want us to put the kid?"

"Take him over to the office," Paul answered. "We'll be over in a minute."

He explained to Dan that he had commandeered two of the condos in a building located just down from the bar when he had first arrived, and he was using them as an office and communications center; Marjorie Wakeshaw was locked in an upstairs bedroom in one of them. Ridley MacPherson was in another bedroom further down the hall, and there was an officer out on the landing. That way he could keep them separated while only using one man to guard them both—he couldn't spare two. He was short staffed enough as it was. He and Dan would use the living room to question her son.

"You coming?" he asked Dan.

"Sure," Dan didn't think they would get much out of Stevie, but he stood up and followed the detective as he stepped outside and walked toward a dark blue crew-cab that was parked in one of the carports outside the condo unit. They were greeted by an RCMP constable holding an old Winchester rifle.

"Found this with a box of hunting gear when we picked him up," he said as he passed the weapon to the detective.

"Loaded?"

"Nope. Had some ammo in the box."

"Anything else?"

"Rope. A tarp. Just the regular stuff. The kid didn't want us to touch it. Said it all belonged to his dad."

"Okay, thanks." Paul took the rifle and headed for the door. "Well, at least we know he won't be shooting at us."

▶ Stevie Wakeshaw was wedged into an old armchair that had seen better days, his huge fingers digging into the ends of the arms.

He was rocking back and forth, his small head nodding in time with the movement above his wide shoulders. Tears ran down his cheeks.

"I gotta get Dad," he sobbed. "I gotta get Dad."

"It's okay, Stevie." Dan moved over to stand in front of him. "Your dad's fine. I saw him just a while ago."

Stevie looked up at him and wiped the back of his hand across his face. "You did?" he asked. "Is he mad at me? That guy took my radio." He pointed at the constable that had given them the rifle. "And he took my dad's gun!"

"It's okay. He's just checking it out. He'll give it back—and your dad's got his knife with him, hasn't he? His hunting knife?"

Stevie stared at Dan for a minute, sniffed a couple of times and then nodded.

"You remember what his knife looks like, Stevie? Was it a big curved one or a straight one?"

Stevie frowned but didn't answer.

Dan pulled the folding knife he always carried out of its sheath, opened it up and held it out. "Does it look like this?"

This time there was a small headshake, but again no answer.

"Was it bigger? I have to find it, Stevie. Your dad needs it. Will you help me?"

"Dad needs it?"

"Yes, he does." It seemed that "Dad" was going to be the key to getting anything out of the childlike Stevie.

"Okay."

"How about if I draw you a picture. Can you tell me if it looks right?"

That drew a smile and the nod was eager. It appeared that Stevie liked pictures.

Dan turned to the detective. "You got any paper?"

The man disappeared into the dining room and reappeared with a notebook and pencil. Dan crouched down beside Stevie and drew a rough sketch of a knife with a long handle and a curved blade, something like the one he and the coroner had discussed when they were talking about the weapon that had been used in the murders.

"Did it look like this?"

Stevie shook his head, the frown back in place. "Straight," he said, using his hand in a downward gesture to illustrate a straight line.

"How about this?" Dan sketched out a simple dagger.

He was rewarded with a smile and a nod and then Stevie reached out a finger to touch the paper and indicate a longer blade.

"Longer?" Dan asked, changing his sketch to reflect the different proportions.

The smile and nod were repeated.

▸ Dan passed the sketch to the waiting detective and stood up. "Thanks Stevie. I'll go look for it."

Paul joined him, and they moved into the kitchen.

"If that's all he's got with him, its not the murder weapon," Dan said as they looked at the sketch. "That was curved. The coroner said he thinks it would look something like a big linoleum knife, but with a long handle so he could take a real swing. You think you've got enough to hold them without it?"

"Right now? Twenty-four hours. Might be able to stretch it to seventy-two. Stevie's gonna be a problem. No way he can look after himself, so we're gonna have to find some place that can take him in."

"Yeah, that's what I figured." Dan sighed. "Listen, this is all yours now. I hate to leave it like this, but I've done all I can do. Any chance any of your guys are headed back to Rupert? I need a ride."

"Jones has to get back. He'll be leaving in about half an hour. You can go with him."

The two men shook hands and Dan headed for the door. He could feel Stevie's eyes watching him as he passed the living room door, and he lifted his hand in a wave.

"It's okay, Stevie," he said. "We'll find him."

He only hoped that was true.

THIRTY-EIGHT

► A breeze from the southeast danced across the water, an early harbinger of the storm that was slowly building out toward Haida Gwaii. It ruffled the tops of the waves as Dan made his way down the ramp to the dock at the Rushbrook Marina. He could see *Dreamspeaker* sitting quietly against the end of the float, and beyond her the rigging of a fish boat danced up and down. Charles Eden must have arrived as he had promised, which meant that Walker and Joel were almost certainly there too.

Dan carefully lifted the long cardboard box he was carrying over the stern rail and climbed up onto the deck. Claire, Charles Eden, Walker and Joel were all sitting watching him. He walked up to Joel and held out the box.

"I think this is yours," he said.

Joel looked at him for a moment, then reached out his hands and placed the box across his knees. "Thank you," he said.

Walker nodded. "We both thank you."

"You want a coffee?" Claire had been watching the exchange with a quiet smile on her face. "There's a pot made."

"That would be great." Dan found himself a place to sit on one of the bench seats. "How long have you guys been here?"

"An hour. Perhaps a little more." It was Charles Eden who spoke. "Joel and Walker took a little longer than they had planned for their exploration."

Dan looked quizzically at the two younger men, but neither of them had anything to add to the statement.

"And you?" Charles continued. "Did you catch the man you were chasing?"

"Not personally, although I wish I had. That bastard damn near killed me. It was lucky the creek was shallow enough right there that I could crawl out with what was left of the dinghy over my head."

"But he is caught?" Charles persisted.

"Yeah. He is now. The guys phoned me a couple of hours ago. They caught him walking across the road. I guess he must have gone up one of the creeks and scrambled up the bank somehow. He said he'd just been out checking for deer. No sign of his kayak, so he may have sunk it."

"But he'll go to jail, won't he?" Claire had returned with a cup of coffee and had heard the last part of his statement. "Surely he won't get away with all those murders—and he killed that nice man we met, the kayaker."

"Kent McGilvery." Dan filled in the name. "No. He didn't do that. Turns out Ridley MacPherson was the one responsible for that. He's the only one who's talking right now, but he told us he found out that McGilvery had been talking about him kayaking while he was up at Kitsault, and he figured it was going to get back to his bosses that he had been playing when he said he was working. He saw McGilvery out on the water and went out to give him hell and things got carried away—not too surprising when we know what a short fuse he has." He looked at Claire and smiled. "Anyway, they got into an argument and MacPherson ended up hitting Kent on the head with a paddle. When he realized what he had done, he slashed the life jacket so it wouldn't float and dumped Kent in the water."

"That's so sad," Claire said. "Do you think he was involved in the other murders as well?"

"No. He's certainly a bit unstable, but I think Marjorie was using him. She lured him into an affair—maybe with her husband's encouragement—and he was so smitten he did whatever she asked him to."

"Sounds like you think this other guy, Wakeshaw, might walk away." Charles took up the conversation again.

Dan shrugged. "Right now, everything we've got on him is circumstantial. Nobody saw him at the murder sites, and even Walker and I can't swear it was him who attacked us. All we can say was it was a big guy with red hair—and we didn't even see much of that. We never actually saw the kayak on that ledge under the bridge, and if he's ditched it, then we don't have that either. We need to figure out the motive, and we need the weapon. If we could find that, maybe we could nail him, but right now, it's not looking good."

The shrill peal of the radiotelephone interrupted his story, and he made his way up to the wheelhouse. When he returned ten minutes later, he had a frown on his face.

"Who was that?" Claire asked.

"It was Mike. He's been checking out the Wakeshaws for me. Seems they were fired from their previous job because Jim Wakeshaw was using the metal shop to make knives that he was selling to everyone in town. The company didn't report it because they felt sorry for Marjorie and the kid."

"Does that help the police any?" Claire looked puzzled.

"I don't know. It might. There's certainly a metal shop there at Kitsault, so it gives him the means. I asked Paul about it—he's the detective who's handling this—and he says that the only thing the two of them seem concerned about is getting fired if this all comes out. That makes some sense because Mike said they're basically broke—they went into debt getting help for Stevie a few years ago and have never got back on their feet."

Dan's voice trailed off and he stared out over the water. When he turned back, there was renewed excitement in his voice.

"If they thought the whole project might be shut down because of the environmental protests . . . I know it's warped and twisted, but maybe they figured they could stop the environmentalists by making it look like they were the ones murdering the pipeline workers. Put the blame on an environmentalist, in this case a Haida . . ." Dan looked at Joel apologetically, "and the government and police would have to step in. That way the pipeline would be clear to go ahead."

He sat quietly for a moment, running the idea through his mind, and then he stood up and moved back toward the cabin.

"It's crazy, but it works. It would explain the journalist too. She wasn't in his plan but she must have seen something and he had to improvise. She was near the bridge. Maybe she saw them coming up from under it."

He stopped for a moment, still thinking about the possibilities, then continued on toward the wheelhouse. "I've got to call Paul again. It's a long shot, but it just might give him some way to nail them."

"Before you do," Walker interrupted. "Joel and I have something that might help you. Kind of a gift to pay you back for helping us out."

Dan looked at the two of them. They had said nothing throughout the conversation so it seemed an odd time to be offering a gift.

"Walker, I don't need a gift. I'm happy I could help. That's my job."

"Yeah, well I think you might need this one." Walker had his trademark grin in place and he looked at Joel for a moment before continuing. "We found the weapon."

Dan jerked upright and stared at him in shock. "You what?"

"We found the weapon. We were following the guy up the inlet and heard him trying to get rid of it. That was just before he tried to kill you."

Joel nodded his agreement.

Dan shook his head in disbelief. He was having a hard time taking in what he was hearing.

"You found the weapon."

Why did it seem that every time he was with Walker he ended up in situation like this—a situation where he was out of his depth and ended up repeating what the man had said? He had to find a way to stop doing it.

"Do you have it with you?"

"Nope. We left it where we found it. Figured it might not be a good idea for two savages like us to have it in their possession, especially when one of them has a record and the other one was recently suspected in the murders. Besides, it might have some prints on it or something."

"But how do you know this is the weapon?"

"Had to be. It was like a scythe, but smaller. Had a long handle and a kind of sheath of yew wood along the back of the blade. He was bashing it on a rock trying to break it up. The handle is broken and the blade's twisted but you can still see what it was like."

"Jesus, I can't believe this!"

Dan turned to Charles Eden who was sitting quietly with a smile on his face. "You know about this?"

"Yes. They told me about it when they got back to the boat. That's why they were late. We even figured out on the chart exactly where it is. Do you want me to show you?"

"Hell yes," Dan answered as he crossed the deck and climbed over the rail to Charles boat.

Ten minutes later, when he climbed back onto his own deck, Joel and his canoe had disappeared.

"Where's Joel?" he asked.

Walker nodded out toward the harbor entrance. "He said it was time to go home. He's going to visit Emily and make sure she's alright. Said she's part of his family now and he has to look after her."

Dan looked across the water at the distant outline of a canoe and then glanced down at the cardboard box that still lay, unopened, on the seat. "He didn't take his paddle."

Walker smiled. "He said it's yours now. You have earned it, and Chinaay gave him another one."

His announcement was greeted by the harsh squawk of a raven as it lifted off the cabin roof and followed in the direction of the tiny shape rapidly disappearing to the west.

THIRTY-NINE

► They made good time down as far as Klemtu, but then the weather changed and they fought the wind all the way through Milbanke Sound and down Seaforth Channel. It wasn't until they reached Hakai Pass that the rain stopped and the clouds started to thin, and by the time they reached Annie's cove, there were glimpses of blue sky.

It was obvious Annie had seen them arrive, but as they had come to expect, she didn't come out to greet them or acknowledge their presence. She did, however, have the kettle boiling by the time they climbed onto the deck of her boat, and she did seem a little more willing to produce a plate of chocolate chip cookies, although she still counted them out carefully and allowed only two each.

"You planning on hanging around?" she asked Walker in her inimitable growl.

He smiled. "Just until these guys leave. I have to get back to the cabin and get it ready for winter, and I need to stock up on salmon while they're still running."

"Huh." She turned to Dan and Claire. "Guess you two are gonna leave too?"

Was it possible there was a note of regret?

"Yes, Annie. We have to get back to Port McNeill. Claire and I both have to get back to work."

"Better leave soon, then. Big storm coming."

Dan couldn't resist glancing out the window at the increasingly blue sky, but he knew that, like Walker, Annie was finely attuned to the weather. It was unlikely she would be wrong.

An hour later they pointed *Dreamspeaker*'s bow out into the channel. Walker's canoe was already a distant speck on the water to the east of them, and as they turned the sun poured through the open door of the wheelhouse and shone on the paddle that Dan had clipped to the bulkhead. If he hadn't known better, he would have sworn the raven that was painted on the blade winked at him.

ACKNOWLEDGMENTS

It takes many people to bring a book to the shelf, and I have been blessed with the help of some of the best and most generous. Special thanks are due to Albert (Aay Aay) Hans who edited the manuscript for cultural accuracy (and who introduced me to the wonderfully rich and complex world of Haida Gwaii and helped make my time there so enjoyable). Others who assisted in opening my eyes and heart (often unknowingly) to the history, culture, and geography of those beautiful islands include James Cowpar, April White, and Jags (Beanstalk) Brown. Joelle Rabu of Haida House in Tllaal made my stay there an absolute delight.

Thanks are also due to editor Linda Richards, and to Taryn Boyd, Tori Elliott, and all the staff at TouchWood Editions who have done their usual wonderful job in getting the words into print, and the pages between the covers. Jim Tipton, Victoria Schmidt, Carol Bowman, Margie Keane, Janice Kimball, Robert Drynan, Mel Goldberg, Carol Bradley, Antonio Ramblés, Jan Steinbright, Lynne Stonier-Newman, and Pam Harting all helped guide the story with their wise words and input.

Last, but certainly not least, to all the survivors of Residential School, who found the grace and courage to share their heartbreaking stories with me, and to my daughter and grandson who have showed me the world of autism—my heartfelt thanks.

R.J. MCMILLEN has spent over thirty years sailing the Pacific Northwest on a thirty-six-foot sailboat she and her husband built, visiting the remote coastal communities where her family worked in the early 1900s. *Green River Falling* is her third mystery. Find out more about the Dan Connor mystery series at rjmcmillen.com.